Doubleday Canada Books
by ERIC WALTERS

We All Fall Down
United We Stand
Safe As Houses
Wave
Alexandria of Africa
Tell Me Why
Beverly Hills Maasai
Shaken
End of Days
The Taming (with Teresa Toten)
Walking Home
Say You Will

REGENESIS

ERIC WALTERS

DOUBLEDAY CANADA

Library and Archives Canada Cataloguing in Publication

Walters, Eric, 1957-, author
Regenesis / Eric Walters.

Sequel to: End of days.
Issued in print and electronic formats.

ISBN 978-0-385-68309-8 (pbk.).--ISBN 978-0-385-68310-4 (epub)

I. Title.

PS8595.A598R44 2015 jC813'.54 C2015-901947-8
C2015-901948-6

Cover design: Jennifer Lum

Printed and bound in the USA

Published in Canada by Doubleday Canada,
a division of Random House of Canada Limited,
a Penguin Random House Company

www.penguinrandomhouse.ca

10 9 8 7 6 5 4 3 2 1

IN THE BEGINNING . . .

My novel *End of Days* tells the epic story of an asteroid's twenty-six-year collision course with Earth and its devastating result—the extinction of all life on the planet.

Initially the discovery of the asteroid's trajectory is kept secret and an undercover, multi-governmental organization is formed to try to avert the collision. The International Space Agency, under the direction of Professor Daniel Sheppard, harnesses the greatest minds and resources of the planet in a valiant effort to save life on Earth.

Like all secrets, the story of the asteroid, the consequences of its impact, and the secret agency working to prevent it is first revealed through rumours—before the terrifying truth is confirmed. As fear builds, society breaks down. People abandon hope, their jobs, their children, and basic morality.

Unknown and unseen, a second front develops under the direction of Joshua Fitchett—not only the world's richest person but its greatest genius. He believes there is no hope of diverting the asteroid. Instead, he devises a plan to save humanity. Children from around the globe are trained to possess all the skills and knowledge necessary to survive with the hope that one day they will repopulate the planet.

One hundred children, under the leadership of Billy Phillips, a "street kid" are sent into orbit, to occupy a space station until the time arrives when the planet can once again sustain human life.

At least that's the plan. However, the best-made plans don't always go as expected.

Welcome to *Regenesis*.

CHAPTER ONE

T PLUS 3 HOURS

Billy sat at the porthole looking back at the space they had travelled through since leaving the Earth behind. The sphere continued to discolour—browns now overwhelming the blues and greens like a dirty, dusty fog drifting down from the northern parts of the globe toward the equator. It was more than that, though. It was a funeral shroud descending upon an entire planet. It was a process slow to the eye but in real time happening as quickly as a jet racing across the sky. Cutting through the browns were blotches of reds and oranges. These were places where the force of a collision, asteroid chunks slamming into Earth, had released energy, causing forests to burst into flames. So many pieces—estimates had been close to three hundred fragments, some close to two hundred metres in diameter as they entered Earth's upper atmosphere, and thousands, even tens of thousands, of smaller pieces—had rained down on the planet.

There was a dull thud and Billy worked not to react, to remain calm and unruffled. They had been hit again by a random chunk of rock that had missed Earth but managed to strike their ship. Small chunks wouldn't hurt. A bigger chunk could rip open the side of their vessel. Even a small puncture would be enough to kill them. Air escaping out and brutal cold breaking in. If that happened, at least they wouldn't have to wait long. Death would be quick and certain and silent. There was no sound in space.

It was important that the others didn't see or sense his concern. Billy was only sixteen, but he was still the official and unofficial leader of the group, not just here but on all five ships.

"Another small piece of the asteroid," Professor Sheppard commented.

Billy turned slightly to face him, nodded in agreement, and then turned his gaze back out the porthole. Soon the angle would prevent him from seeing the planet, and he would see only the space that surrounded it. He wanted to—*needed* to—see it as long as possible. Somehow, watching made the real seem a little bit less real. Truly, though, how could anybody actually comprehend what was happening?

Of the 101 people aboard the ships, only one was older than Billy. That was Professor Sheppard. He was a last-minute passenger, sent into space never to return. He was too old—almost seventy-five—and their mission would be too long to ever think he'd return to the surface. He'd die in space. His role was to advise, to offer his own expertise on the mechanics of space travel, to help the rest of them survive long enough to return to the planet and spread life once more. But that would have to wait. Now, down below on the surface, there was only death.

Another thud, louder than the last.

"It's unnerving enough to be hurtling through space without those fragments colliding with us," Professor Sheppard said. "This could have been avoided if the ships had launched a few days earlier."

"The first ship was launched four days ago, and a full day of prep between launches was necessary to get all five ships launched," Billy explained.

"But why not launch the first ship ten or even twenty days ago?" Sheppard asked.

"Supply issues. Rockets don't work without rocket fuel."

Sheppard laughed. "That's right. I authorized the release of that fuel. But I could never have conceived of the possibility that I would be sitting on that fuel when it was ignited."

"Do you regret coming along?" Billy asked.

"Probably from the first moment I put on the spacesuit I had doubts, but no regrets. This is where I want to be. Perhaps even more important, this is where I need to be."

"You're still uncertain about my crew," Billy said.

"Do you blame me?"

Billy thought back to a few weeks earlier, when he'd first been told of the plan—to launch one hundred children and teenagers into space to await a time when conditions on the planet had settled down enough to allow them to return—and he remembered how crazy he'd thought the whole idea was.

"I guess not," he said. "But believe me, you'll soon be convinced." He paused. "How many . . . so far?"

"I don't understand," Professor Sheppard said.

"On Earth, how many people have died?" Billy asked.

"It's difficult to know. There are different factors and scenarios. I don't have access to full data, and the number and angles of entry of the asteroids are correct only within a certain set of probabilities. I'm hesitant to give numbers without complete information."

"All I'm asking for is a guess," Billy said.

Professor Sheppard looked unsure. For him, mathematics was something of purity, of certainty, in a world that was never pure or certain.

"It's not like I'm going to hold you to it, or I can check," Billy said. "Just make an educated guess."

Professor Sheppard didn't answer right away. Billy understood that the mathematician in him needed to fully weigh all the alternatives. Numbers weren't something he freely "threw out," because the concepts of "educated" and "guess" seemed so contradictory to him.

"My best estimate would be that, so far, close to 800 million people throughout Europe, northern Africa, and North America have perished," he said. "That would be from the initial direct hits, the pulses of energy generated into surrounding areas, and the secondary effects, including firestorms and tsunamis."

Sheppard said it all with clinical calm, which was the way Billy received it—a non-reaction to a non-reaction. Two people talking about an abstract number—800 million—as if it weren't people but simply a number. Really, how could any of that register? There were so many deaths that Billy didn't—*couldn't*—think of them as individuals.

Then he thought of real people. "Do you think the tsunamis have hit New York yet?"

"The whole East Coast of North America would already have been hit by a series of waves of various sizes, with the most severe still to come."

"So there could still be people alive in New York?" Billy asked.

"Probably nobody in an area less than ninety metres above sea level would be alive. That means that almost every person in New York, Boston, virtually the entire Eastern Seaboard, has perished."

Both of them thought of the images they'd seen on TV over the preceding weeks of the mass migrations away from the coasts and toward the south, away from the territory where it was projected the asteroids would hit—a swath of land running from the Middle East across northern Africa and Europe, across the Atlantic, and halfway across North America.

"And of course those numbers don't include the very real possibility that a large fragment hit within 160 kilometres of the city, and then the entire city would have been pulverized, knocked flat, everybody killed almost instantaneously in the energy pulse it would have released. It would then be conceivable that closer to 1 billion people have already perished in the initial bombardment."

Billy shuddered.

Professor Sheppard, who was never one to pick up social cues readily, suddenly got an insight into why Billy was asking about New York.

"Do you have family in New York?" the professor asked.

"Not family, but like a family . . . a group. Street kids."

"If a fragment hit it would have been quick, almost instantaneous. I don't know if that matters," Professor Sheppard said.

"It matters. I just wish that it could have been different, that I could have helped them. I was their leader."

"You're still a leader here, but with a purpose."

In some ways it was the same, Billy thought, but in many ways it was different.

"The group back in New York was made up of kids who'd been orphaned or abandoned in the years leading up to the asteroid strikes. We were just trying to stay alive," Billy said.

"Isn't that what we're all doing up here as well?" Professor Sheppard asked.

Billy laughed. That surprised both of them. "I guess it is. It's just that these kids here are so . . . so *different*."

They *were* different. While they had also been abandoned by their parents, they had been discovered, tested, observed, and those with innate abilities had been raised in a series of learning hothouses around the planet. They had been supervised, cared for, given everything possible to allow them to focus on their studies. Among them they had all the skills, knowledge, and abilities necessary not only to survive but to replicate some of the greatest accomplishments of mankind. But for the time being Billy didn't care if they spoke a dozen languages or played musical instruments or could quote from Shakespeare. He just needed them to have the skills to ensure everyone's survival while they hurtled through space.

"Do you . . . *did* you have family?" Billy asked.

"A sister, her husband, and a nephew. I didn't even have a chance to say goodbye to them," he said.

"I didn't say goodbye to my family either. Not the street kids or my real family. My parents and brother died in a car crash."

"I'm sorry to hear that."

"It was a long time ago. And if they hadn't died I wouldn't be here, I guess. I'd be down there, back there, either dead or waiting to die," Billy said. "How long do you think it's going to be, you know, until it's over for most people?"

"Again, it's hard to give any accurate projection with a high degree of certainty because of all the variables that—"

"I just want your best guess," Billy said.

Again, Professor Sheppard hesitated as he calculated the numbers, trying to work through the known, probable, and unlikely variables. Working with numbers always seemed to calm him.

"Projecting the wind speed of currents in the upper atmosphere, the debris and dust scattered by the collisions, the smoke caused by fires and the transference of winds from the northern to the Southern Hemisphere . . . I estimate that the plume of smoke, dust, and ash moving from north to south will completely envelop the earth within two weeks. This will block sunlight from reaching the surface and completely destroy the process of photosynthesis."

"So no plants will grow," Billy said.

"None. And without food all animals will die within three to six weeks."

"But people who have stockpiled food will survive longer," Billy said.

"Those who survived the explosive power of the fragments, mainly in the Southern Hemisphere, will more likely die of starvation than as a result of the impact itself. The initial death count of 800 million will be relatively stable for two to three weeks, after which a massive extinction phenomenon will happen within thirty days. Virtually all life forms, roughly 99 percent, will be wiped from the planet, including close to 9 billion humans."

"How many people will survive longer than that?"

"I've heard estimates that there are more than three hundred well-established survival colonies, built under ground, under the ocean, or in fortified bunkers in the mountains."

"I didn't know there were that many," Billy said.

"It looks as though each government had that option as a backup plan. It's similar to how Joshua had a backup plan for your group."

Really, Billy knew, there were two groups—those on the five spaceships and another 1,600 people living deep in a mine shaft in Idaho, the place where they had been launched from.

Joshua Fitchett was the mastermind of both these groups—the one in space and the one in Idaho. He was a genius. Some people argued that after da Vinci, he was the smartest man to ever live. Others thought he was so far above da Vinci that there was no point in comparing the two. As well, he had used that genius to become the richest man who ever lived. And it was that combination of genius and wealth that had allowed him to do what he had done. He had not only given Billy and his fellow space travellers the best chance to survive, but also probably initiated the best possible chance for mankind's survival.

"Do you think Joshua and our people on the surface survived?" Billy asked.

"We won't know for certain until we make radio contact."

They both knew that contact wouldn't happen for days, or possibly even weeks. The radio antennas on the ground had been taken down pending the impact, so no radio communication was possible. As well, the spaceships would soon be taking shelter in orbit on the dark side of the moon, out of contact, hidden from view and asteroid chunks and radio communication.

"But from the little I saw of that facility while I was there, I feel certain that nothing short of a direct hit would have caused it to be breached," Professor Sheppard said. "I believe they survived."

Billy thought of all those he'd left behind on the surface—or more accurately, six hundred metres below the surface. They were burrowed in, beneath solid rock, in an area large enough to hold housing, hydroponic farms, and all the facilities and resources needed to allow sixteen hundred people to live, not just now but into future decades, if necessary. He wished he were down there rather than up here—assuming there still was a "down there" to be part of. Only time would tell.

Billy and the professor looked up as Amir, their eleven-year-old pilot, entered the small cell where they sat.

"Sorry to bother you," he said.

"No bother. You have a report?" Billy asked.

"The first of our ships has reported a successful entry into orbit around the moon," he said.

"Excellent. One down and four to go. Report in as each enters orbit," Billy ordered.

Amir turned to leave, but Professor Sheppard called him back.

"When will this ship be entering into orbit?" he asked.

"Less than forty-eight hours."

Professor Sheppard looked at him anxiously. It was strange enough to request and receive information from a little boy, but even more disturbing when the information seemed to be wrong—perhaps deadly wrong.

"The usual passage for an Earth-to-moon transit is more in the neighbourhood of seventy-two to seventy-five hours," Professor Sheppard said.

"Yes, normally, but due to the closeness of our launch to the impact time we were forced to travel at an accelerated speed. We are travelling at approximately 115,000 kilometres per hour."

"That's too fast!" Professor Sheppard exclaimed.

"No, my calculations are based on our current speed and the distance from Earth to the moon."

"I'm not questioning the equation in which time equals distance divided by speed," Professor Sheppard said. "I'm saying that the speed we are travelling is too fast to enter into a lunar orbit. The gravitational pull of the moon is insufficient to capture our craft at that speed, and we will shoot past and off into space!"

"I am *aware* of the speed necessary to enter orbit," Amir said. "We will engage the ionic engines with backthrust to decelerate so we can slow our approach to a speed under orbital velocity." He looked and sounded annoyed at having to explain this, as if his expertise was being questioned.

"Oh . . . good . . . sorry."

"You'd better get back to your post," Billy said.

"I can do that. Unless he wants to fly the ship?" Amir said, pointing to the professor.

"Me? I can't fly a spaceship."

"Just offering." Amir gave him a little salute and turned and marched out.

"I'm sorry if I offended him," Professor Sheppard said.

"That's okay. He was just kidding you. He does that a lot." Which was unlike most of the other members of the crew. "They're all experts in their fields, but it takes a little while to get used to having experts who haven't reached puberty."

"It is a little unnerving."

"You just can't think of them as regular kids," Billy said. "They're not like any kids I ever met before I got involved in this project."

"How did you get involved?" Professor Sheppard asked.

"I was kidnapped."

This time Professor Sheppard laughed out loud. "Me too! They wanted my expertise to try to divert the asteroid." He paused. "I guess that expertise wasn't worth anything."

They both peered out through the porthole back through space to the planet they'd left behind. Maybe it was just his imagination but Billy was positive the brown haze had dropped down farther than the last time he'd looked, only a moment before.

"How many people will be alive in a month?" Billy asked.

Sheppard had to stop himself from qualifying his answer. These figures had already been calculated. "Approximately 175 million people, plus or minus 5 million."

"So close to 9 billion people will have died."

Sheppard nodded.

"And within two months?"

"Less than 75 million," Sheppard said.

"And a year from now?" Billy asked.

"Estimates are less than 1 million, and every year after that the number will halve. So 500,000 at year two, 250,000 at year three, 125,000 at year four."

"And at year twenty?" Billy asked. That was the length

of time they were potentially capable of staying in space, hovering above the planet.

"It might be only two or three thousand . . . or only us . . . well, the rest of you. I don't foresee *me* living to the ripe old age of ninety-four. I will not set foot on Earth again."

Billy almost said that it was quite possible none of them would ever touch down again, but he couldn't allow that message to leave his lips, even if Sheppard was the only one present to hear it. He had to remain positive, lead through example, banish doubts. Even if he was filled with doubts himself. Sometimes being a good leader was nothing more than being a good actor—or a good liar. He knew he could play those roles because he'd played them before.

"Rather strange to be talking about all this as it were only numbers," Professor Sheppard said.

"It *is* only numbers," Billy said. "How can anybody ever understand what 9 billion lives looks like?"

"It's probably better anyway," Sheppard said. "I think Stalin was right—the death of a million is a statistic and the death of one is a tragedy. What's happening on the surface of the planet is a statistic."

"And a tragedy," Billy said.

He stared harder, trying to pierce through the distance and the haze to see Earth's surface. Then he thought better of it. There was no way, and no point in looking back. He had to focus on the future. He turned away and then stood up.

"I'm going to bed. Best to get some sleep while we can," Billy said.

"I'm not sure I can sleep. I'll just stay here and watch. And, Billy, I want to thank you for what you said to Fitchett, for allowing me to come along."

"Before this is over you might be cursing me instead of thanking me," Billy said. "Goodnight."

CHAPTER TWO

T PLUS 53 HOURS

The lights in Billy's sleeping capsule started to glow softly. They were programmed to simulate sunrise in Idaho at this time of year. It would take thirty minutes for the "sun" to be fully up, and if Billy wasn't up by then a gentle alarm—the sound of simulated rainfall—would start. But there would be no need for the alarm. There was no need for the lights. Billy had been awake for hours, thinking, planning, and worrying. Floating around in space was Professor Sheppard's lifelong dream, but it was more like Billy's nightmare—even if, so far, none of the nightmarish scenarios had come true.

As planned, their ship had established its orbit of the moon—exactly on schedule, as predicted, and piloted by Amir. Sheppard had been hopeful but hesitant right up until the ship slipped into its lunar orbit. Billy had tried to act nonchalant, but Sheppard's anxieties had rubbed off on him.

By then, the other four ships had already safely and uneventfully entered orbit. Billy's ship was the only one to have experienced contact with fragments of the asteroid. Thank goodness they'd only been small chunks and had inflicted no damage—at least, none that Billy had noticed.

Already dressed and sitting at a desk, once again he hit the switch for the mechanism that would allow him to walk instead of float. He didn't really understand how it worked but he thought of it as a magnet being activated. It was really much more complicated than that. Billy just knew that through connections in his shoes and the hull of the ship, adjusted for his weight, he was able to move around the craft, walking as if he were on Earth instead of in space, in zero gravity.

Of course, technically there was no such thing as zero gravity, only more or less gravity. Every object, large or small, had gravitational pull. Earth had sufficient mass to stop a person from floating away. Larger spheres, like Jupiter, would exert so much force that a human would be flattened to the ground, squashed like a pancake, while on the moon that same person would be able to jump six metres into the air before gently floating back to the surface. Here, travelling through space, there was almost no gravity, and if Billy wasn't belted in place or wearing the shoes, he would float around, moving by pushing or pulling against the sides of the ship.

Some of the younger children aboard were thrilled to float about the cabin. It felt to them like swimming without water, almost like flying. Others were disoriented and nauseated.

Billy found the floating strange, and a little bit disorienting. He liked his feet on the ground. He *needed* to have his feet on the ground, in more ways than one. Thank goodness for the shoes. They kept motion sickness to a minimum and gave a patina of normality to his movement. The workings of the special shoes had been explained to them all by Joshua. He had invented them, and many of the other things they'd need on their flight. For Billy, it was enough to know that they worked, and that other members of the crew understood the theory and practice so they could fix them if anything went wrong.

Billy just wished that Joshua were here with him, by his side, instead of back on Earth, six hundred metres beneath the surface. Joshua Fitchett was the founder of this program, the brains, imagination, money, and force behind its creation. But more than that, he was Billy's mentor, his friend, his guide, and his teacher. Billy trusted him more than he did any person he'd ever met.

It was such a strange relationship—the elderly billionaire genius and the young street-smart kid gang leader. They couldn't have been more different, and they couldn't have been more connected. Of course, it was now a connection that had to stretch over almost four hundred thousand kilometres. But Billy could still "hear" Joshua talking, telling him things, sharing ideas, sharing his confidence. Billy just wished they could talk now, share a few words over the radio. But that wasn't possible, and Billy knew he had to focus on what he needed to do, and what he could do.

Slowly, his shoes gripped the metal floor and he moved

from his room, down the central hallway. On each side were closed sleeping capsules holding the dozing crew members. Sleep was good. There was nothing they could do right now. He entered the command centre—the cockpit of the spaceship. Amir was at the controls.

"Good morning," Amir offered to Billy as he settled into the co-pilot's seat.

"Did you sleep at all?" Billy asked.

"I got a few hours in the transit toward the moon, and at least three or four last night."

"Sleep-deprivation can impair your judgment and functioning," Billy warned him.

"I don't have much need for either today," he said. "I'm just an observer. Besides, it's hard to sleep when the view is so amazing."

Billy looked out the front porthole. The surface of the moon stretched out before them. It was deeply cratered, shades of grey and black and brilliant patches of white. The "dark" side of the moon, the face hidden from the Earth, was oriented toward the sun and was bathed in light. It was beautiful, and surreal, and eerie.

"They say seeing is believing, but I still don't believe it," Billy replied.

"I've been staring at it for hours trying to remember it's real and not the simulation I've been studying. Do you know how many times I've done all this in a simulator?"

Billy shook his head.

"Thousands."

"That's reassuring," Billy offered.

"And I hardly ever caused it to crash and burn." Amir chuckled to himself.

"Not as reassuring."

"But those crashes were in the first hundred or so simulations. None of us has crashed in years," he said as he gestured out the window.

Glittering in that same light were the four other ships in their convoy. Over the past few hours they'd been repositioned so that two were now paired much closer together, although not as close as they were going to be.

"Mind if I join you?" It was Professor Sheppard.

"No, please do," Billy said.

"You can have my seat," Amir offered as he got to his feet and then floated into the air.

"Not necessary."

"I need to grab something to eat, so please," Amir said. "And as I offered before, take it out for a spin if you want."

"My apologies for doubting you," the professor said.

"No worries. It won't be the last time."

Amir pushed off the wall and floated across the room, doing a little spin as he exited through the door.

"I know I could do that, but I think walking is more my speed," Professor Sheppard said.

He moved slowly across the room. Not only was he not floating, but he awkwardly shuffled over and plopped down into the seat. "I'm not sure it's possible to teach an old dog any new tricks," he said.

"You're doing fine. Everybody is doing fine. Are you here to watch the docking?" Billy asked.

"I've seen ships dock with the space station before—of course, on camera—but to see it live is something not to miss. And to have multiple dockings is even more exciting."

"Only two," Billy replied. "Those four ships are going to come together to form two pairings."

"But why wouldn't all five ships come together so there needs to be only one docking with the space station?" he asked.

"We're not docking with the others. We'll be arriving before the other ships," Billy explained. "We're going to make sure that there are no complications, no damage to the station."

"There shouldn't be any damage if it was parked in orbit correctly, using the Earth itself to shield against any asteroid collisions."

"That's the hope. Still, systems have to be initiated. The station has been in hibernation for the past six months," Billy said. "If nothing else, we have to turn on the lights and turn up the thermostat so it's warm and running. And it's not a bad idea to make sure that the atmosphere is breathable and the artificial gravity has been engaged."

"I guess that makes sense," the professor said. He looked as though he was thinking things through. "Still, even with this ship going first, wouldn't it be wise to have a third docking to merge the four paired ships into one?"

"I think they want to minimize that. I've been told that ship-to-ship docking has some dangers," Billy said.

"It does, but docking with two spaceships of equal size is still much safer than each ship attempting to dock with a space station that is much larger and relatively stationary."

"I didn't know that," Billy said.

"So will the two pairs come together to form one spaceship prior to docking with the space station?" Sheppard asked.

"That isn't the plan."

"But wouldn't that make more sense, given the risks involved?"

"The plan calls for them to remain in two separate pairs that dock independently with the space station," Billy explained.

"I don't think that's the wisest course of action. While both ship-to-ship and ship-to-station dockings are successfully completed more than 99 percent of the time, the ship-to-ship connection is more than twice as successful, on average."

"That's interesting."

"But now that you know the risks, shouldn't you override the existing plan?" Sheppard asked.

Billy shook his head. "We're going to stay with the plan."

"But now that you know the risks you need to re-evaluate—"

"We go with the original plan."

"But by following the plan, you're putting lives at a greater risk. In this case, with the information I've given you, you can make a better decision. Isn't that why I'm here? To give you information you can use? And isn't that what leadership is about? The ability to make new decisions when faced with new information?"

Billy paused. He knew the right answer. He just wasn't sure how to phrase it. "I know that Joshua was completely aware of the statistics you've given. Wouldn't you think?"

"Probably."

"His corporation ran a space program. He was aware."

"Perhaps he simply overlooked this one variable."

Billy laughed. "You obviously didn't know Joshua that well. He overlooked nothing. Ever. He made this decision for a reason."

Sheppard shook his head sorrowfully. "Then I don't understand why he would want to put lives at greater risk."

"Some lives," Billy said.

"Lives are lives. Especially when there are so few." Sheppard looked flustered.

"That's the reason," Billy said. "If something happened to two ships, what would be the result?"

"Potentially forty lives would be lost."

"And if four ships were connected and they had a docking accident, what would happen?" Billy asked.

"Then potentially eighty lives would . . ." He let the sentence trail off. "That's it. He didn't want to risk that many lives."

Billy nodded. "To survive we need the expertise of sixty people who are spread out among the ships. We can afford to have one of the three separate crafts come to tragedy without jeopardizing the entire program. There are a hundred of us. The critical number for survival is more related to the skills of sixty people."

"So by keeping the ships separate he's not putting all his eggs into one basket, so to speak," Sheppard said.

"Joshua never does. He always has a backup plan. Everything is done with redundancy. On each ship there are duplicate experts in the fields we'll need to survive."

"Including a duplicate leader?"

"I'm sure other people would step forward if I wasn't able to lead, but I doubt that will be necessary."

"Have I missed it?" Amir asked as he reappeared.

"I think your timing is perfect," Billy said.

All three peered out the window as the ship closest to them fired one of its thrusters. It moved off to the side and accelerated toward one of the other ships.

"It's moving into position," Amir said.

"It's moving too quickly," Sheppard said.

Billy had thought the same thing, but hadn't said anything. "Do you know the pilot on that ship?"

"Tasha."

"And . . . how old is Tasha?" the professor asked nervously.

"Twelve. And she's an excellent pilot," Amir added, sounding a bit defensive.

There was another burst from a thruster and the ship shifted again.

"We're too far off to the side to see if it's coming in on line," Sheppard said.

"I can fix that." Amir reached over and hit a couple of buttons, and a screen came to life on the control panel. It was a camera attached to the ship that Tasha was piloting, and it showed the other ship and its docking sleeve—the target for the first ship.

"It's lined up almost perfectly," Billy said.

"I told you she was good. The numbers on the left of the screen represent distance in metres." The numbers were rapidly changing as the ship closed in, going down from one hundred to ninety to eighty.

"Don't you think it's too fast?" Sheppard asked.

"She'll use her retro-thrusters to decelerate," Amir explained.

Almost instantly they could see the burn of three rockets at the front of the ship—yellowish-white exhaust fumes—and while the numbers on the screen slowed they continued to go down.

"Twenty metres," Amir called out. "Fifteen . . . twelve . . . eight."

The camera image showed the two ships coming together, closer and closer, and then finally the image was consumed by darkness.

"Just like in the simulations," Amir said.

"Simulations?" Professor Sheppard asked.

"Of course. She's done this hundreds and hundreds of times. All the pilots were selected because they scored the highest in initial testing, and they received extensive additional training. Tasha was the *second* best."

"And I'm assuming it goes without saying that the best is standing here beside me," Billy said.

"Well, if I told you, that would be bragging . . . but really, if it's the truth, is it bragging?" Amir asked.

Billy picked up the microphone. "This is Ship 5 to Ships 1 and 2. Do you read me?"

A voice came back almost instantly. "Affirmative."

"That was very skilled. Good work."

"Just following my training," Tasha replied over the radio. "Roger and out."

"It was nice that you complimented her," Professor Sheppard said.

"Doing your job isn't something to be complimented on," Amir said. "She was just doing what she needed to do."

"Human kindness is always appreciated," Professor Sheppard said. Amir looked confused. "At least, it is by me."

"The next two ships are moving into position," Amir pointed out, ignoring what the professor had said.

All eyes shifted to the window in front of them. The two remaining single ships—3 and 4—started to move together. As with the first docking, one ship fired its thrusters and got into position, and then the two ships became one. A second successful docking, and again Billy radioed over his compliments.

For the next six days the ships would remain in place, in geostationary orbit above the moon, using it as protection from the remaining asteroid fragments. Of course, that also meant that they wouldn't be able to see Earth or communicate with it. There was no ability to curve radio waves around the moon. And there was no possibility of seeing what was happening on the face of the planet.

CHAPTER THREE

T PLUS 5 DAYS

Billy looked down on the dark lunar surface. Christina was at his side. Together they'd been sitting there silently, alone in the control room, staring at the moon for hours, waiting and watching. She would wake and then fall asleep in the chair again. It was reassuring to have her at his side, a little bit of life and warmth in the vast ocean of cold and sterile.

They had really only known each other for a few months. Perhaps because she was closest to his own age of the children and teenagers there, Christina had been assigned to be Billy's guide when he'd first arrived at the colony in Idaho, brought there against his will. Or perhaps it was her calm demeanour that had suggested her for this role—nothing seemed to rattle her or shake her composure. She had shown him around and explained how everything worked, and how the children there had been chosen for their specialized knowledge and skills. One of her own special gifts was languages—she spoke Arabic, English, French, Spanish, Italian, German, and Latvian. Latvia was a place Billy had never even heard of, and he'd felt more than a little intimidated by her.

Now, though, it felt to Billy as though Christina had always been with him. Or, more accurately, as though he had always wanted her to be there. Sometimes he found himself just looking at her as she slept. It made him happy.

As the moon continued its rotation around the Earth, its "dark side" was now turning toward the sun. He was witnessing lunar sunrise as the first rays of light started to come over the horizon. Little by little, and then all at once, the surface became illuminated. Deep creases, high mountains, flat planes—the oceans seen by ancient astronomers—and, of course, the craters. The craters were what really drew his attention.

Professor Sheppard entered and cleared his throat to signal his arrival.

"Good morning," Billy said.

Christina opened her eyes and offered a gentle smile.

"Did you sleep well?" Billy asked.

"Like a baby. How about you? Did you sleep at all?"

"I got a few hours. I wanted to be here to watch the day begin."

The professor came to the window and looked down at the surface. "I still don't believe it. Seeing isn't believing when it's this awe-inspiring."

"I just wish I were looking down on the surface of Earth instead."

"Three more days," Professor Sheppard said, "although it might be years before we can actually see the surface."

"So you're certain that the entire planet will be covered by the time it comes in sight again?" Billy said.

"If the progression continues at the rate we've witnessed, then perhaps there might be a slice over the Antarctic still visible, but even that is doubtful. Then, depending on the dispersion, density, and reactions of the weather systems, it might remain shielded from view for at least five years, but possibly much longer."

"And that cloud is what will cause the mass die-off," Billy said.

"No sunlight means no photosynthesis. No photosynthesis means no food production. No food production and mass starvation will take place."

"And when it finally clears, the surface will be covered with craters, like the moon."

"Except you'll hardly be able to see Earth's craters from space."

"But we can see those on the moon clearly," Christina said.

"Our orbit is low, and there is no atmosphere to distort the view, or land features to hide them."

"How many craters do you think there are on the moon?" Billy asked.

"They've all been mapped and noted. There are close to six thousand impact craters that are twenty kilometres in diameter or larger. And if you count the smaller impact craters there are over a million."

"And on Earth?" Billy asked.

"Prior to this bombardment there were just under two hundred impact craters mapped on Earth."

"But Earth is bigger. Shouldn't there be more craters, not fewer?" Christina asked.

"Earth has a much greater diameter, so it's a much larger target. In addition, that size gives Earth a greater gravitational pull, so it is much more likely to attract any asteroids passing by. It's estimated that the Earth has been subject to twenty times as many impacts as the moon," Professor Sheppard explained.

"But why are there so many more craters on the moon?" Billy questioned.

"When we look at the moon we are basically seeing every single impact that has taken place over the past 4 billion years. It is a living—or I should really say dead—representation of every impact that has ever taken place on the surface. But the Earth is able to heal, or at least hide its scars. Statistically, 72 percent of impacts would have happened in oceans or other bodies of water. And each impact on land is subject to weather, water, and plants. Craters are worn down, filled in, grown over, or erased by volcanic activity."

"But it isn't as though that takes place overnight."

"You're right. In many cases it would have taken hundreds of millions of years to completely erase the crater. But an overwhelming number of impacts on the Earth would have taken place between 2 and 4 billion years ago, during the heavy bombardment period."

"Again, I don't know what that means," Billy said.

"The period of the creation of the solar system was rather messy. There was debris scattered throughout space. Let's see if I can provide an example." Professor Sheppard glanced around. "Imagine this room is the solar system."

"I always pictured it as being bigger," Billy said, with a grin.

"Now imagine what the floor would look like if you took handfuls of sand, gravel, pebbles, and rocks and threw them randomly across the surface."

"That would be a mess."

"Next, take a broom and clear away a circular path, an orbit around the room."

"That first sweep, making the first path with the broom, would accumulate the greatest number of pieces of debris," Billy said.

"Exactly!"

"Subsequent orbits would still gather some debris, but the amount would never be as great," Billy added.

"Right. The debris within the inner solar system became less with each individual impact."

"And while the moon was hit far less, we see all those impacts," Christina said.

"Many more of the intercepts, the coming together of the moon and the debris, resulted in direct impacts. The moon, with no atmosphere, has no protection from smaller chunks. With the Earth, many of the smaller asteroids that were destined to hit it either were burned up by the atmosphere or experienced airburst."

"Airburst?"

"That is when an asteroid explodes above the surface."

"I didn't know that could happen."

"A number of pieces of this asteroid would have been airburst ignitions as well. The most fully documented event of this type happened in a remote area of Siberia in 1908. An asteroid exploded at an altitude of five to ten kilometres above the surface. The explosion resulted in trees being destroyed in an area of over two thousand square kilometres, and half of that area experienced complete incineration."

"How many people were killed?" Christina asked.

"They believe no more than a few people, because it happened in such a remote area. If it had happened over Moscow, London, New York, or Beijing it would have resulted in millions of deaths."

Billy laughed slightly. "Who would have thought that millions of deaths would ever look like a minor event?"

"That was one asteroid somewhere around fifty metres in diameter causing localized destruction. This . . . this was an extinction event for the planet."

"And in all those hundreds of millions of years, we were here for it," Billy said.

"We were here for *one* extinction event. There have been many over the years. So many times, life began and evolved and developed and was then stunted, frustrated, and almost eliminated. Still, life finds a way. The last event was about 65 million years ago, and it caused both the death of the age of dinosaurs and the birth of the age of man."

Billy looked at him in confusion.

"That last event caused the death of over 99 percent of all species. Those deaths left an opening that was then exploited by some evolving species. It was at that point that mammals, ultimately leading to man, started their march to a position of dominance."

"It seems strange to think that an asteroid caused us to rise to become the dominant species and then tried to eliminate us," Christina said.

"Pride goes before a fall. We were so sure of our dominance that we didn't see the end coming from above."

"Now you sound like those religious nuts, those Judgment Day people, as if you believe the asteroid was an act of God," Billy said.

Professor Sheppard laughed. "Those Judgment Day fanatics considered me an agent of the devil. I was, for many years, the man they most wanted to kill."

"Why would they want you dead?" Christina asked.

"They considered the asteroid to be sent by God to end man's wicked reign on earth. And as the head of the research institute trying to stop it, I was the chief agent of the devil."

"That's just crazy," Billy said.

"Desperation and fear and false hope can make people do crazy things," the professor said. "Reverend Abraham Honey, their leader, went from being the preacher of a little church in Texas to one of the most influential people on the planet. In the end he had close to a billion followers."

"I just don't know how that many people could be fooled," Billy said.

Professor Sheppard shrugged. "I try not to rule out anything, although the greatest irony of all is that many theorists believe that life itself was sparked by the seeds sown when an asteroid crashed on earth, releasing its frozen kernels of life."

"And which do you believe?" Billy asked.

"I seem to fall somewhere in the middle. If there is a God I believe he put the machine in motion and then sat back to allow the mechanics to act out as they were programmed. Gravity, inertia, and all the rules of physics and science were put in place, and then they governed the way space functioned."

"Einstein said that God does not play dice with the universe," Christina said.

Billy had no idea what that meant, but Sheppard spoke. "For a purported atheist, Einstein certainly spoke a great deal about the role of God in the universe. I tend to listen, though, when one of the three greatest minds in the history of mankind speaks."

"Who do you think the other two are?" Christina asked.

"While there is no consensus about the exact ranking, most would nominate Einstein and Leonardo da Vinci for the first two, and our very own Joshua Fitchett as the third."

"Joshua got us into space and is saving humanity, so I don't have much question about who should be in first place," Billy said, defending his mentor. "Could either of the other two have done that?"

"Certainly not," Professor Sheppard said, "although Joshua had the benefit of building upon their genius. Would space travel have been possible without the work of Einstein?"

Billy didn't know what to say. So much of this was beyond his knowledge.

"So if there is a God, you believe he sent the asteroid? You must think God is pretty cruel to set in motion a piece that will exterminate almost all life on the planet," Billy said.

"Perhaps he was being kind. If this asteroid had hit even one hundred years earlier in the history of man—a very short history—then not only would we have been unaware of its approach, but we would have been completely unable to avoid that extinction. Now, look around," he said, gesturing around the ship. "We are alive. A little piece of life. Noah's ark with a chance to restart humanity."

"That's small consolation to the billions who are dead, or will be soon."

"It wasn't meant as consolation. But think about it. For the first time in the history of mankind, the vast majority of the inhabitants stopped trying to kill one another and started working together to try to survive."

"Unsuccessfully tried to survive," Billy said.

"We are that success. We are alive. There are people on the planet who are alive. The way we were going, our end was going to be just as certain without the asteroid. Whether it was through nuclear warfare or environmental disaster, our time on the planet was limited. Did you know the time of the dinosaurs lasted thirty thousand times longer than as the time of man?"

"I didn't know that," Billy admitted—once again realizing that there was much he'd never learned.

"The asteroid only accelerated our downfall, and perhaps, just perhaps, gave us a chance to become better, bigger, brighter than we were destined to be."

"That's . . . that's almost romantic," Christina said.

"Certainly positive. Certainly hopeful. And perhaps you're right, just a little bit romantic, although I don't think anybody has ever called me that before . . . perhaps it's the moonlight."

"The moonlight?" Billy asked.

"Lots of old songs equate the light of the moon with romance. Well, both that and crazy behaviour—lunacy."

"Some people might think this whole plan, us up here trying to survive, is lunacy. Do you?" Billy asked.

"If you'd asked me that question a few weeks ago I would have said that this whole project was so completely impossible that it was beyond my capacity to even imagine any of it."

"And now?"

"I believe it is the best possible plan."

"I've really enjoyed hearing you talk about all this," Christina said. "It's like being back at our collectives. We had wonderful teachers."

"I was a teacher, a university professor," Sheppard said. "Don't get me wrong, I was above all else a researcher, but I did enjoy helping young people to understand science. Science is my life."

Billy didn't need to hear any more. Instantly a plan came to mind. He turned to Christina. "Could you please leave the professor and me alone for a few minutes?"

She looked confused but almost immediately got to her feet. "Of course."

She left, and the airtight compartment door closed automatically behind her, sealing the two in, not just alone but completely isolated, where they couldn't even be heard.

Professor Sheppard seemed to hardly notice. If something important was to be discussed, he certainly didn't seem to realize it.

"I hardly knew any of the things you were talking about," Billy began.

"There's so much *I* don't know that it boggles my mind," the professor said.

"But I don't know even more. Do you know how far I went in school?"

Professor Sheppard shook his head.

"Grade seven. I didn't even graduate. I can read and write, and I always did well in class, but I'm not like you or everybody else on these ships that I'm supposed to lead. I'm less educated than *everybody* on this mission."

"But you showed you can be a leader, back there, on Earth."

"I was a leader, but leader of a bunch of street kids. What we needed, what they needed, was different. I knew almost everything that we needed to know, and if I didn't know I could figure it out—I *did* figure it out—faster than anybody. If I hadn't been able to, we wouldn't have survived down there."

"But you think this is different," the professor said.

"This *is* different. For starters, down there I earned the leadership."

"I understand. You feel that because Joshua simply appointed you, your leadership can be questioned."

"My leadership was questioned every day before. I had to fight for it, watch out for challenges, be aware of those trying to take it away from me," Billy said.

"I don't think that will be the case with this group."

"It can't be," Billy said. "Not yet. But there are only two ways to lead. You're either respected or you're feared." He paused. "I don't want them to fear me. Up here I know less than everybody. I didn't know hardly any of those things you were talking about. Amir tells me things too, and I nod my head and pretend I know what he's talking about. It's the same with the others. Sooner or later they're going to know that I'm not as smart as they are."

"I'll be shocked if they haven't already realized that they know things you don't know," Professor Sheppard said.

That had crossed Billy's mind too. And he felt it in the defensive attitude the crew took when challenged about their age. Age did not, for many of these children, seem to come into their thinking. It certainly did not seem to inspire any kind of automatic respect.

"They know things that *I* don't know," Professor Sheppard said. "Do you think I know how to dock a spaceship? Lord knows I can't speak the languages or play the musical instruments, and I don't have the item-specific knowledge base that many of them have. This isn't about knowledge; it's about leadership. You were put in this position because one of the smartest people who ever lived felt you could handle it. There seems to be only one person on this mission who questions that leadership, and that's you."

"They don't question it now, but this is potentially a two-decades-long mission. How long before they challenge me?" Billy asked.

"Hopefully they'll challenge you every day, but that doesn't mean they're not going to follow you. As far as I can tell, these children were *raised* to follow direction. As long as they agree that you are their leader, they will do whatever you tell them to do."

Billy thought he understood, that he agreed. So long as no one else stood up to lead them.

"I want you to think of these children—as well as me—as mountains, as peaks. They were raised, educated in their collectives, in a very specific manner. There wasn't time to teach them about everything, even if that were possible. Instead they were given intensive, extensive teaching in one very, very specific area that matched their innate abilities. They have great heights in very narrow areas, but in everything else they fall off to practically nothing. You, on the other hand, are a plateau."

"A plateau?"

"I'm trying for another geographic metaphor. A plateau is a high, long land formation. It can be as high as a mountain, but it isn't a peak. Its heights extend over a great distance. That is you. You don't have the specific knowledge of any of the people here, but nobody, including me, has the breadth of knowledge that you have about human interaction, about leadership, about so many things. Those on the ship, including me, we are, in terms of knowledge, tall and thin. We are specialists, and you know what they say about specialists."

"I don't."

"A specialist is somebody who knows more and more about less and less until he finally knows all there is to know about nothing." He laughed at his own little joke. "You, young Billy, are the ultimate generalist. You are the normal one."

"Not on this ship. Normal means like everybody else."

"Then you're not normal. You are a specialist in being a generalist. And that's the thing that most qualifies you for leadership."

"Now I just have to convince everybody else," Billy said.

"Oh, no, they're already convinced. Now you have to convince yourself. I understand. Believe me, I understand. You have to remember that, at one point, just a few short weeks ago, I was the leader of mankind. I, Daniel Sheppard, a very mild-mannered university professor, was put in charge of hundreds of thousands, no, millions of people in our efforts to save the planet. How preposterous does that sound?"

"It does sound a little strange."

"Do you think that's stranger than you being in charge of a hundred young people?" Sheppard asked.

"One hundred young people above the moon in spaceships getting ready to dock with a space station that is preparing to spend a decade or more orbiting Earth?" Billy asked.

"Okay, we'll agree that is rather strange too," Professor

Sheppard said with a laugh, and Billy felt the pressure lift. He felt better.

"I want you to help me," Billy said.

"You know I'll do whatever I can, for as long as I can."

"I want you to be a teacher."

"I love being a teacher. Shaping young minds, having discussions. This group could certainly use a widening of perspectives."

"Not for them. For me," Billy said. "I need you to be *my* teacher."

"I'd consider that an honour."

"But it has to be our secret. Nobody, except for maybe Christina, can know about this."

"I understand. They need to see you, and only you, as the leader."

"That's pretty smart for a mountain peak," Billy said.

"I'm an old mountain peak. I've learned a few tricks over the years."

"They will see you as my trusted lieutenant," Billy said. "Somebody who can be counted on."

"And you *can* count on me . . . well, at least until I die, or my mind goes and I'm not just an old man but a doddering old man."

"Until then. Do we have a deal?" Billy asked.

They shook hands.

CHAPTER FOUR

T PLUS 16 DAYS

The original plan had been for the ships to be parked behind the moon for seven days. Billy had revised the plan to double that length of time. Their scans of space had revealed that debris continued to travel past the edges of the moon—or was absorbed by the moon and its gravity—for longer than expected. Billy didn't agree to reposition the ships until he was more certain that they would be safe. He and the others would be in space for years to come; whether it was on the space station or on these ships, it didn't really matter. In fact, the ships were designed to be self-sufficient, especially if docked together, for up to a year. Nobody wanted to think that would be necessary, but it was possible.

Amir sat at the controls, Billy at his side, Professor Sheppard and Christina behind, and then it seemed as though all of the ship's other occupants were either peeking in through the door or standing in the corridor behind it.

"It's time," Billy said quietly.

He was surprised when a cheer went up all around him. He wasn't sure if it was celebration or anticipation or both. He had already become aware that for children who were raised to follow routine, any change in plans could be very disruptive. He had already decided, with Professor Sheppard's help, that he would always weigh and temper what he said and what he didn't say. They needed to know what plans had been made, but he would keep specific time frames more general and less defined. If they had not known that the original plan was to leave the moon after seven days, stretching the wait to fourteen would not have created the ripple of anxiety he'd seen on his ship and felt from the others.

Despite everything—their knowledge, their training, their skills—they were still nothing more than children. And he and Christina—along with Sheppard—were their parents. Of course, he and Christina were parents who were only a few years older than some of them, but those few years meant so much. To a nine-year-old, the two of them were wizened sixteen-year-olds. For some of the very youngest ones, Billy, Christina, and Sheppard seemed almost to be the same age because they were all *so* much older.

Amir fired the thrusters and their ship started off. The motion, the change, couldn't be felt but could be measured against the background; it appeared as though the other two ships on the horizon changed their position. Below, the moon was dark, the features hidden, giving no reference to draw their movement against. There was no sound in space, and few reference points for movement, direction, or even what was up or down. Billy had learned those were just relative terms. The floor was down simply because they had decided to walk on that surface. The ship could be rotated to make any surface down or any surface up.

The plan now was simple. The two docked ships would stay in place, hovering above the moon, locked into position where the moon's mass continued to provide them with protection from any stray fragments of the asteroid's collision with Earth. The third ship, the one they rode, was now going to start the journey back toward Earth, toward the space station.

The next step was now in place. The ship was in motion and would orbit until Earth came into sight. That orbit would continue for at least one and a half full revolutions. First they would see Earth but be separated from the other ships in such a manner that radio communication would be impossible.

While they were exposed on that side of the moon, the next decision, the next step, would be determined. Would there be so much debris that they'd need to move back to the shielded position, or would they be able to move out of lunar orbit and back toward the planet of their birth? Either way, they would continue this orbit of the moon at least once. Even if they were leaving, they needed to communicate their mission to the others and then continue the rotation, using the moon's gravity to slingshot them toward Earth on the next pass.

The natural urge was to continue forward, to make the next step in a journey of thousands of steps that would take them back down to the planet. Billy would authorize that step only if he felt it was the right one. Sooner didn't make it better, and he knew that patience wasn't his strength. That decision—and it was his decision alone—would be made after all the information had been gathered, after everybody had contributed their opinions, and after he and Professor Sheppard had sat down and privately discussed all the information.

The other ships disappeared from view. They were now behind them. If he had wanted to, Billy could have seen them out of the side or rear portholes, but he already knew what was behind. He needed to know what was in front of them. They would remain in contact for the next few hours, until the horizon of the moon came between them and all radio communication would cease.

A few hours later, after they continued their orbit, they would once again come within sight of—and possible communication with—Earth. But what would Earth look like, and would there be anybody left to communicate with?

Billy made a point of touching base with the other crew members, offering reassuring words, kind words, making everybody feel safe as well as necessary, even important. Those were the leadership things he would normally do without even thinking about them. They were as natural to him as water was to a fish. Now he tried hard to be a fish that was aware of the water.

Billy thought a lot about water. Each day, each person received his or her daily ration. It was a precise amount based on body mass and activity level. Back at their base on Earth, before they blasted off, everybody had as much of everything as they wanted. Not here. Food and water were completely regulated. In a way, they also drew the amount of air they needed based on those same factors, body mass and activity level, but that didn't feel regulated.

When Billy was little, when his parents and brother were alive, they'd spent part of each summer at a little lake in the tri-state area, where New York, New Jersey, and Pennsylvania came together. There, in a trailer much smaller than this ship, he and his family spent their holiday time. They'd run and play and laugh and sing stupid songs and swim.

The other night he'd woken up from a dream about being back there at the lake, Lake Mohican. He was paddling around and his family was on shore. He seemed to get farther and farther away from the shore, and they kept getting smaller and smaller, and no matter how hard he tried to get back to them, back to land, he couldn't. They got so small that he couldn't see them at all, and finally he couldn't even see the shore.

He'd awoken with a start. The dream had been so real that he'd turned on the lights and half expected to be in that trailer, or at least in his home. The trailer was gone. So was his home. So was his family. For all he knew, even the lake didn't exist any longer. He was in space in another tin can. The only moisture here was the sweat that soaked him and slicked back his hair. His family had gotten away from him. They were gone. He'd never reach them. He could only hope that one day he would get back to the shore.

"We'll be coming within sight of the planet in under two minutes," Amir announced over the P.A.

Crew members who had gone back to other tasks took note, and once again there was a surge toward the control room. Nobody wanted to hear. They wanted to see.

Billy excused his way through the crowd until he could get back to the door and into his seat. The spot was already taken by Professor Sheppard, and Billy stood behind him. Sheppard tried to get up to make way, but Billy placed a hand on his shoulder.

"I'd rather stand," he said.

"No," Sheppard said. "This is your seat. I'll be the one to stand."

Slowly the professor got to his feet. But Billy didn't sit. He turned so that he could face his crew. He had something he wanted to say to them. More to the point, he knew they needed something said to them. He had been working with the professor on what he was going to say.

"Can I have your attention, please?" Billy began, and everybody fell silent.

"Below us is the moon. It stands in the way of us seeing our home. In 1969, man came here for the first time. It seems like a really long time ago to all of us. Even in the history of mankind that seems like a long time ago. In the history of our planet it was just a minute ago. In the history of our universe it was the blink of an eye. According to history, when that first astronaut, Neil Armstrong, stepped onto the moon, he said, 'That's one small step for a man, one giant leap for mankind.'

"Before Armstrong there were many steps along the way, from the first flight of the Wright brothers to the first astronauts escaping Earth's atmosphere and entering space. I try to think what it would have been like for those first space travellers to look down and see the Earth beneath them. To travel away from the planet and see it getting smaller and smaller. To orbit the moon, as we have, and to see the Earth appear. A little blue ball in the darkness of space. We stand on the edge of history."

That last line was completely the professor's.

"I want to thank all of you for your hard work. I am so fortunate to have such a capable crew. Give yourselves a round of applause."

They clapped and offered congratulations to one another. The sombre and solemn looks of concern were replaced by happiness. If ever there was a group of young people who needed to learn to relax and be natural, this was it. Of course, in some situations—this situation—their anxiety was understandable.

"I know that everybody will do their job. You all know what needs to be done. You are the best, and I am honoured to be part of this mission. As soon as the planet comes into sight and we come into radio communication range, I want to know, and I want you all to know, what is being said on Earth," Billy said.

"What frequencies do I try, and how frequently?" Jason asked from the radio console.

"All frequencies, at five-minute intervals, until we go back behind the moon," Billy said.

"What do you hope you will hear?" Jason asked.

"I just want to hear from those who have survived. To know that we're not alone."

There was another round of applause—this time spontaneous.

"Roger," Jason said.

"We're coming around," Amir said. "In five . . . four . . . three . . ."

Billy leaned forward and tried to see over the horizon, and then they came around the curve and there it was. The third planet from the sun was visible across the expanse of space. But the blue planet was no longer blue. It was brown. Different shades of brown.

What they couldn't see was that their orbit around the moon had coincided with the Earth's orbit in such a way that they were looking at the Western Hemisphere. For the next few hours, as they could see Earth, the part of Earth that they wanted to hear from was aimed toward them. There, somewhere beneath the haze, was North America in general, and Idaho specifically, and even more specifically the underground colony that they'd left behind.

"As predicted, it looks a little different," Billy said. He was speaking to everybody in the room, everybody on the ship. "No surprises. Jason, are you hearing anything?"

"Three seconds from Earth to us," Jason said.

A radio message travelled at the speed of light—300 million metres per second—so it could reach Earth in less than three seconds. A return message, once sent, would reach the ship just as quickly. Technically, they could have already had their first contact.

"I want all sensors on full sweep," Billy said.

The crew would be scanning space for debris and aiming sensors directly at Earth, trying to analyze the extent of the dust cover as well as trying to see through it. Most of that data would be gathered but not fully analyzed until they were back around to the far side of the moon.

The crowd, the crew, dispersed as everybody who had a job to do went to do it. The only two without a specific task seemed to be Billy and the professor. Billy had also asked Jennie, whose area of expertise was climatology, to stay in the control room to answer some of his questions.

Billy sat down next to the professor and looked toward the planet. "Is there anything there that you didn't expect?" he asked.

"On some subconscious level I just expected it would be the blue-and-black ball that I've always seen pictures of," Professor Sheppard said. "But I knew what we were going to encounter."

"Sorry you were disappointed, Professor," said Jennie with a smile. "I guess brown is the new blue."

Billy turned to Jason. "Well?"

Jason nodded. "I'm already receiving messages sent out from surviving settlements. As well, I've sent a message and received a reply from our friend."

Billy felt a swell of relief. What hadn't been spoken of was that Jason's first communication—with their *friend*—was with the unmanned space station circling the Earth, the place that was going to be their home. It had been pre-programmed to change its orbit from a hiding spot behind the planet—the way they had hidden behind the moon—to escape from the asteroid fragments. It was now locked in orbit between them, and directly above the Idaho colony.

Jason had sent a signal to the space station's array of automatic equipment asking for a status report. That message was more important than anything Billy was going to say. More important, even, than anything that was going to be received from the Earth. Their future home had survived the asteroid, using the massive bulk of the planet to hide behind. Its delicate hull, so vulnerable to being pierced and destroyed, had remained intact. It was still there, still alive, still inhabitable. Well, at least still capable of sending back that message.

"So far, so good," Billy said.

"Hopefully this isn't a false positive," Jason replied.

Nothing could be known for certain until they did an external inspection, and until they actually docked and entered the station.

Only the people present in the control room knew about the call to the space station. Billy needed to have control over what information could and should be shared. The truth was necessary—but too much truth, too soon, or delivered to the wrong people, could be problematic. Billy knew that to be true, whether it was a gang of street kids scuffling to survive on the streets of New York or a group of super-genius prodigies struggling to survive in space.

As they continued their orbit, the Earth became more visible through the control centre window. It seemed so small, so far away, and so surreal. A brown sphere hanging there, no strings attached, in a sea of black. Billy had seen pictures. This wasn't what it looked like in any of the pictures he'd ever seen before.

"Any thoughts?" Billy asked the professor.

"I have nothing but thoughts. Do you realize that in the history of our planet, approximately 40 billion people have ever lived?"

"I didn't know that."

"And here we are, two of twenty-one people who are able to watch it unfurl in front of our eyes."

"I guess that makes us either lucky or unlucky," Billy said. He looked at the Earth again. "Jennie, I didn't expect that the colour would be so blotchy."

"The weather systems are distributing the dust and smoke and soot," she explained.

"The Southern Hemisphere is so much lighter. It looks as if I could almost see through to the surface," Billy said.

"It will ultimately be more uniform in colour, I expect, as the dust cloud becomes more evenly distributed across the entire planet."

"And then it will fade away slowly," Billy said.

"That depends on the potential sources of ongoing eruption," Jennie said. "Do you see the red spots?" They were faint but visible. "Those are volcanic activity. The impacts have created some volcanic activity around the Pacific Ring of Fire."

"Was that expected?" Billy asked.

"Nothing was completely expected. We're watching an experiment in process that is both difficult and complex.

It's hard to fully understand anything, and impossible to understand everything. Dust, debris, ash, and smoke are being thrown up into the air, and that will continue as long as there is a source. The volcanic activity provides more sources."

"So this will delay our ability to see the surface? To return to the surface?" Billy asked.

"I'm not certain of that. What I know is that the thicker the layer of dust and soot and ash, the less sunlight will reach the surface."

Jennie was probably not even aware that she was nervously chewing a fingernail. It seemed to Billy then that understanding the truth and accepting it were not necessarily the same things.

"So the more photosynthesis is interrupted, the bigger the mass die-off. The greater the number of extinctions."

"That is the general theory," the professor said. "We'll be watching as it plays out over the coming years. I just wish I could live long enough to see how this whole thing finishes. How fascinating it's going to be."

"Fascinating isn't the word I was thinking of," Billy said. He turned to Jason. "I don't suppose there have been any messages so far for us from the surface?"

"There have been over seven hundred messages."

"Seven hundred! How is that possible?"

"Automated messages have been flowing out from across the hemisphere," Jason explained.

That made sense. "What locations?" Billy asked.

"Cities. They're in at least twelve different languages, although I am able to understand only English, French,

Spanish, and Portuguese. I've recorded the others and will ask for them to be translated."

"Christina can help. And any messages from our colony?" Billy asked.

Jason shook his head.

"Understood," Billy said. "We came around a week later than planned, so we can't expect they would instantly be sending out messages to us. We have another five hours before our rotations are no longer in sync. Keep listening."

CHAPTER FIVE

They sat around the table in the large room. At night it was the boys' dorm. During meals it was the galley. Now it was the conference room. Every space on the ship had to serve multiple purposes. The only private room belonged to Billy and Christina. Even Sheppard, the late addition, shared the dorm room with the boys. Billy as the leader and Christina as his partner had that privilege of privacy. So they were the only "couple." Ultimately, as the children aged and the project developed, that would change.

Billy sat at one end of the table with Professor Sheppard at the other—that way they could make eye contact and communicate without being obvious about it. The rest of the crew sat along the other two sides.

Their ship had continued its rotation, probing, testing, and recording data as long as they were able to see Earth. Once again their orbit had moved them into a position where the moon itself was between them and the planet. Now was the time for analysis and reporting on what they'd found.

"While we've gathered information about the planet and the space station, I want to begin with the data collected about the open space between the moon and Earth," Billy began.

"That's my area," Katie said.

Katie was one of the youngest crew members, and she sat with her head and shoulders only slightly above the table.

"We used radar and wide-spectrum radio waves to look at the debris still occupying the area," she said.

"And?"

"There is a remarkable lack of debris. The asteroid pieces have either impacted on the planet, passed by, or been captured by Earth's gravity."

"So the open space is clear, but there are chunks that have taken up orbit?" Billy asked.

"Exactly."

"Do you know if they present a danger to the space station?" Billy asked.

"That's not my area of expertise."

"Whose is it?" Billy asked.

An even younger girl at the end—her name was Sophia—raised her hand. "The pieces are dispersed and small and statistically not significant."

"What are the odds of one of these statistically insignificant pieces hitting the station?" Billy asked.

"Very, very low. The station is in such a high orbit that

the fragments are orbiting below it, or weren't captured by Earth's gravity at all."

"Excellent. Reports on the station itself?" Billy asked.

"It has responded to all messages and requests," Jason said.

Orders had been sent to have the station rotate, open its solar wings to gather power, and shift its rotation to a more southern orbit. All requests were fulfilled, almost instantly and without incident.

"Is there any question that it's alive and ready for habitation?" Billy asked.

"It's ready," Jason said.

"Any disagreement?" he asked.

There was a general shaking of heads.

"Then we know what to do next. Finally, reports from those who were focused on Earth itself," Billy said.

"We exposed it to radar, a full spectrum of light analysis, and radio waves. We were able to see through the haze to the surface," Sophia reported.

Billy thought about how the words and the squeaky little voice didn't seem to fit together.

"And?"

The earth science specialists looked from one to the other. None seemed ready to talk.

"I know you need to analyze the data more fully. What can you tell me with certainty?" Billy asked.

"The surface temperature has plunged dramatically." Scott, the eldest, spoke for all of them.

"How dramatically?" Billy asked.

"By approximately seven degrees Celsius."

"At the poles?" Professor Sheppard asked.

"Worldwide through all latitudes, the temperature has, on average, dropped by seven degrees from the expected temperature," Scott answered.

"And the oceans?" Billy asked.

"We're only able to look at the temperature on the water's surface, but that has been, on average, close to four degrees lower."

"So the oceans will have had a moderating effect on adjacent land?" Billy asked.

"We weren't able to sample that from this distance, but that's the assumption," Scott said.

"Has there been an expansion of the polar ice caps?" Billy asked.

"The Arctic polar ice field has already expanded over 10 percent, while sea ice has extended out from the Antarctic by hundreds of kilometres," Sophia replied.

"Then the temperate zones must be rapidly retreating toward the Equator," Billy said.

"I don't think anybody predicted temperatures would drop this quickly. Basically, nuclear winter has already arrived," Professor Sheppard said.

"Can you give me any indication as to how this is affecting Idaho?" Billy asked.

"It's both in the north and away from ocean influences. The temperature drop there will be significant," Scott reported.

Nothing he had said was surprising or unexpected.

Ideally, the base would have been in a more southern climate, but there were many practical reasons for locating it in Idaho. It needed to be inland to escape the very real danger of tsunami activity. It had to be in an area of hard rock to support the expansion of the existing mine. It had to be able to host facilities to launch the spacecraft. It had to be isolated. And finally, it had to be property that Joshua Fitchett owned and could access without drawing attention from the outside world.

"Was there any communication from the colony?" Billy asked—although he already knew the answer.

"Nothing. No messages," Jason said.

"Possible reasons?"

"We did leave our position one week later than planned," Jason noted.

"But we were within radio range for almost eight hours, and you were sampling Earth messages, correct?"

"Every five minutes, as ordered," Jason said.

"So either we missed the message or they didn't send," Billy said.

"Or the asteroid shower may have damaged or destroyed their radio array."

"And you assume that the repairs have not taken place," Billy said.

"Or that it isn't safe to travel to the surface, or that their ability to travel to the surface has been compromised. Or that a direct hit has destroyed the facility," Scott added.

There was a sudden, uncomfortable silence around the table.

"We won't even consider that at this point," Billy said. "The odds of a direct hit are less than one in over ten thousand, and fatal damage is even more unlikely. We're not even going to look at that possibility, because, quite frankly, it is irrelevant in deciding our next step."

Billy had said the words, and they were true, but it was almost impossible to keep the emotion from his voice. If the colony had actually been destroyed, not only were they alone, but they were isolated from the only people who could help them. It couldn't be possible.

"I can see no reason to delay our departure," Billy said. "We will continue our orbit, communicate with the other ships, and then, as we come around again, fire our thrusters to escape lunar orbit." He paused. "We're going home."

The ship maintained its lunar orbit until, on reaching the far side, Billy was able to communicate with the other two ships to tell them his intentions. Those ships remained in geostationary orbit until they once again came around to the far side. Then they fired their engines to exit orbit and headed toward earth, toward the space station.

T PLUS 19 DAYS

With each passing hour the brown ball they were aiming toward had become larger and larger until now, only a few hours out of Earth's orbit, it dominated the entire view.

Professor Sheppard, Amir, and Billy were together in the control room. The three had practically lived in there for the past three days. The passage across 384,000 kilometres of open space had been completely uneventful. As predicted, there was no space debris. Whatever had been there had moved on. It had travelled through one side of the inner solar system and had either been captured by the sun or continued out through the other side.

As they neared Earth, Sheppard couldn't help but calculate all the angles and speeds necessary for them to acquire an orbit. Too fast or on too great an angle and they'd simply bounce off the atmosphere, escape Earth's gravitation well, and overpass the planet. If that happened, then returning for another pass at the planet would rob them of fuel and take days. The alternative was worse, though. If they arrived too slowly or on too shallow an angle they'd plunge downward, burning up as they encountered the atmosphere.

Sheppard knew all the mathematics. He also knew that Amir knew all those same things and there was no need to check or even ask. It was amazing how much respect the professor had developed for their eleven-year-old pilot over the past two weeks.

The plan was simple. They would achieve an orbit and then use their thrusters to start chasing down the space station. Once they found it in its geostationary orbit, they would match speeds until they were able to dock.

"Here's where it gets interesting," Amir said. He sat intently at the helm, controlling the thrusters to change the angle of entry and using the ionic engines to slow the rate of speed. There was no way of gauging a change in speed, but the Earth, outside their window, seemed to shift slightly as the attitude of the ship changed.

Billy was aware of *what* was being done but had neither the skills nor the technical knowledge to know exactly *how* this was being done. It didn't matter. His job was to lead, not to perform specific tasks. He had to believe his crew knew what they were doing—he had no choice.

The angle continued to change until the Earth finally seemed to stop directly beneath them.

"We've achieved orbit," Amir announced.

"That looked very easy," Billy said.

"It's always easy when you know what you're doing. Docking will be more challenging."

"Where is the space station located?" Billy asked.

"It is almost completely on the other side of the planet from us."

Billy strained to look out and down to the planet. The surface was obscured by a swirling brown haze. "If I could see down to the surface, what would be below us?"

"The Indian Ocean would be to your left and the continent of Australia would be coming up on your right."

"Australia would have been one of the last places to be engulfed in dust," Billy said.

"It would have been like a curtain being drawn across the face of the planet, starting with the top and working down until finally even the Antarctic was covered," Professor Sheppard said. "A radar scan would be able to pick out the features of the land masses."

"I'm sure we'll get a full report once we settle into the station," Billy said.

Beneath them there was a sudden, bright flash of light that burned for a few seconds and then was gone.

"Asteroid fragment entering the atmosphere," Amir said without being prompted.

"That's going to be happening a great deal as multiple fragments in unstable lower orbits are drawn into the atmosphere and burned up," Professor Sheppard said. "Under normal circumstances, each year the Earth would encounter 400 billion particles entering its atmosphere."

"Did you say billion?" Billy asked.

"Yes. Most of those particles are no bigger than a grain of sand or a small pebble. The pebble-sized pieces are those shooting stars we would have seen on a clear night."

Billy's thoughts once again returned to Lake Mohican, he and his family lying on the beach looking up into the clear sky, so many stars it seemed unreal, looking for those little bursts of light. Billy could almost hear his brother squeal, the voice of his father, the laughter of his mother as they reacted to each little mega-burst. Now, here he was in space, watching those same collisions from the other side. And his family was all gone. Almost everybody's family was gone.

It seemed strange, but the farther from Earth he'd gotten the more he thought and dreamed of his family. Down on Earth, he'd never had the luxury of grieving or dreaming because his energies were focused on surviving the nightmare that he was living. Now here, on the other side, those memories kept flooding back. He found himself looking at the picture of his family that Joshua had given him—salvaged from their home, which had been burned down long before the day of the asteroid. It was all he had of them, so he held it near and close. He carried it in an inside pocket and often pressed his upper arm against it ever so slightly so he could feel it there. It gave him reassurance and comfort and a reason to go on. A little bit of them was living as long as he lived. He wasn't going to let anybody kill the part that remained.

There were times in the past when things had seemed impossible, when Billy had thought that he would have been more "fortunate" to be with them when they were killed. It would have been so much easier. He kept fighting through, somehow surviving, beating the odds, keeping his family alive in his memory, in his genes, and now in the picture in his pocket. He'd beaten the odds again, one of a handful of people still alive when soon there would be 9 billion victims. He couldn't allow himself to think of any of that. Not even of his family. He had to keep his head in the game and stay focused.

"Of course, those small grains of dirt and sand and gravel all add up. It's estimated that in any normal day, fifty tonnes of meteoric mass enter Earth's atmosphere," Professor Sheppard said.

"And now?" Billy asked.

"It's only a rough guess, but we might expect ten times that much, including many larger pieces anywhere up to a dozen metres in diameter or more. Those large chunks would either have an aerial burst or actually reach the planet."

"So in some ways it's similar to the heavy bombardment period," Billy said.

"Exactly!" Professor Sheppard said. "We're witnessing the same phenomenon on a smaller scale, and we have a front-row seat."

"This stuff really excites you, doesn't it?" Billy said

"How could it not? We are witnessing something that scientists have only been able to predict or hypothesize. It is happening before our eyes!"

"I don't think most of the planet shares your enthusiasm for witnessing the process," Billy said.

"That was insensitive of me," he said. "I didn't mean it that way, of course, and really, I have witnessed planetary bombardment before."

Billy gave a questioning look.

"It was long before your time, in the beginning of my career, and of course it didn't take place on Earth."

"You must mean the Comet Shoemaker–Levy 9 impacts on Jupiter," Amir said without looking up from the controls.

"Exactly. In a span of a few short days we witnessed a 'string of pearls,' twenty-two fragments hitting the surface of the planet. Some of the impacts created disturbances in the atmosphere of Jupiter that were larger than the diameter of the Earth. These threw up debris clouds that would have extended hundreds of kilometres above the surface of the planet, and even back into space."

"Why were there so many fragments?" Billy asked.

"Jupiter is a giant. It is 122 times larger than Earth. In

fact, if you put all the planets in the solar system together, Jupiter would still be two and a half times as large."

"And with size comes gravity," Billy said.

"Thank goodness for those of us on Earth. Jupiter has always acted as a bodyguard for our planet. Its gravity is so strong that our solar system almost acts as if it's a binary system."

Billy gave him a questioning look and Sheppard knew he had to explain further.

"A binary system has two suns. In the case of our solar system the sun, along with Jupiter, has a somewhat similar effect. It captures stray comets and asteroids that enter our atmosphere before they can possibly impact with Earth. That was the case with Shoemaker–Levy 9. The comet entered our system and was captured by Jupiter's gravity. It became a satellite orbiting the planet, but it was in an irregular orbit, doomed ultimately to crash. It was shattered into pieces by the gravity of Jupiter in a close pass."

"Almost like an aerial burst," Billy suggested. He was trying to take the information they were giving him and synthesize it into something he understood.

"In this case, it was an orbital burst. It fragmented while in space, above the atmosphere of Jupiter. We were then able to predict, from speed, angle, and altitude around the planet, that the fragments would plunge to the surface in the next close pass. With that knowledge, we had every eye trained, every telescope aimed, ready to witness the predicted collision. It was the first time human eyes had ever witnessed an impact."

"Second," Billy said.

The others looked at him.

"In 1178 a monk saw an asteroid crash into the moon," Billy said, remembering something Joshua had told him.

"That's right! I forgot about that incident!" Professor Sheppard exclaimed. "I assume others have been witnessed, but that one was documented. Imagine seeing something like that happen when it defied the scientific and, more importantly, the entire religious framework of his era and his existence, and then writing about it. That was a brave and wise monk. It wasn't until more than five hundred years later that Galileo looked at the universe with a telescope and started to make sense of it all."

"Does it make sense to us now?" Billy asked.

Professor Sheppard shook his head. "Not completely. We make guesses and models. That's all we're doing now when we look down on the planet."

Billy looked at the swirling clouds of dust and debris that obscured the surface below.

"Then all our plans to stay up in space are based on guesses and models," Billy said.

"All of them."

"And the planet could settle down enough to be habitable in two years or twenty years."

"Or two hundred," Professor Sheppard said. "The suggested time span of one decade is an approximation. I heard that figure was plus or minus five years."

Billy shook his head. Ten years was going to be difficult. Fifteen years unbearable. Two hundred years—well, anything beyond his own lifespan seemed impossible.

"My grandmother used to say you should prepare for the worst and pray for the best," Professor Sheppard said.

"We're prepared for whatever we need to do," Billy said, "step by step. And the first step is to get to the station."

"We'll get there, Captain. In fact, we're tracking the station down now," Amir said.

"I've lost track of the whole procedure," Professor Sheppard said. "What happens next?"

"We chase after the space station, which is now on the other side of the planet, so we can move into position to execute docking procedure," Amir explained.

"What's the time frame?" Billy asked.

"I could make it happen extremely quickly, but instead we'll use minimal thrusters and rendezvous within six hours."

"Excellent. I'm going to catch a few hours of sleep. Could you please have somebody wake me when we're within sight of the station?" Professor Sheppard asked.

CHAPTER SIX

T PLUS 21 DAYS

The race to dock with the space station had become a crawl. In order to track down the station the ship had been speeding around the planet, but now they needed to slow down to match its speed. The station, in geostationary orbit, was travelling at a rate of 3.1 kilometres per second in order to stay positioned exactly atop the colony in Idaho. In an hour, both ship and planet would have moved over 10,000 kilometres. As well, the planet itself was speeding through space at more than 100,000 kilometres every second. Yet, with nothing to judge its speed against, the station appeared to be hanging there, motionless.

The speed of the station didn't matter. The speed of the planet didn't matter. Even the speed of the ship didn't matter. What did matter was the speed of the ship relative to that of the station—the closing speed. In order to dock, these two had to be travelling at the same speed, give or take a metre or so per minute.

Billy couldn't help but think of what the professor had said about the dangers involved in docking a ship to a station. But he simply had to have faith in the plan, in the pilot, and in their mission.

They continued to close in, the distance now measured in metres and the speed differential at less than five metres per second. It was still too fast to dock without destroying the ship and damaging the station.

Billy was mesmerized by the station. It was a bizarre combination of cylindrical and boxy structures connected with narrow passages, and it had long solar-panelled appendages extending out and away. It looked like an insect, its multiple wings stretching out as if it were about to take flight and fly away from them. How could something that looked so delicate possibly support them, keep them alive, for what could stretch out to be a decade—give or take five years? Billy didn't want to think about decades, or years, or months, or even days. All that mattered was the next fifteen minutes.

On his way to the control room, Professor Sheppard was doing a quick calculation. He was almost seventy-five, and a ten-year orbit would take him to eighty-five. Life expectancy for a white male in New Jersey, where he had spent most of his professional life, was just over eighty years. Factoring his parents' lifespan into the equation—his mother had died at seventy-two, his father at seventy-five—made the prospect of still being alive when they returned to Earth seem increasingly far-fetched. But he wanted to live. That hadn't always been the case. Sheppard had lost his will when it became inevitable that the planet would not survive. As the head of the failed project to save the planet, he felt it was his duty to die, like a captain going down with his ship. But now, to be a witness to history, to do his small part to help save humanity—he wanted to hang on as long as possible.

"I almost overslept," he told the others when he arrived. "I dreamed about what it would be like to see my station in space, and now there it—" He stopped and turned to face them. What he saw was not at all what he'd expected. "My station is there, but there are others, so many others, all connected."

"Joshua arranged for other orbital assets to be harvested," Amir said.

"There's the European space station, and the Russian . . . I see two units owned by private corporations . . . and numerous satellites. How did that happen?"

"We had a spacecraft that captured abandoned or unused assets in space and brought them together for our use," Amir explained.

"But that satellite, the one on the far right, that's one of our satellites. I mean the International Aerospace Research Institute. It went offline a few months ago, some sort of malfunction."

"I believe we arranged that malfunction," Amir said. "We needed its solar-generating capacity, and Joshua decided that it wasn't going to benefit your efforts."

"But . . . but . . . that's stealing," the Professor said, and then instantly realized how foolish he sounded.

"With some of the platforms, our technicians arranged for false signals to be beamed back to Earth so the receiver believed that the asset was not working but was still in the place in orbit where they expected it to be," Amir continued.

"And instead you were out here in space with a gigantic butterfly net capturing them," Professor Sheppard said.

"We had two teams," Amir explained. "One used a big arm, something modelled on the old U.S. space shuttle. It had a big pincer and it just grabbed them and moved them into position. I was part of that team. On the far station, attached to the European space station, you'll see one of the ships we've used already. It is docked and locked in position."

The professor tried to figure out where he should look, but there were so many segments that he couldn't pick it out.

"So you've been in space before, correct?" he asked Amir.

"This is my ninth trip."

"And you said there was a second team?"

"Yes, they put the pieces together, floating around like space construction workers. In addition, they attached to the main station segments that were constructed on the surface and sent into space. We have two members of that team on board our ship. They can fix whatever goes wrong structurally with the station. At least, that's the hope."

"It appears that my station is the central section," Professor Sheppard said.

"It is the largest section and it forms the hub," Amir confirmed.

"Unbelievable after unbelievable," the professor said.

"To not only see my station in space but see it as only part of an intricate complex is almost beyond words."

Sheppard had been the chief designer and the primary consultant on the International Space Station. He had overseen the manufacturing and assembling. He had spent extensive time aboard the station on the ground as each new segment was added. He'd practically lived on board during the construction and spent many nights sleeping in the astronauts' quarters. Lying in one of those bunks, he'd dreamed about what it would be like when it was in orbit around the Earth, what it would be like to be in space.

Finally completed after almost five years of work, the station was then disassembled and the segments were launched separately into space, where they were reassembled in orbit. The reassembling, of course, he'd witnessed only from the command centre via cameras from space. He had been there for each step, helping to solve the problems as they evolved. That was so long ago. Almost thirty-five years. He couldn't help but feel very . . . well, very old.

Being there for those final stages had left him with a strange set of contradictory emotions. Of course, he'd known that the launch had to be done, that it was the culmination of his efforts, but he'd still felt a sense of loss before the ultimate triumph. Sheppard had never married. Never had children. Never even owned a dog. This station was as close to a child as anything he'd ever known, and watching its success from so far away was as close as he'd ever get to the experience of having a child grow into adulthood and then leave him forever. Now, after a thirty-five-year separation, he thought, he was having a supervised visit with his grown and aging child.

The space station was never meant to have survived this long. Sheppard felt both proud and apprehensive. Something that was past its expiration date—something he had made himself—now needed to last another decade or two. He had to hope that each weld, each joint, each nut and bolt, each section of metal was stronger than anybody had projected.

"Coming in for docking," Amir said.

Amir had manoeuvred the ship through the long tendrils of the space station's solar wings and was now in line with one of the docking stations.

"The secret is to come in with enough power to seal the connection," Professor Sheppard said.

Amir gave him a sideways glance. "I've done this before. I know what I'm doing. But if you really want I'll give up the controls."

"Simulations aren't necessarily the same as the real thing," Sheppard said.

"I found that the over five hundred simulations and four actual dockings at the station were really remarkably similar," Amir said.

"You've done this before?" Sheppard exclaimed.

"I've been on the station before, remember? And four of those times I piloted the docking. This will be my fifth . . . and I do need to concentrate."

"Sorry." Sheppard felt abashed, and more than just a bit useless.

Amir focused on the controls. Sheppard knew there was no point in even trying to decipher the multiple indicators, so he simply looked out the front screen. As they closed in there was finally a sense of movement of the ship relative to the station. In slow motion the ship moved into position.

The docking port was directly ahead and they continued to move forward until the ship kissed against the station. Sheppard felt a bit of forward movement and then the ship rocked slightly. Amir got up from his seat and manoeuvred some more controls. He was making the connection airtight before they opened either the hatch of the ship or the entry point into the station.

"Locked, sealed, and ready for entry," Amir said.

"Nice work," Billy said.

For a few seconds the three were silent, unmoving. They were here, but now they needed to take the next step. To leave the ship behind would be to enter into their new home—a home they were going to occupy for years to come.

My final home, Sheppard thought.

"Time to go," Billy finally said.

"I need to stay here in the control room for now," Amir said.

Billy looked confused. "But I thought you were going to lead us into the station."

And just then Sheppard felt much less useless and maybe even a little bit younger. "I can go. I know the docking sequence," he said. "In fact, I *wrote* the docking sequence."

The professor could lead them in—that was more than slightly reassuring to Billy. Together they left the control room and headed down the corridor.

Sheppard opened a small hatch that led to a steep, ladder-like set of stairs. Carefully the old man went down them backwards, and Billy followed. They were on a level that Billy hadn't even been aware of. The ceilings were low, and both men were forced to bend over slightly to move and not bump into the wires and tubing overhead.

Sheppard stopped in front of a small circular hatch located just above the floor. Billy looked up and thought that they must be directly below the control room. That made sense.

"I've done this protocol dozens and dozens of times," Sheppard said. "Of course, that was always on Earth. If a mistake was made or a leak was present, it didn't mean anything. Here, depending on the size of the leak, we could lose our atmosphere in seconds and suffocate."

"Good to know," Billy said weakly.

"Could you go back and seal the last hatch, please?"

Billy did what was asked. Swinging the door closed, he spun the wheel to engage the seal. This meant that the rest of the ship was protected from anything that might happen in this section. It also meant that they were sealed in, unable to escape whatever happened on their side. Not so reassuring.

Sheppard was working a small control panel above the hatch. As he worked he was quietly muttering to himself, and Billy realized he was talking himself through the protocol.

"Seal is solid, at least according to the dials," Sheppard

muttered. "As well, my readings indicate that the atmosphere within the station, on the other side of the connection tube, is almost equal to that of the ship. There will be a slight rush of air from the ship to the station as I open the internal connections." He turned to Billy. "I know this may be silly, and you are the commander, but would you mind if I am the first to enter the station?"

"I think you deserve that. I'm more than happy to be the second person to enter our new home."

"Thank you for understanding."

The professor tried to turn the wheel to open the hatch but it was locked in place too firmly for him to muscle open. Billy put his shoulder into it, breaking the seal, and the wheel spun freely. He then stepped back and gestured for the professor to go forward, but he stopped him just as he was about to open the hatch.

"Jason, Amir, we're going in," Billy said into the comlink clipped to his shirt. "If there are any issues, take the ship away to assess the situation. Do you read me?"

"Roger that," Jason said.

"Got you, Commander," Amir added.

Billy released Professor Sheppard. He opened up the hatch, and as he had predicted, a rush of air flowed out of the ship and into the connecting corridor.

"If I can't open the hatch at the other end I might have to come back to get you," Professor Sheppard said.

He bent down to fit in and then moved into the crawl passage. He had deactivated his special shoes and he floated rather than crawled. It reminded Billy of the opening at the top of a playground slide. He bent down and peeked in, but his view was blocked by the body of Sheppard as he slowly floated forward, pulling himself toward the hatch of the space station.

"I'm there," Sheppard called back, his voice echoing along the passage. "I'm going to try to open it."

Billy involuntarily held his breath. If the passage opened into space, if there was a leak, this would be his last breath. Really, though, he didn't have to worry about suffocation. The temperature flood would kill him. In direct sunlight the temperature outside would be more than 120 degrees Celsius, and in the shade it would be, at most, minus 200 degrees.

A puff of air came toward Billy and he felt an equal rush of relief. Air wasn't leaving the ship for space but entering the ship from the station. The docking was complete, the lock done, the seal solid.

"I'm going in," Sheppard called back. "I'm entering the space station!"

Billy watched as the professor moved through the passage and then disappeared. He thought about whether he should follow or go and get others or simply wait. His decision was made for him.

"Billy!" Professor Sheppard called. "Can you please come and join me?"

Billy ducked down, deactivated his gravity shoes, and floated through the hatch and into the passage tunnel. He knew this was better than crawling, but being anchored to the ground gave him a sense of security and normalcy that floating didn't. He pulled himself quickly along the corridor to the second hatch, the opening to the station, and hesitated. He thought about the fact that once he entered through this door he wasn't going to be leaving for years, possibly a decade, possible fifteen years, possibly forever. This wasn't just a station. It was going to become his home. Or his prison. Or his coffin. But what choice did he have?

Billy floated through, grabbed the side, activated his shoes, and stood up. He was shocked. Professor Sheppard was in front of him, his hands up in the air. Three men stood there, two of them with pistols, and those weapons were aimed directly at him!

CHAPTER SEVEN

Billy raised his hands, surprised that he was even able to do that, so shocked was he by what he was seeing.

One of the men rushed toward Billy, his gun still aimed directly at him, grabbed him by the arm, and threw him to the floor.

"There's no need for any of—"

The second man reached out and smacked Sheppard, propelling the little man halfway across the room, where he hit the wall and crumpled to the floor.

"There's no Jason here to protect you, old man!" he yelled out.

Jason? How did they know about their communications specialist, and how did anybody think a twelve-year-old boy was going to protect him from anything? . . . Wait! Before he came on the ship, Sheppard used to have a bodyguard named Jason—Jason Parker, Billy realized.

Sheppard pushed himself up to his knees. He was bleeding badly. "Just put the guns away. If you fire accidentally and a bullet pierces a wall we'll all be dead."

The man walked over, grabbed Sheppard by the shirt, and pulled him back to his feet. He pressed the gun right against his head. "Nothing accidental is going to happen," he snarled. "This bullet will stay in your skull."

The first thing Billy noticed from his position on the floor was that all three men had their feet planted firmly on the ground. They were wearing the same gravity shoes as the members of his crew. What did that mean?

"We're not a threat," Billy said. "We can leave."

"You'll do what we tell you to do."

"Who are you?" As Billy asked this, he slowly moved his hand to turn on the com-link without them noticing. Whatever happened to him and the professor, he had to make sure the ship and the people on it would be safe. He needed the crew on the ship to hear what was going on in the station.

"Do you want to tell them, Professor?" the larger of the two men demanded.

"I . . . I don't know how you got here," he stuttered.

"But you should know who we are," the largest of the three said. He was obviously the leader, the one Billy needed to focus on, the one he needed to talk to.

"You look familiar but I just don't know."

"That's because for you we were nothing more than background. Necessary for you and your kind to live, but otherwise expendable," he snapped.

Billy now knew who they were. It wasn't just what the

man had said, it was the way they looked. "You're security for the Space Agency, like Jason Parker was for Professor Sheppard."

"The kid has never met us but he remembers us," the second man said as he stood over Billy.

Slowly, without asking permission, Billy rose to his feet. He tried not to be threatening in any way. Who was he fooling? He was no threat to three men with two guns, and maybe that was his only advantage. They were bound to underestimate him.

"We were assigned to other so-called leaders in the agency," the head of the group said. "Then, when it all fell apart, nobody was thinking about saving the lives of the people who had saved their lives a hundred times over."

Sheppard looked at them, long and hard. "Were you assigned to specific people or part of general security?"

The larger man shook his head and scowled. "We were in the same room with you hundreds of times. We were assigned to Dr. Proust and Dr. Founder."

Professor Sheppard knew both men well. "Where are they?"

"Back on the surface," he said. "Probably dead or dying. Where they were going to leave us."

"Did all you scientists have a backup plan?" the smaller armed man asked.

"I don't know what you mean," Professor Sheppard said.

The larger man laughed. "So it's just a cosmic coincidence that you're here on the very space station where Proust and Founder were planning on going."

"I had no idea about their plan," Sheppard said. "Are you sure they were . . . ?" He stopped himself. "Of course. How else would you have gotten here?"

"I was their pilot," the third man, the unarmed man, the man who had been silent, said. "They arranged for me to fly them here, but then . . ."

"It was them or us," the larger man said. "It's not like we put a bullet in their heads."

"That might have been kinder," Sheppard said, before he realized what he was saying.

"It was the same kindness they were going to offer us. The same kindness you obviously offered to Jason."

"Jason? Jason is fine. He made a decision to—"

"Stay on the ship," Billy said, cutting him off. "He's one of nineteen crew still on our ship."

"There are that many of you?" the man asked.

Billy had to decide how he was going to play this out. "Did you think this was being set up for only three people?"

Nobody answered, but it was obvious that was what they thought.

"We do, however, have extra space and the provisions to absorb three more people on the station," Billy added. "I'm sure you have skills we can use."

"I'm a trained shuttle pilot," the third man said. "I've been in orbit and I can—"

"Shut up!" the leader ordered. He turned back to Billy. "This is our station. Possession is nine-tenths of the law, and those with the weapons make the laws. Why should we allow any of you onto our station?"

"Well, I can think of a few reasons," Billy said. "I have my com-link on. Jason, I know you can hear me. I'd like you to acknowledge that by dimming the lights of the station."

There was a delay of a few seconds as Billy heard Amir and Jason arguing about what was taking place. Only Billy could hear their confused discussion as they tried to figure out what was happening on the station and why he'd want that order to be executed. Billy needed Jason simply to do what he was asking, because if he didn't he had no way of backing his bluff. It seemed like forever to Billy. The lights dimmed off and on twice.

"Could you also seal the hatch to our ship, seal all entry points to all the other stations, and turn off the life-support system for the station itself," Billy said.

"I don't have that control," Jason said, with only Billy able to hear his response.

"Excellent," Billy said, ignoring his answer. "Do everything as requested. And acknowledge receipt of my orders by again dimming the lights."

"What are you doing?" the man demanded as the lights dimmed again.

"Showing who really has control of the station."

The man rushed forward, grabbing Billy by the shirt and pushing the barrel of the pistol into his stomach.

"Tell him to turn on the systems, now!"

"Jason, you already have your orders," Billy said. "If you don't hear me give a counter-order, put the station into hibernation."

"Do you want to die?" the man demanded.

"I think the better question is do *you* want to die," Billy said.

He was working hard to try to remain calm, in control. Sheppard looked shocked. The lights dimmed again.

"If we shoot you, you'll be dead long before us," the man snarled.

"Not really. And in the long run, what does an extra seven or eight hours mean? It would be better to go fast than slow. I think a bullet in the gut would be better than suffocating," Billy said. "Kill me and you'll find out exactly how that feels . . . running out of oxygen . . . you'll probably get sleepy, lose consciousness. I imagine it will at least be painless."

"Your death will be extremely full of pain," the larger man said. "I can assure you, I can make it slow and full of so much pain that you will be begging for death to finish you off."

The more he spoke, the more obvious it was that a showdown was inevitable. Billy didn't know what this man was going to do, but he focused on his voice to avoid showing fear of the words.

"It doesn't matter," Billy said. "Nothing matters now. Our ship will just come back after we're all dead and the mission will go on without any of us. Is that what you want?"

The man looked hesitant, which meant Billy had been convincing. Billy could see surprise and confusion in the man's eyes. Apparently he was used to having his threats taken seriously, to having people fear him and cave in to his demands.

The man released him and aimed the gun at Sheppard's head. "Maybe you're not afraid for yourself, but what about him? He dies first."

"And then we all die after that. This is *his* station. He knows how to make everything work. Why do you think we brought him up here to begin with?" Billy asked.

"You brought him?" the man asked.

"How else did you think he got here?" Billy asked. "Look, you have to make a decision. We all live or we all die. It's your choice."

There was no answer as the two armed men looked at each other. The third, the pilot, wasn't part of this equation. He was neither their partner nor their peer. He held no power.

"Decide or the decision is being made for you," Billy said. "Jason! In sixty seconds break the dock and the seal and leave. Come back when you're sure nobody is alive on the station."

The smaller of the two men rushed forward and slammed the open hatch closed, turning the wheel to establish the lock.

"Well?" Billy asked.

"What's to stop us from simply destroying the station ourselves?" the large man asked. "We could just put a few shots through the walls, making this station unusable."

"Making only this part of the station unusable. The rest of the units have already been sealed off," Billy said.

That, of course, was a lie. Billy had to hope they didn't go check and call his bluff.

"Well?" Billy asked. "Do we live or die?"

"You seem awfully willing to die," the smaller man said.

"Everybody I know is already dead. It doesn't matter much to me one way or the other."

Billy said the words so convincingly that he almost believed them himself. Maybe he did believe them. He wanted to live, but he was more than prepared to die.

"You have a deal," the larger man said.

Billy reached a hand forward and the man thought they were going to shake. Instead Billy turned his hand over, palm up. "Give me your weapons. Now."

More hesitation, and the men exchanged looks.

"You have less than ten seconds. The weapons are useless in here anyway. Besides, do you need them to protect yourselves from us? Are you afraid of me or the old man?"

"Maybe the other nineteen people on your ship, including Parker."

"Nobody is going to harm you. We don't work that way," Billy said.

"Yeah, right. That's how all people work. They will do what they need to do. Or will you try to convince us that you are just a bunch of innocents trying to help each other?"

"Believe what you want and do what you have to do," Billy said. He reached his hand out again. "Last chance—for all of us."

The larger man let the gun swing around on his finger, then snapped on the safety and handed it to Billy. The second man did the same.

"Thank you," Billy said. "Jason, can you please cancel

my orders, turn on the life-support systems, open the hatches, and send a crew of five station scientists over to initiate the systems here."

"So how come you're the one giving the orders and not him?" the large man asked, gesturing to Sheppard.

"Because I'm the one in charge here," Billy said.

The man's expression reflected nothing but doubt.

"He's telling the truth," Sheppard said. "I'm only along for the ride."

"It's a little more than that. Do any of you have a problem with that?" Billy asked.

The leader didn't answer right away, and the other two shook their heads. Finally the big man talked.

"I guess I don't care who I talk to. I just want to stay alive."

CHAPTER EIGHT

Sheppard led the way. He knew the main section of the space station better than he knew the back of his own hand because he'd been responsible for its construction. The three men trailed behind. They wanted to exchange words quietly among themselves, just as Billy needed to pass something on to Sheppard.

"Just follow my lead in the conversation," Billy said.

"What are we going to say?"

"I don't know yet. Try not to reveal too much."

"I understand. Things that are said can't be unsaid," Sheppard added.

The door to the conference room opened automatically as they approached. Inside was a large, rectangular stainless-steel table surrounded by a dozen chairs. This was the station's multi-purpose space, an area that served as conference room, galley, and exercise room. In the corners were stationary bikes and rowing machines.

Billy deliberately ushered Professor Sheppard to the head of the table, the spot that announced who was in charge and would dictate the discussion. He stepped away, waiting to see who would take the opposite side, and wasn't surprised when the biggest man took that seat. The leader's right-hand man sat immediately to his right, and the third man, the nervous little pilot who hadn't had a gun, took a neutral position in the middle of the other side. Billy sat down on that same side, one empty seat between them, but still suggesting a bridge.

"We need to talk," Billy said.

"I thought we had a deal," the right-hand man said.

"We don't have a deal," the largest man said. "All we have is a truce. You want to talk about the terms of our surrender."

"Not surrender. Partnership," Sheppard said. "We are all on the same team now."

The leader couldn't hide a flash of contempt that was lost in his next neutral expression. "What do you want to talk about?" he asked.

"Maybe names would be a good place to begin. I'm Billy Phillips." He stood up and offered his hand first to the man beside him.

"Lars. My name is Lars Elliot."

"I'm pleased to meet you. You're a trained astronaut?" Billy asked.

"I'm a pilot . . . I was a pilot with the Swedish air force before all this, and I flew four missions with the European Space Agency."

"So you've been in the European space station before?" Sheppard asked.

"I made all my shuttle runs to the station and stayed there a total of three weeks. That was our destination, where I was supposed to bring Doctors Proust and Founder."

"Until we found it wasn't where it was supposed to be in orbit," the leader snapped.

Billy moved around the table and offered his hand. "Your name?"

"Ivan. Ivan Demetry," he said.

"I remember you," Professor Sheppard said. "I do remember you." Judging by his tone of voice it was not a pleasant memory.

"And you are?" Billy asked, turning to the third man.

"Miller. Sam Miller."

"Australian?" Professor Sheppard asked.

"If you go back far enough. I was with the International Aerospace Research Institute from the very beginning. I was there that first night when you were brought into the program."

Sheppard looked shocked. He tried to think back, almost thirty years. He had been woken up in the middle of the night by armed men dressed in black, holding their weapons on him. They'd practically carried him to a waiting car and onto an airplane, drugged him, and flown him halfway around the world to Switzerland. There he'd learned about the asteroid, the plan, and his role, which would eventually grow into leadership of the entire project.

"I was sitting beside you in the car and across from you

on the plane."

"I'm so sorry, but it was all just a blur. Literally. I was so confused and scared, and you wouldn't let me have my glasses. I'm practically blind without them."

"That was part of the plan."

"So do you know Parker?" Sheppard asked.

"I know him from before. He and I worked in the same agency before any of this happened. He's one of the best," Sam said.

Sheppard knew that Parker—his bodyguard and friend—had worked for the CIA before taking up his assignment with the Aerospace Research Institute.

"When you found out that the station wasn't in its geostationary orbit you must have been rather surprised," Professor Sheppard said.

"Surprised isn't the word I would use. Shocked and disturbed. I thought I'd made a terrible mistake, that we'd entered orbit with no place to go."

"I have to admit that I was more than a little surprised myself when I saw all of the space assets that had been assembled here," Sheppard said.

"You didn't arrange this?" Lars asked.

"I didn't arrange anything. Parker arranged for me to be taken across the country on the night that the centre fell. I was totally unaware that other groups and plans and subplots were in play all around me," Sheppard said. "And here we are in one of those plans."

"You want us to believe that you had no knowledge of this?" Ivan questioned.

"I admit that most of what happened shakes simple belief, but I had expected to go down with the ship."

"Maybe you should have," Ivan said.

"Maybe all of us should have," Lars said.

"This from the man who was going to pilot the ship to safety," Sam added.

"I guess I deserve that. Who arranged for all this to happen?" Lars asked.

Sheppard looked to Billy for an answer. He couldn't follow a path that wasn't being walked.

"We are a part of a larger initiative," Billy said. "It was designed to allow life to survive above the planet until it is deemed safe to return to the surface."

He deliberately didn't mention the other ships, the fact that they were all children, or the colony below the surface of the planet.

"So you think that we can survive up here?" Ivan asked.

"This system was designed to allow us to survive for years and years if necessary. How much of the extended station have you explored?" Billy asked.

"We've seen the hydroponic facilities, and we are aware of the solar capacity and the air-purification capabilities," Lars said. "Not to mention these gravity shoes. Who designed them?"

"Our founder is known for his creativity with many things."

"Long-term living in space without some form of gravity would cause major problems. These are a crucial invention."

"There is much more involved in this. We have the people and the skills to allow all of us to live for as long as necessary," Billy said.

"All of you? All twenty of you?" Sam asked.

"All of us," Billy said. He weighed his next words. "All 101 of us."

There was stunned silence.

"Or now all 104 of us," Billy added.

"And we're all going to be living together on this station?" Ivan said. He didn't sound as though he believed it was possible.

"Living together in harmony," Billy said.

He deliberately did not say that their mission was also designed to repopulate the planet, or that, with the exception of Sheppard, they were all children, with Billy being not only the leader but also the eldest. He wanted these men to continue to believe that they were outnumbered, and that those numbers included people like Sheppard's former bodyguard, Jason Parker. Billy hadn't known Parker long, but he knew that he was somebody not to be taken lightly. Even the threat of him had an impact. These men could respect the threat of size and power, if nothing else.

Neither of these two men was to be taken lightly either. They were self-described security agents. That meant they were trained to kill, and something about Ivan made Billy suspect that he had killed before and would not hesitate to kill again.

"Can you tell me what became of the two people you were assigned to protect?" Billy asked.

"We are unsure of their present status," Sam said.

"You left them to die," Billy said.

"As they were prepared to leave us. We were given no choice. You would have done the same." Ivan shrugged.

"No, I wouldn't have," Professor Sheppard said.

"And yet you're here and alive, while billions are dead or dying," Ivan said.

"That was—"

"Not his doing," Billy said, cutting him off. "He was kidnapped once and we kidnapped him again to assist us in this project."

"This project?" Ivan questioned. "Who do I assume is behind it all?"

"You can assume a group of very smart and very rich people led by one brilliant man," Billy said. "What matters isn't the creation of the project but the future of it. You're here, in our station. We could force you to leave. We could have killed you," Billy said.

"And we could have killed you," Ivan said.

"You were dead either way. Now I am offering you the chance to be part of our group."

"And what do we need to do?" Sam asked.

"Follow the rules, follow orders, do your job, help secure our joint future."

"And if we don't want to follow orders?" Ivan asked.

"Then you are free to leave," Billy said.

"Leave?" Lars asked.

"Get into your ship. Fly away. Please be certain to close the hatch door on your way out."

Lars, the pilot, held up his hand. "I'm in. I want to live."

Sam nodded his head in agreement. "I'm agreeable to your offer."

That left only Ivan.

"And how is that you, a boy, are able to make this offer?" Ivan asked.

This was the question Billy had known was coming. "I am able to make that offer because I am the leader of our entire expedition, all the people who will live on the station."

"Do you expect us to believe that?" Ivan asked.

"He's telling the truth," Sheppard said. "Billy is our leader."

Ivan scowled. "So you are asking us to follow your orders, to do what you ask?"

He stared directly at Billy. Billy didn't look away or look down or even blink. He returned the direct glare.

"That is exactly what I'm saying."

Ivan didn't look away either. "We will do what you ask . . . for now."

CHAPTER NINE

T PLUS 27 DAYS

The control room was bustling with activity. Billy, Sheppard, Lars, Amir, and Sam stood watching. That was pretty well the extent of what they could do. Off to the side, Jason—the newcomers now knew this wasn't the security officer but a twelve-year-old boy. When they became aware of the deception they were confused—and Ivan had seemed angry—but they had not reacted in any way. In some small measure Ivan might have even respected using that deception against them.

Jason was in radio communication, guiding in the first ship, piloted by Tasha. The two ships had been ordered to break free of the moon and come to dock with the station forty-eight hours after the first ship left. As they came around the moon and communication with the station became possible, they were told that all was well.

And, indeed, even the unexpected element—the three new passengers—seemed to be working out fine. The men had agreed to be part of the enterprise. They didn't change their minds when they found out the other passengers were all children, but it certainly confused them. And made them bolder. Especially Ivan. He had a smirk on his face most of the time, even when given directions by Billy. And he seemed to have considerable disdain for everybody else, including the professor.

Billy knew Ivan's type. He'd dealt with them before. If he wasn't kept in line he'd end up completely out of control. Billy wondered what the result would be if there was a confrontation. He'd sized Ivan up. He was bigger, stronger, more experienced—a trained guard, a mercenary. Billy knew that in a straight-up fight, he wouldn't stand a chance against Ivan. Billy always had a knife strapped to his leg so that was his advantage. He had to wonder if Ivan might be carrying a weapon as well.

"This station is about to get a whole lot more crowded," Jason said as they watched through the front view screen as the first ship approached.

"The station was designed for a hundred people—I don't think four more will make much difference," Billy said.

"Four . . . wait, you mean Sheppard, right?" Sam asked.

"He was a last-minute addition, but we're glad he's here."

"I think we all are. I know Ivan doesn't think much of him, but Sheppard was always fair to people. Dr. Proust had nothing but good things to say about him."

"That didn't stop Proust from working behind the scenes so they could get to the space station without the professor knowing."

"Without any of us knowing," Sam said. "He had us all in the dark until the end."

"Really? You didn't know anything?" Billy questioned.

"Nothing. I wish I had. Maybe things would have worked out differently, and it would have been the doctor up here with us instead of Ivan." He paused and leaned in closer. "Don't trust him."

Billy didn't answer. He didn't trust either of them. Lars was probably different, but not so different that Billy would make an exception for him—at least, not yet.

The first of the two paired ships was readying itself for docking. The entire station was alive with the excitement of being joined by the others. They were about to be reunited with friends, professional colleagues, and in some cases kids they'd grown up with at the same collective.

"On board that ship, there's nothing but kids, right?" Sam asked.

"On all the ships," Billy answered. "Other than the professor, I'm the oldest person on the platforms."

"Not counting Ivan or Lars or myself, of course. You know, it might be beneficial to have some older eyes in place to handle any problems that arise."

"Don't be fooled. These kids were raised to handle problems, or stop them from happening in the first place," Billy said.

"They're certainly, shall we say, going to be unusual," Sam said. "Really, not like kids at all. Do they play or do any kind of kid things?"

Billy thought about it, trying to bring an example to mind. "No, not really."

"And the pilot of this ship?" Lars said.

"Tasha," Billy said.

"She's only twelve years old?"

"Almost thirteen," Amir chimed in.

Lars shook his head. "Do you know what I was doing at twelve, or almost thirteen, years of age?"

"Sports, video games, and probably thinking about twelve-year-old girls," Sam answered.

"All of those, but thinking more about fourteen-year-old girls . . . my neighbour. Her name was Carolyn. Sometimes I wonder what happened to her."

The words had barely come out of his mouth when they all realized what had undoubtedly happened to her. She was either dead or waiting to die, like almost everybody else they'd ever met or known or passed on the highway or never met at all.

If Sheppard's estimates were correct, there would now be over 1 billion people dead, and another 2 to 3 billion facing death from starvation, illness, or injury, or at the hands of people who were also desperate to survive and trying to hoard vital resources. Within the next two weeks, the death toll would probably reach 5 billion—more than half of the world's population.

"I lose track," Lars said. "How many days has it been since it happened?"

"Twenty-seven days," Professor Sheppard said. "I've been thinking about the entire timeline. Previously, human history was divided into two periods—BCE, before the Common Era, and CE, Common Era."

"With the birth of Jesus Christ being the dividing point," Lars added.

"Exactly. Previously, the abbreviation BC signified before Christ and AD was Anno Domini, Latin 'in the year of our Lord.' Scientists, non-Christians, and non-religious people preferred the abbreviations BCE and CE," Sheppard said.

"And you're suggesting something else?" Billy asked.

"I believe we need a third abbreviation: AAE. This would stand for—"

"After the Asteroid Era," Billy guessed.

"Exactly! This needs to be seen as the third era of mankind, with the impact of the asteroid being the defining moment of that divide."

"So what does that make today?" Billy asked.

"This would be the twenty-seventh day of Year 1, AAE. It's the start of a new era in the history of mankind," Professor Sheppard said.

"I don't think anybody would argue with that," Lars added.

Sam unexpectedly laughed, and they all turned to him. "People will argue about anything and then use force to back up those arguments. That's probably the thing I've learned from all of this. Even the threat of extinction wasn't enough to bring us together."

"Maybe this will," Billy said. "Here, on this station, we can work together. This could be the beginning."

"You didn't strike me as that much of an optimist," Sam said.

"Look around. We're here, a few of us, around a hundred people out of a population of 9 billion. We're the ones who are alive, who have survived. Do you know what the odds of that are?" Billy asked.

"Approximately one in 10 million," Professor Sheppard said.

"We're all just one in 10 million, and yet we lived and we beat the odds. We survived. Doesn't that sound like a reason for optimism?" Billy asked.

Ivan rose to his feet. "We have survived. So far. Tomorrow is another day and another question. I will stay a pessimist. It's what's got me this far." He walked out of the room, the door self-sealing behind him.

"He's always looking for the black cloud to surround any silver lining," Sam said. "He's always been that way." He paused. "But don't worry. I have my eye on him, and on your back." He motioned around to them. "All of your backs. Professor Sheppard, you have to know that Parker was a dear friend of mine, and I have made it my personal responsibility to honour him by protecting you."

"I don't think I have quite the same need for protection up here," Sheppard said.

Nobody answered, but they were all thinking the same thing: Ivan seemed to be the only thing that they needed protection from.

"Tasha, you're clear for docking," Jason said.

They all turned back to the viewing window. Caught up in their discussion, they'd lost track of what was about to happen before their eyes. Amir watched the indicators while Jason worked the radio and called out the distance and speed. Billy didn't know exactly what the numbers meant, but Jason's calm was reassuring.

The ship slowly eased into the docking ring. There was a slight nudge as the much bigger station absorbed the momentum of the ship.

"Capture complete," Amir announced. "The ship is being locked in place and the seal secured."

"That was textbook perfect," Lars said. "I couldn't have done better myself. Actually, the last time I came into that dock I had to come back around. And your pilot's only twelve?"

"Yes, but you have to remember that she hasn't been wasting her time with sports or thinking about Carol," Billy said.

"Carolyn," Lars answered. "Her name was Carolyn."

"Request from Tasha," Jason announced. "She's asking permission to come aboard."

"Professor?" Billy asked.

Sheppard looked surprised.

"It only seems fair that you be the one to welcome them aboard *your* station."

Sheppard smiled. It *was* his station. "Please welcome Tasha and her crew and passengers to the station, and give them permission to board."

Billy got up. He had asked Sheppard to give permission, but he was going to be the one to be there as they came through the hatch for the first time.

Billy was far from the only person waiting at the hatch. At his side was Christina, who had assembled a crew to welcome the new passengers aboard, bring them to their quarters, and help orient them to the station. Others were there simply to greet friends, people they had grown up with who had been placed on another ship. There were reasons behind the assignment of individuals to specific ships. There was always a plan involved in anything Joshua Fitchett designed and executed.

Christina was in charge here, keeping track of everyone, directing the efforts to welcome and settle the newcomers. She felt comfortable in that role, confident. She had received training in human behaviour—she was a sixteen-year-old who specialized in linguistics and human psychology. In fact her ability to talk to people and her caring were a big part of who she was, as hard-wired into her makeup as mathematics was in Sheppard's. And at that moment she was feeling glad about one thing: what she felt she was supposed to do and what she really wanted and was able to do were the same thing—it was all about making these special children feel welcome right from the beginning.

Billy and Christina exchanged a wordless message. It was reassuring to both that the other was there. Christina was not so reassured, however, when she caught sight of Ivan standing off in a corner. He was watching everybody and everything. Her training told her that this aloofness was a red flag. Ivan might turn out to be a complication. She would have to spend more time around him, start to get a better sense of what made him tick. But first things first.

The hatch was unsealed and the first member of the crew, a young girl, appeared. Spontaneously the assembled crowd burst into applause, and she smiled and laughed in response. She seemed so happy, almost elated. An uncharacteristic display of excitement for one of these children, Christina thought, and she found herself smiling too. One by one the crew and passengers emerged. Billy greeted each one. His intention was to welcome and reassure them, but also to establish his status as leader. Christina knew that was important.

She was proud of Billy in that moment, proud to be his partner. She wasn't even sure how that had come to be—somehow they had just known that they were meant for each other. Christina thought about what that kind of connection meant, that love. It was like the idea of family. She had no memory of her own family; she had been taken when she was very young to be raised in a collective, to learn and develop her own remarkable skills. These feelings were still new for her, as they were for almost all the children who would make up the crew on this space station. This, for all of them, would be their first experience of family, and she was determined that it would be a positive, supportive, happy one.

For starters, they would all continue to live together in assigned groupings. The five ships would now become the permanent dormitory for half of the station's occupants. Ten people would stay in each ship, for a total of fifty. Forty-five more—in most cases the younger of the children—would be housed in two dormitories on the main station's second floor, close to the galley, dining area, and activity room.

Amir, along with four others, had already taken occupancy of the small ship that he had previously piloted, already docked at the station. This ship also had one more occupant, Professor Sheppard. He and Amir had struck up a relationship as they found they had many common interests. The professor had been given a small conference room off the ship's control area to use as his bedroom. It wasn't big, but it was private, and it gave him a place to be alone. Being alone, Christina could see, was going to be both a much-desired luxury and a privilege.

The remaining three men, the unexpected guests, were staying in the cramped sleeping quarters aboard the ship they had come on. They hadn't been happy to relocate out of the spots they'd already staked out in the dormitory, but there was no choice. The larger space was needed for the larger numbers—two dormitory rooms, divided by gender. The ship that they'd arrived on was by far the smallest vehicle, but Billy wanted a way to keep them separate. They were grown men. Men they couldn't trust.

Billy also had one more reason for this separating them, he had shared only with Christina. With the men contained in their ship, he had the ability to isolate them completely, to close the hatch and seal them away. And if necessary, he could discharge the ship, blow the seal and send them away; he could even evacuate the atmosphere and kill them. He hoped he wouldn't need to pursue that option, he'd explained to Christina, but he wanted it available. He didn't trust any of them, but he trusted some of them less than others.

Christina watched as a small boy now emerged from

the ship—his name was Rohan—and burst into tears! Billy, clearly startled, almost stumbled backwards. Rohan rushed to him and threw his arms around Billy and buried his face in his shoulder. His tears, rather than subsiding, became full-fledged sobs. Christina was stepping toward them when she was stopped by the next child—a girl, slightly older—who also emerged in tears.

Christina's mind raced. Had something bad happened, or was it still happening? She rushed toward the child, took her by the shoulders, and bent down so she was looking directly into her eyes.

"What's wrong?" she asked.

The girl started sobbing louder, crying harder.

"What happened?" Christina demanded, this time a bit more forcefully.

The child's eyes got bigger. She stopped crying for a second and yelled out a few words. "Scared . . . I was scared."

Christina was taken aback. She had almost never seen the children scared, or crying, or for that matter, laughing or happy. For them, this was an extreme emotional outburst. But she understood that what they were really doing was acting like a bunch of normal kids—kids who'd been left on their own on the far side of the moon. And abandonment, perhaps, was a feeling that they understood better than most. No matter what skills they had, what they'd learned, what they were capable of doing, they still had the needs of kids, including a need to feel cared for and safe.

As soon as all the new passengers were safely on board—welcomed, reassured, and shown the facilities in their new home—Billy and Christina sat down together to talk about what had happened.

"You know, as surprising as that was," Billy said, "at least I could kind of understand what they were feeling. Most of the time I'm not really sure what goes on in their heads."

"I agree, it was a bit outside of their normal behaviour. But I think we should feel glad that they trusted us with their feelings. I think it shows growth," Christina added.

"But it makes me realize that I've never considered fear as a factor in their job performance," Billy said. "I mean, I just assumed that Tasha would pilot the ship into the docking station without incident."

"Which she did."

"Right, she did. But what if she had felt afraid? What if her emotions had got the better of her? Could she have piloted effectively if she were crying? Would her hand have been steady enough if she were shaking? Would her focus have been as clear if she were afraid?"

Right then they decided that they had to separate those they could trust to act reliably from those who could be more emotionally fragile. And then they had to help those others to become less afraid, to feel secure and safe. Not just for their sake but for the sake and safety of everybody on the station. It was more than their lives. The lives of everybody on the station were at stake, perhaps even the survival of their species.

In the next few days Billy and Christina would meet with every single passenger. They'd talk to them, offer reassurances, try to make them feel safe, but also assess each one, and then, with Christina's help, make decisions about their stability.

CHAPTER TEN

YEAR 1 AAE–DAY 31

With the successful docking of the second ship, the population of the station was now complete—there were 104 individuals, four more than planned. Four more adults than planned.

The new, energetic activity level was a bit disruptive for Billy but much more so for Sheppard, who not only valued his privacy but was used to living a life that was both focused and isolated. Sitting in the conference room now, door closed, outside sounds sealed away, he was feeling calmer. Billy, Christina, and Ivan were in the room too, and they would be joined by individual members for one-on-one interviews.

Billy's decision to include Ivan in these meetings had shocked and confused Sheppard. But Billy had thought long and hard about his choice. He needed outside eyes, another person to help him assess the emotional status of his entire crew, and he had only two options—that person was going to be either Ivan or Sam. Their professional experience in security had involved watching people and making assessments, judgments of who was in control, who was friendly or dangerous. And just as important, they could be detached enough to give their honest opinion.

Sam was the natural choice, the expected choice, the more friendly of the two. In contrast, Ivan presented an air of displeasure, defiance; he looked as if he was constantly judging. And that was what made him a better choice. As well, inviting Ivan gave Billy a chance to keep him where he could see him, gain more information about him, and perhaps co-opt him so that a conflict would be less likely to happen.

The door slid open and Tasha walked in.

"Tasha, it's good to see you," Billy said. "It was reassuring to have you at the controls of the spaceship."

"Thank you. I was just doing what I was trained to do."

"Regardless, you did a very good job. You stayed calm and focused."

"A pilot needs to be focused."

"Some of your crew members weren't quite as calm," Billy said.

Tasha didn't answer at first. "I wasn't aware. My focus was on the controls. I was piloting the ship, not the crew."

There was no deceit in what she was saying. In the command room, working the controls, reading the dials and gauges, communicating with Jason, she had probably been oblivious to all that was going on around her.

"Are you pleased with your new quarters?" Christina asked.

"It's my old quarters with fewer people. It's very satisfactory," she answered.

"We're sending a scouting ship out to take readings from different sectors of the planet next week. Are you interested in piloting the ship?" Billy asked.

"I'd like that."

"And you feel confident in your ability?"

"Yes, I think that I am very qualified to—"

"I would rather go out with Amir," Ivan said, cutting her off. "He's a better pilot."

Tasha didn't answer.

"I trust him. You I don't trust with my life," he said defiantly, pointing a finger at her.

Billy knew what Ivan was doing, trying to ruffle her, because he'd done it with a few others before—he had, in fact, told Amir that he trusted Tasha more. He wasn't interested in making friends.

Ivan stood up and walked over until he was standing right overtop of her. "Do you think I'm wrong?"

She shook her head. "I don't think you're wrong. I *know* you're wrong."

Ivan chuckled and a smirk escaped onto his face. "This girl I like."

"Why are you testing me?" Tasha asked. She was the first person bold enough to question them.

"We're reviewing everybody," Billy said.

"And did I pass the review?" she asked.

"With flying colours," Billy said. He looked at the others at the table and they all nodded in agreement.

"We know that the pressures of our situation affect different people in different ways. We need to have complete confidence in our key people—people like you."

"I'll do whatever is needed," she said. "So will it be me or Amir piloting that ship?"

Billy laughed. "It will be both of you at different times. There are going to be many flights." He paused. "But never will the two of you be together."

She understood what that meant. They would be the two key pilots, and they wouldn't be risking both of their lives at once.

"You're free to go," Billy said.

She got to her feet. She was one super-cool, confident twelve-but-almost-thirteen-year-old.

"Do you want me to send in the next person?" she asked.

"Not yet," Billy said. "And, Tasha, you have my complete confidence. I want you to know that."

She smiled. "And you have mine."

Tasha approached the door, which opened automatically. They waited until she had left and the door closed behind her.

"How about if we take a short break before we continue the interviews?" Billy suggested.

Everybody got up and stretched.

"I'm afraid I need to use the facilities," Professor Sheppard said.

"I'd like to check on some of the younger children as well," Christina said, and the two of them excused themselves, leaving Billy and Ivan in the room.

"So what is your assessment?" Ivan asked.

"Tasha has my complete confidence."

"I meant your assessment of me," Ivan said. "Isn't that why I'm here?"

"You're here because I value your ability to figure people out, and your opinion is important."

"I *am* able to figure people out, and my opinion *is* important," Ivan said, "but that's only part of the reason you have me here. You're trying to assess me."

"Aren't you trying to figure me out as well?" Billy asked.

"Of course, but now you're just avoiding my question. What is your assessment of me?" Ivan asked again.

Billy thought about lying but knew it was pointless. Instead, he would give part of the truth, which was often more effective than an out-and-out lie.

"I think you are a very capable person. You've made a career of assessing and analyzing everything and everybody."

"You would know what that is like," Ivan said.

"You can be ruthless, and you'll do whatever needs to be done. You're dangerous, but not impulsive. And you're not somebody who should be taken lightly."

"And you don't trust me," Ivan added. "Keep your friends close and your enemies closer. Is that what this is?"

"Do you think of yourself as my enemy?" Billy asked.

"I think I'm one of the few people who *could* be your enemy," Ivan said. "But I'm not an enemy."

"But that doesn't mean you're an ally, either," Billy observed.

"It's hard to be an ally with somebody who has considered blowing the space lock and killing me and the others on my ship," Ivan said.

"I wouldn't do that," Billy said.

"You say you *wouldn't*, which simply confirms your awareness that you *could*. That is why you left us in the ship, correct?"

"I left you there to keep you isolated from the children."

"And yet you choose to make me a part of the assessment of those same children."

"I need an outside eye. I trust your assessment skills," Billy said.

"But still you don't trust me," Ivan said.

"I trust your skills. Do you blame me for not trusting you yet?"

Ivan smirked. "No. I could have killed you back then. I still could. Like that," he said, snapping his fingers.

"But you didn't and you won't. You know your life is dependent upon me."

"I'm not so sure of that. If you cut the head off a snake the body goes dead quickly enough."

"There are a hundred people in this snake."

"And without you they would all obey me out of fear. Fear of me and fear of not having somebody to lead them. I've been able to assess this."

For the first time Billy felt that he'd overplayed his hand. He shouldn't have involved Ivan, or been alone in this room with him. Slowly, without noticeably moving his upper body, Billy slid one hand down his leg toward a knife concealed in a sheath in his sock. Without a weapon he was outsized, outmuscled, and outmatched. Even with the knife he probably couldn't win. Without it, he had no chance. He started to pull it free.

"But I'm not going to do that," Ivan said. "My best chance of living is to live in peace."

That statement should have relieved Billy. It didn't. He knew that the best way to attack somebody was to lower their defences. That had to be what Ivan was doing now. Silently he removed the knife and drew it up to his lap, hidden beneath the table. The knife, almost fifteen centimetres long, was thin and sharp. He knew what it was capable of doing. He'd both been stabbed himself and stabbed somebody else. He preferred one much more.

"I do not blame you for doubting me," Ivan said.

Suddenly Ivan's hand held a knife—a big knife—the blade glistening in the light. He slammed it down on the table in front of him.

"Mine is on the table. Maybe you should put yours there too. Nobody is going to be stabbing anybody today," he said.

Ivan slid his knife the length of the table so that it was well beyond arm's reach of either him or Billy.

This was the time, the few seconds when Billy had a distinct advantage. His opponent wasn't armed any longer and he was. He could act swiftly, cleanly, put the knife in him and end it all. Or try to continue in a different direction.

Billy pulled the knife up so it was visible. He held it in his hand, slowly turning the blade so that it caught the light. He looked over at Ivan. He had hoped to see fear, uncertainty, something other than Ivan's expression of total confidence. He placed the knife on the table and slid it away so that it joined Ivan's, far out of reach.

"I am glad you decided to do that," Ivan said. "As I said, I greatly prefer not to kill you."

Ivan pulled out a second knife, and before Billy could even think to respond, he also slid that knife away and out of reach.

"Two knives are better than one," Ivan said. "Especially when your potential adversary knows you have one of them." He paused. "You are not like these children, but you are not like any sixteen-year-old I have ever met."

"I guess I should take that as a compliment."

"Not a compliment. Just fact. You are not like them. You are like me. You will do what needs to be done. So will I. We are both better allies than enemies. I will help you, and you will help to keep me alive. Agreed?"

"Agreed."

Ivan reached out and the two shook hands.

Billy had agreed, but that didn't mean he trusted him. He would keep his eye on Ivan. The same way Ivan would keep his eye on Billy.

CHAPTER ELEVEN

YEAR 1 AAE–DAY 35

Billy looked down on the planet. Well, at least at the clouds that obscured the planet. They had radar that could pierce the clouds and "see" the surface, but no way of truly knowing what was going on down below.

In his head was a running count. How many people were dead and how many were still alive? They had almost reached the point at which, if Sheppard was to be believed, as many had died as those who still remained alive: over 4 billion dead, with another 5 billion clinging on to some sort of life.

What exactly did 4 billion dead people look like? What did 4 billion of anything look like? The numbers were too large and the concept too frightening to ever allow the mind to fully comprehend!

While the original deaths had been from the impacts themselves—the tsunamis, fires, and airbursts—now the threats were disease, starvation, sickness, and freezing temperatures. The nuclear winter caused by the clouds had seen the surface temperature drop even more dramatically than anticipated. The entire planet was almost twelve degrees colder than three weeks before. There would be major crop failures—because of not only the temperature drop but also the whole breakdown of the photosynthesis process, as the sun's rays were bounced back up by the same cloud cover that blocked his view. Mass starvation was taking place as food stocks were exhausted. Those who didn't starve to death would succumb to illness and disease brought on by malnutrition. The temperate zones, the places where people could live in a reasonable climate, had continued to race away from the poles and toward the equator, moving faster than most people could migrate. People—scrambling for dwindling resources, on the move, scared and uncertain amidst a complete breakdown of society—were now the biggest danger. If the world had been in chaos waiting for the asteroid strike, it was beyond anything imaginable now. People would kill for a loaf of bread—or be killed for possessing it.

Up here they had food and water and warmth. Billy knew that down below there were safe havens—maybe hundreds of them—where people had gathered to try to weather the storm, to wait for some new form of normal to evolve and emerge. He didn't know how many, but he was concerned about only one. Directly below them was the Idaho colony.

After five weeks there was still no word. At least no word they could filter out and find. The radio waves were filled with messages. Not just the automated ones, but tens of thousands of others. All around the planet, messages were being sent. Some announced that the senders were "still alive," but most were pleading calls for help. Help that not only wouldn't be offered but couldn't be offered. Anybody who hadn't prepared was dead, probably sooner than later. Even the vast majority of those "safe spots" hadn't prepared nearly well enough, and their inhabitants too would die, just not as soon. He couldn't help but wonder if that was ultimately to be the fate of his mission too. Could they stay up in space long enough to allow this to pass, or were they just going to experience a more prolonged life leading slowly to the same death?

"This is control to Billy," Jason called out.

Billy came out of his head and back to the room. "I'm here."

"The crew is preparing to leave in less than ten minutes. You said you wanted to be advised."

"Thanks. Let them know not to leave until I speak to them."

Billy exited the conference room and was immediately surrounded by the rush of activity that always filled the common areas. The station was large, but not large enough to allow any sense of privacy in any part of the station shared by others. He needed to move quickly, but that wasn't possible. He was continually stopped by children who wanted to share a message, to ask a question, or simply to be subconsciously offered reassurance by speaking to him. He knew how important it was for him to appear calm, relaxed, patient—to have time for them even when he didn't.

Although he didn't want to keep those on the ship waiting, on his orders they weren't leaving until he got there, so realistically he had as much time as he needed.

Billy's interaction with those in his charge had changed since he'd seen them behave more like who they really were—brilliant, talented, skilled children. They reminded him now of the children in the street family he had led, before he was "invited" to join this project. More than their leader, he felt like a parent. He and Christina had become the sixteen-year-old mother and father to a brood of ninety-eight children. And if they were the parents, then Professor Sheppard had become the grandfather. Some had actually started calling him "Grandpa" or "Grandpa Shep." And it was apparent that Sheppard, far from taking offence, enjoyed it.

All the children had been raised in their collectives with staff in place of parents. Billy's own parents had been ripped away from him, but he still had inside of him the gifts they'd given him—time, attention, love, and acceptance. He was now trying to offer these to his children.

Of course, if he and Christina were the parents and Sheppard was the grandfather, what did that make Lars and Sam and Ivan? He had to be careful to monitor these relationships. Despite their talents, most of the children were emotionally younger than their years. They were innocents, naïve, unable to read situations and people. They could be easily tricked or fooled or used or abused. He had to make sure that didn't happen.

Lars seemed harmless enough, and he shared common interests with many of the children. He and Amir and Tasha were all pilots. Lars had an undergraduate degree in earth sciences and a doctorate in physics, and he spent time with the children who were specialists in those areas. He was a good resource for them and for the mission.

Sam and Ivan were different from everybody else, and different from each other. Sam seemed to have a ready smile and happily offered encouragement to the children. He'd mentioned that his biggest regret was that his job prevented him from having a family. Ivan hardly ever smiled. He was constantly on alert, looking, assessing. If Sam was relaxed then Ivan was like a tight spring, ready to go off. Sam talked about his parents and sisters and how much he missed them all, and how sad he felt about what he knew was happening. If Ivan even had a family he never mentioned it, or in fact, anything personal about himself.

Arriving at the docking station, Billy was surprised to see Ivan sitting at a table in the corner with Tasha. They were engaged in a game of chess. Tasha was lost in the game. Ivan looked up and gave Billy a subtle nod of his head. Billy changed directions so that he could talk to them.

Tasha was playing white and Ivan black. Somehow it seemed appropriate that Ivan would be with the darker forces. The game was well under way and it appeared to be fairly even, judging by the number of pieces each still had on the board. Billy's father had taught him to play the game when he was young, but he'd never really taken to it.

"It looks like a good game," Billy said.

"It will be a good game when I win," Ivan said.

"If you win," Tasha added.

"I will win. You do not think far enough ahead to win."

"Check," Tasha said.

Ivan moved his knight to block the check and protect his king. "That is an example. Why would you make such a move? Now you have a choice of which piece you will lose."

"Not much of a choice," Tasha said. "I can lose my rook or a pawn."

She moved the rook and Ivan used his next move to take the pawn. "You know, even though we are just pawns, we are all important in our ways," Ivan said.

Tasha looked confused. Ivan wasn't talking to her, in any case.

"This girl is a good chess player. Not as good as me, but very good."

"I can beat you."

"Perhaps. But not today. Checkmate."

Tasha looked down at the board and quickly saw there was no way out. She turned her king onto its side and then offered her hand. There was a slight flicker of pleasure on Ivan's face as they shook, which made a nice change from his usual stony countenance.

"It's good you have come to see them off," Ivan said.

"Tasha, I hope you understand why I asked Amir to take out this mission," Billy said.

"He's a good pilot."

"And he's piloted this ship before. He's docked with this station half a dozen times."

"I'll be ready for the next one, if you want," Tasha said.

"In the meantime we will play more chess," Ivan said. "Who knows? If we are up here long enough, she might even beat me sometime."

"I'd like you two to join me for the pre-flight meeting," Billy suggested.

Ivan showed a flicker of surprise. Billy liked trying to catch him off guard. Ivan knew that.

Billy ducked down and entered the ship through the narrow passageway that connected it to the station. He hit the switch to deactivate his shoes and swam down the passage. It was faster, easier on the knees, and truth be told, he was starting to enjoy it sometimes. He sometimes watched the younger kids floating and spinning and playing in the common room. It was three storeys tall and left lots of open space. He had to admit that it did look fun, and he was always happy when they acted like kids.

Funny, it reminded him of a time when he and his parents went to the zoo. There was a family of otters—a mother, father, and three young ones. There was a slide in their pen—part smooth concrete and part mud. The three little ones kept sliding down—over and over again, back and forth, sometimes alone, sometimes all in one tangled mass of fur and feet.

Billy had just sat down at the glass—he couldn't have been more than four or five, because his brother was still in a stroller beside him—and watched. At first his parents had tried to convince him it was time to go because there were "so many animals to see," but he had not wanted to see any of them. Finally, his parents had just sat down beside him, and they stayed there for hours—all of them laughing. Even his brother in the stroller. And he remembered his very favourite part: the mother and father otter joined in, all of them taking turns sliding down, spinning and turning and splashing. Billy made a mental note to join those kids floating in the common room.

Of course, it was essential that they spend most of their time walking and not floating. It wasn't just that walking was more functional for working—their bodies needed to have gravity, even artificial gravity, imposed upon them. Professor Sheppard, and Joshua before that, had warned him of the dangers of spending long periods of time without gravity.

Entering the ship, Billy reactivated his shoes and took to the floor. Tasha and Ivan were close behind. The three of them crowded into the little control room that doubled as a conference room. Already seated at the table were Amir and Jason, who would monitor radio signals from the planet; Professor Sheppard, who was there for the briefing but not to go on the trip; and the three mission specialists.

Vula was twelve and specialized in earth sciences. Samuel was nine and an expert on atmospheric phenomena. And the third mission specialist was Jennie, almost fifteen, the climatologist. Jennie, although she was the oldest, was the one whom both Billy and Ivan had assessed as the most fragile. She was deliberately put on this mission with four very strong crew members. It was hoped that rather than her nervousness infecting others on the ship, their confidence would rub off on her. Her skill set would be crucial in determining when they would eventually be able to return to the planet. That was probably a decade away, but as always Billy was looking to the future.

Amir was seated at the head of the table, and as they entered he got up to yield that seat to Billy.

Billy put a hand on his shoulder to stop him. "You're the captain, and that's the captain's spot."

Amir replied with a smile as Billy took a seat to his right. Ivan took the last available seat, and Tasha stood off to the side.

"Please continue," Billy said.

"We haven't started," Amir said. "We were waiting for you."

"Then my apologies for keeping you waiting."

"Professor, would you start the briefing?" Amir asked.

"Certainly. Let's begin with the rationale for your mission. As we are all aware, the station is in geostationary orbit. Rather than orbiting the Earth, we are orbiting *with* the Earth. We are permanently positioned over the northwest section of the United States."

That was to allow them to be directly above the Idaho colony. Everybody on the ship knew that except Lars, Ivan, and Sam. Everybody on the ship knew that this fact was not to be divulged to them. Billy wasn't sure why he had insisted on keeping this from them, but he knew that having information they didn't was a potential source of power. Maybe even more than that, the shared secret was a way of banding all of them together and keeping those three on the outside.

"By virtue of being geostationary, we are completely blind as to what is happening on most of the planet. We need to not be blind. One option is to allow the station to orbit independently," said Professor Sheppard.

"Which involves greater danger, technical complications, and a massive use of fuel," Amir said.

"A second option, and our first choice, is to send a scout ship to capture information and to complete a survey of the entire planet, which is what we are doing today. You will be looking at atmospheric and climatic conditions, measuring surface temperature, and using radar to penetrate to the surface," Billy said.

"We'll be looking for the degree of variation over different parts of the planet," Samuel said. "I can't believe I'm actually getting to take all the theory I've been taught and see it in action, live and in person!"

"Well, I'm not as crazy about the live and in person part," Vula added, a bit anxiously. "I'm not sure how much I'm going to love being on the ship again. But I really can't wait to come back with the data and start analyzing it. Samuel's right—it is going to be amazing to give our training a practical application."

"And this will be just the first snapshot," Professor Sheppard said. "Every four weeks another survey will be taken."

"We expect that Tasha will be piloting the next mission."

"Looking forward to it," she said.

"Amir, can you talk about the orbital pattern, please?" Billy asked.

"We will be travelling in a high orbit to avoid the debris

field currently in the areas closer to the surface. Our route will take us in a north–south direction so that each orbit will travel over the poles. Our orbital speed will be slow, and with each pass we will adjust our course to allow a pass that covers a ten-degree arc of the planet," Amir said. He continued, "And while this will involve an ever-larger slice of the planet as you approach and reach the equator, the monitoring equipment is capable of capturing very precise measurements."

"What will the duration of the mission be?" Jennie asked.

"Seven days planned, with a potential for an additional two days if necessary," Amir said.

"What would make a longer trip necessary?" Ivan asked.

"If we see something that is different or troubling, or if we have equipment failure and need to make more passes. We are equipped so that we will not be forced to return to the station," Amir explained.

Jennie looked uncomfortable, and Billy made a mental note to check in with her.

"That sort of flexibility is necessary," Billy said. "And speaking of flexibility, do you have space to accommodate another crew member?"

"Two extra spots are possible. Are you going to come with us?" Amir asked.

"My place is on the station, as is the professor's. I want Ivan to accompany you on this mission."

"Ivan?" Professor Sheppard questioned.

Everybody looked surprised, including Ivan for the split second before he hid his feelings and his expression locked back to neutral.

"I think his presence would be a positive influence on the mission." Billy turned to Ivan. "You should go and get a few personal items and a change of clothing for the trip."

Billy waited for Ivan's response. Was he going to object or question or—?

"I will return quickly." He got to his feet and left.

This was exactly the response Billy had wanted and hoped for. He wanted to establish his position of authority and see if Ivan would respect that or try to question him. And there were other reasons why he wanted him to be on the ship.

Billy wanted Ivan on the mission in part to separate him from Tasha. Billy wanted Ivan to assess the children objectively, and his connection to Tasha seemed to be stronger than Billy had anticipated.

Christina had assessed Tasha as susceptible to influence. She also detected a slight anti-authoritarian attitude. That wasn't necessarily the worst trait, as it fostered the type of independence they would ultimately need, but it could also be a danger. Forewarned was forearmed. Christina would watch her, and that was reassuring to Billy. He'd already learned that in a world where trust had to be earned, Christina was beyond that. He would trust her with his life. He would also willingly give up his life for her. She was something special.

So far, Ivan had done nothing to make Billy question his trustworthiness. He had done as he was asked. His analysis of the situations that arose on the station had rung true. Billy had not had occasion to mistrust him, but still he did. Billy was concerned that Ivan was telling him obvious truths to obscure and disguise the less obvious lies.

As well, sending Ivan away on this mission separated him from Sam. It was important to keep the two of them apart. Billy needed to play one against the other, because together they would be far too strong for him to deal with. So far, that strategy was working. It was clear that Sam trusted Ivan even less than Billy did.

"I'll arrange for additional supplies to be brought on board so that the length of your mission isn't compromised. We'll let you get on with your final technical details," Billy said. "You all understand how important your mission is to the overall success of our project. I want you all to know that I have complete faith in the captain and members of the crew."

He looked from person to person, stopping very deliberately and looking each one in the eyes.

"I look forward to frequent updates on your mission and to the complete analysis of the data that you are going to collect," Billy said. "I wish you all well."

He stood up and shook hands with each member of the mission. Again, deliberately, he looked directly into each person's eyes, bending slightly for Samuel, the youngest crew member. He took a few more seconds with Jennie.

"Jennie, I couldn't be more pleased that you are a member of this mission. Your role is crucially important, and we are fortunate to have somebody with your level of expertise aboard."

"Thank you so much for saying that." She looked happy. He had given her a little boost of confidence.

CHAPTER TWELVE

YEAR 1 AAE–DAY 37

Sheppard and Billy settled into the conference room, the closed door separating them from the noise and activity of the common area.

"Is there any word from the ship today?" Sheppard asked.

"Not yet. Every day they report in at seventeen hundred hours. Do you want to be there when they do? Is there anything you want to ask them?"

"Nothing specific. I'm just curious about the extent of the regional differences they've noticed so far."

"They've reported that the farther south they investigate, the less the density of the cloud cover," Billy said.

"As expected. It's reassuring when the data match our own models and predictions. And temperature?"

"Continues to drop. Does your model predict just how low the temperatures can go in a nuclear winter?" Billy asked.

"That will be determined by the thickness of the cloud

cover. Thicker clouds reflect back more of the sun and prevent radiant heat from reaching the surface. We were able to make predictions based on the thickness of the cover, but there is no defined floor."

"Floor?" Billy asked.

"The floor is the bottom, the point at which the temperatures will not fall any lower. The data Amir and his crew are collecting will provide us with accurate information about the thickness of the cover, and then I'll be better able to make those predictions. Or perhaps Jennie will."

"If you could work with her but allow her to take the lead, I'd really appreciate it," Billy said.

"I will offer my assistance."

"Thanks, Professor. I know it will boost her confidence if she is in charge. Now, I would appreciate it if you could offer your assistance to me—can we continue your tutorials on the space station?"

Billy was trying to learn more about how food, water, and air were produced within the station. He needed to know more about what made everything work. While there were experts to keep the systems running, he needed to know enough to help make decisions.

"I'd like that. I've been discovering so much more as I continue to explore," Sheppard said.

"But you designed the station."

"I designed the core station, but with the addition of the other space stations, as well as a good many clever alterations, it has changed quite a bit. Investigating it has been a wondrous adventure for me. Our little world is not that little."

"It seems pretty little to me," Billy said.

"You have to understand that I've lived most of my life inside buildings and laboratories and concrete bunkers, so this isn't very different. You've lived your life in the outdoors."

"Sometimes there was too much outdoors."

Billy had spent years on the streets of New York City, and when he was indoors, it was in abandoned houses and apartment buildings, or even below ground in the sewer system. In many ways life on the space station was beyond any luxury he could have imagined. He had a soft bed, clean water, food, and warmth.

"I've actually stopped thinking of this as a station and started to think of it as our world," Professor Sheppard said.

"A very little world."

"Well, you can think of our station as a little world, or you can think of Earth as a very large space station. We are both independent, closed systems travelling through space."

"What do you mean by a 'closed system'?" Billy asked.

"In thermodynamics, a closed system is an environment that doesn't exchange mass or energy with its surroundings. The Earth, and any other planetary object, is considered a closed system."

"But the Earth is gathering fifty tonnes of space debris every day," Billy said.

"Technically it's still a closed system, but that's a theoretical concept and not a possible reality." The professor paused. "If you think it through we are actually here in this station because the closed system of the planet was ruptured by the addition of the mass and energy of the asteroid."

"Is the space station a better representation of a closed system, then?" Billy asked.

"Again, both theoretically and practically, yes. On the space station we are operating within a true closed system. We cannot add mass—we don't bring in any food or water that is not produced onboard—or lose mass, by expelling our waste, for example."

"It still amazes me that we can produce all the air we need," Billy said.

"It's the most essential of our 'rule of three' needs," Sheppard said.

Sheppard had explained this term in a previous session. A human could survive three minutes without air, three days without water, and three weeks without food. All of those were provided consistently on board. Of course, in space there was one more need to consider: exposed to the extremes of heat or cold outside the station, a person would survive only three seconds in space.

"We are fortunate to have the large-scale hydroponic facilities," Sheppard pointed out.

Walking through the gardens in the hydroponic facility felt to Billy like walking through a field. He could almost feel the wind blowing off the plants. And Sheppard had taught Billy how hydroponics—the practice of growing plants in water without soil—not only provided the passengers with food, but allowed interactions necessary to support life. Humans breathed air and produced carbon dioxide. Plants took that carbon dioxide to use for their own survival and released oxygen. So the production of food, the plants that grew to feed them, also helped them to survive in the most basic way.

In addition, the station had two more sources of clean air. One was a sophisticated scrubbing system that took carbon dioxide out of the atmosphere and released oxygen. Sheppard was impressed that this system—which he had designed and implemented—needed to function at only 30 percent of its capacity due to the very effective production of oxygen in the hydroponic facility.

A third source of oxygen had not yet been used, and Billy hoped it would never be needed. Caches of certain inorganic chemical compounds were stored in different locations around the station. These chemicals, when combined, would produce breathable air. In the event of a massive puncture and air loss—assuming anyone survived—they'd have the ability to fix the puncture and then regenerate an atmosphere. This was their emergency backup plan.

As well, emergency oxygen canisters were strategically placed around the station. Not unlike the oxygen tanks used by scuba divers, these held a supply that would last two or three hours, depending upon the size and physical exertion of the user. Each tank was attached to a spacesuit that would protect the wearer. These were very different from the suits that would be used in a spacewalk, but they would provide the user with enough protection to survive—at least as long as the oxygen lasted.

Billy knew where every emergency tank and suit was located. He knew the layout of the entire station. He had memorized it and drawn it, detail by detail, time and again, until he could produce a model that contained each emergency hatch, each alternate route if one section needed to be closed down, and each section that could be sealed as a safe haven. He knew how the station would be evacuated if there was a catastrophic failure. This was all part of being prepared. In an emergency he would have to act—and direct other people—with potentially only a few seconds or moments to decide.

While parts of these details were known by many of the crew, only Billy, Christina, Amir, and the professor knew all of the plans. Billy knew that this circle of knowledge had to be expanded to a few more trusted people, and then he'd have to schedule drills to test them in action—sort of like the school fire drills he remembered, from back in the days when there were actual functioning schools.

"There is, of course, one other major way in which both our station and Earth are not actually closed systems," Sheppard continued. "We are both dependent upon the sun as our source of power and energy."

The space station was given life by the massive solar-panelled wings that spread out in all directions. Computer-programmed so that they were continuously rotated to capture the maximum solar radiation, they were the heart of the entire program. They provided the energy that heated and cooled the atmosphere, drove the scrubbing system, and powered the lights that allowed them to see and allowed the hydroponic gardens to grow.

As he had with all parts of the program, Joshua Fitchett

had overdeveloped their essential resources. The panels operated on seven different circuits and produced almost three times the power that was necessary for them to survive. Over time, individual sections or whole grids could, and probably would, fail. They could survive in spite of those potential failures.

The surface of the planet itself was now undergoing catastrophic failure. The sun's rays weren't able to penetrate through the clouds of debris to reach the surface. Without that radiation, the temperature of the planet had continued to plummet, and photosynthesis had broken down. Since the space station continued to rotate with the planet, it had night when North America had night. On Earth, however, neither the moon nor the stars were visible. And daytime barely existed on the surface; high noon was now no brighter than deep dusk.

Sheppard had explained that there would be enough light to see but not nearly enough to drive photosynthesis. The death of all plants would lead to the death of all life forms. By now, almost all animals would be either dead or living on the verge of starvation. Predators, carnivores, would continue to dine on the carcasses of the dead until those became too few or too rotten to consume. Humans who had stores of food would continue to live off those reserves until there was nothing left of their supplies, unless they could somehow replenish them. There would be hydroponic gardens at some of the surviving colonies. Other survivors would go out and take what they needed from anybody who had anything. Predators would take many forms.

Billy's thoughts once again returned to their colony below the surface. He thought about it often.

"How do you think our people are doing down there?" he asked.

Sheppard shook his head. "I've been so occupied up here that I haven't thought much about them. That facility was so well constructed, so deep, that I'm sure they're fine."

"I just wish we could confirm that with a communication."

"We continue to listen for messages?" Sheppard asked.

"Our receptors are aimed directly toward their communications array."

"Then we have to assume that the fault is in their ability to send messages. My first assumption would be that their communication array has been destroyed."

"Why wouldn't they simply have replaced or repaired the array?" Billy asked.

"The next assumption is that they didn't have the equipment necessary to make the repairs."

"No, that's not the way Joshua operates. Every plan has a backup, and there's backup for every piece of equipment and all supplies. He probably even has a backup for the backup for the backup."

"Then logically we would next look at their ability to get to the surface. If there was a collapse or partial collapse of the elevator or—"

Billy's personal communication device beeped. He thought about ignoring it, but realized the message was coming from the control centre.

"Billy here."

"We just received a message from the away team. There's been an incident on the ship."

"Incident? What kind of incident?" Billy demanded.

"They didn't say, but they're returning to the station immediately."

"I'm coming down. Get them on the radio so I can find out more details," Billy said.

"I'm sorry, but they dropped over the far side of Earth and they're out of communication range."

"How long before we can get them on the radio?"

"Five to seven hours."

"And they gave no more details about the incident on the ship?"

"No, sir. Nothing more."

"How long before they dock?" Billy asked.

"Another two hours after they re-establish communication."

"Thank you. Keep me informed if there are any new developments. Out."

CHAPTER THIRTEEN

YEAR 1 AAE-DAY 38

"I want you to wait right here," Billy said to Sam as they stopped at the door to the clinic.

Sam nodded. "Nobody in and nobody out without your permission. Especially not the young lady."

"Thanks."

Billy had already developed a rapport with Sam. Sam seemed to be able to read him and follow orders almost without being asked. That was both reassuring and troubling at the same time.

Billy entered. It was completely quiet. Christina, sitting beside the bed, gave him a smile that helped to brighten the dimly lit room. In bed was Jennie. Her eyes were closed. She looked to be asleep but most likely was just sedated.

"How is she doing?" Billy asked quietly.

"She's fine . . . now."

They had both been there when she was taken off the

ship, screaming and crying and fighting to get free, held firmly in Ivan's viselike grip. For a few seconds, Billy had assumed Ivan was the cause of her distress. Jennie was like a wild animal, and the other members of the crew were obviously distressed. Even Amir, who was always calm, reliable, joking around and funny, had shaking hands—although not shaking badly enough to interfere with a perfect docking.

"Have you seen these?" Christina pulled up the sleeve on Jennie's nightgown. There, clear to the eye, were four long, distinct bruises.

"It's on both arms," Christina said. "Those are finger marks where Ivan was holding her. Did he have to be that rough with her?"

"I haven't talked to him yet," Billy said.

He had spoken to everybody else after Jennie was sedated and transported to the medical clinic. They had all told basically the same story: Jennie had been very calm and quiet at the beginning of the mission, rarely talking, except for a few exchanges related to her job. Then she'd become a bit more agitated. She couldn't seem to settle down, and she would go from person to person repeating the same information and comments and questions, her speech becoming faster and faster. Jason said that it was like she was doing laps. And then, finally, she tried to leave the ship.

She was in the process of undoing a hatch when she was discovered. They tried to calm her, talk with her, but finally they had to physically intervene to stop her. At last, Ivan had to intervene.

The door opened and one of their doctors entered. His name was Saul, and after Billy he was the oldest of the children. Somehow, a sixteen-year-old doctor seemed stranger than kids that age or younger filling other roles.

"How is our patient doing?" Saul asked.

"I was hoping you could tell us," Billy said.

"She's stable and sedated."

"What do you think happened?" Christina asked.

"I'm no psychiatrist, but judging from the reports it sounds as though she had a psychotic break, probably caused by an anxiety disorder complicated by sleep deprivation."

"Could you put that in simpler terms?" Billy asked.

"She got really scared, couldn't sleep, and went sort of crazy because of it. That's when she decided to try to leave the ship."

"Will she be all right?" Christina asked.

"Again, I really haven't had much training in this area, but there's no reason to believe that she can't make a full recovery. I think you, with your training, would be better able to make that assessment."

"And what will be done while she's recovering?" Billy asked.

"She'll remain in sick bay."

"She'll be under supervision," Billy said. "I don't want her left alone for even a minute."

"It will be arranged."

"It already has been arranged," Billy responded.

Without another word, they all understood the reasons. If she had managed to open the hatch of the ship she would have killed everyone on board. Doing the same thing on the station might result in all of them dying.

"I'd like to talk to her," Billy said.

"I can administer a medication to bring her around."

"No, you won't do that," Christina said. They both turned to her. "She needs to sleep. She's gone through enough without having more drugs shot into her. I'll stay right here by her side. I'll watch her until she wakes up."

"Okay," Billy said. "I've posted Sam outside to provide, um, support. I'm going to talk to Ivan."

Billy tapped on the frame of the passage leading into the ship. Ivan looked up from his tablet.

"May I come in?" Billy asked.

Ivan motioned for him to come. "How is the girl?" he asked.

"Asleep . . . well, sedated."

"Good. That was necessary. I wish that I'd had some medication out there on the mission. It would have made it more comfortable for everybody on the ship."

"Especially Jennie," Billy said.

"She was beyond comforting or reasoning with," Ivan said.

"Can you tell me what happened, please?"

"The girl became increasingly erratic, agitated, and irrational. I knew there was an issue, but I didn't expect her to try to take a spacewalk without a suit."

"So you knew something was happening?"

"It was hard to miss—although most of them did seem

to miss it. Even when she was trying to open the door they all acted so . . . so strangely *themselves.*"

"What do you mean?" Billy asked.

"They all just stood there, watching, talking to her, but nobody intervened. It was as if they weren't aware that she was going to kill us all," Ivan said.

"They all knew the consequences."

"But nobody acted. I grabbed her, pulled her away from the hatch with one hand, and completed the seal, cranking it back with the other."

"How close was it?" Billy asked.

"Two more cranks. A few more seconds. How did you know?"

"Know what?" Billy asked.

"That this was going to happen."

"I didn't have any idea or I wouldn't have let her on the mission. But I was concerned."

"Concerned enough to send me along. That's why you sent me on the mission, wasn't it?" Ivan asked.

That wasn't the reason, but it could only strengthen Billy's hand to have Ivan think this.

"I thought your presence might be, shall we say, reassuring."

"Why didn't you give me more warning about her condition?" Ivan asked.

"I didn't suspect anything that severe was even a possibility. We all owe you a big debt of gratitude."

"I'm just surprised I didn't see it coming better. These kids are just so . . . different. I think their lack of reaction, just standing there watching her try to kill us all, was more troubling to me than what she was doing," Ivan said. "Psychotic breakdown I understand. Passively watching somebody try to kill both herself and you is something I just don't get."

"It's taken me a while to get used to them myself," Billy admitted.

"They're just kids. You're all just kids. I just can't believe that anybody was crazy enough to ever think this was a good idea."

"That so-called crazy person is the smartest man who ever lived," Billy said.

"You can be smart and crazy. The two aren't mutually exclusive."

"Joshua and his genius are the reason we're all still alive," Billy said, defending his friend.

"The reason we are alive is one thing. Let's not make him also the reason we're all going to die."

Billy gave him a questioning look.

"I've been reading a great deal about Joshua Fitchett." He pointed down at the tablet. "He was a genius, but he was never married, never had children. In fact he never *was* a child. He was born an adult, so he doesn't understand these children."

"These children weren't children either. They were raised differently," Billy explained.

"They were raised differently, but that doesn't change the fact that they are still children. You don't understand that because you think Fitchett understood. He didn't."

"And you do?"

"I understand that if you push these children too hard or expect too much they'll break down, just like that girl did."

"Her name is Jennie."

"I know her name."

"She has bruises on her arms where you grabbed her," Billy said.

"That wasn't my intent, but it also isn't my concern. I did what needed to be done. I'll always do what needs to be done."

"How many times have you done what needed to be done?" Billy asked.

Ivan looked Billy straight in the eyes, sizing him up. "Are you asking how many people I've killed?"

Billy nodded.

"I've killed exactly the number of people who needed to be killed. Not one more. And you?"

Billy didn't answer right away. He thought about not answering at all.

"I've killed people. Probably some of them didn't need to be killed, but I thought they did at that instant. I always thought I'd rather be wrong than dead."

"Probably wise. For what it's worth, I've never killed a child before," Ivan said.

"But you would if you had to."

"Of course. Wouldn't you?"

Again Billy hesitated. Then he nodded ever so slightly in agreement. "If I had to. I just hope it doesn't come to that."

"More precautions need to be taken."

"Such as?"

"For starters, all external hatches need to be secured so that it is impossible for them to be opened without authorization."

Billy hadn't thought of that. "Go on."

"You are protected as much as possible from external forces, but there is no protection from internal forces. I will give it more thought and present you with a report, if you want."

"That would be good. But nothing happens without my approval. Understood?"

Ivan laughed. "I understand. I also understand why you need to remind me over and over that you're in charge. I'm not questioning your authority, but I will continue to question your decisions if I think you're wrong."

"I'd appreciate you telling me what you think needs to be changed."

"That's good to hear, because none of these kids are going to tell you. They seem very good at following orders but not necessarily that good at thinking."

"They can think. They just don't question. They don't challenge. I'm sure you have no problems with questioning things," Billy said.

"None. I try to be very direct about things. Speaking of which, when were you planning on telling me about the colony?" Ivan asked.

"Colony?" Billy wasn't giving anything away.

"Please. I know all about Fitchett and the Idaho colony. Why did you try to keep that particular piece of information from me?"

Billy didn't have a clear answer to that. "Did Tasha tell you?"

"Tasha is far too clever to give away information, but as I said, these are just children. I heard them talking when they were unaware I was nearby. You know, in some ways, they aren't just children but very naïve children. Did any of them have any real life experiences?"

"Their lives were very protected. That's why they still need to be protected," Billy said.

"And do you think they need to be protected from me?"

"They need to be protected from everything. That's my job."

"You almost lost five members of your crew today, so it sounds as though you need some help with that job, and I'm volunteering. I guess the only drawback to that offer is that you still don't trust me."

"Do you trust me?" Billy asked.

"Probably to about the same extent you trust me. But, realistically, keeping you in control and alive keeps me alive. I trust you to do that, and you can trust me to help you do it." Ivan got to his feet. "I'd like to see Jennie."

"She's not awake."

"I'd like to be there when she does wake up," Ivan said.

Billy wasn't sure if this was a caring thing or if Ivan was simply saying what he thought was a caring thing. Either way, they'd go to see her. Either way, neither did trust the other, but both could pretend for now.

CHAPTER FOURTEEN

YEAR 1 AAE-DAY 65

The common room was filled with chairs. Project members were sitting and chatting, or relaxing and listening to the quartet that was performing on an elevated stage. The violin, cello, bass, and viola played a Bach melody. Billy didn't know this piece—or basically anything that they played—but he knew he liked it. It was soothing and helped produce a calm atmosphere.

Up above the seats, above the quartet, there were people floating through the air. It was almost magical as they spun and twisted and twirled, pushing off the walls and ceiling to propel themselves around the room. Most were alone but some were in pairs, and they almost looked as though they were dancing. Not surprisingly, the very best were all members of the spacewalk team. They were the ones who went outside in spacesuits and did maintenance work on the exterior of the station.

Though they were all enjoying the music and the activity, they weren't here for a concert. Billy had called a meeting, an opportunity for all of them to get together and share information. That way he could control the information that was being passed on. There would always be conversation among people but giving them information tended to control gossip and rumours. As well, he would try to focus the group on positives and read the mood to see how people were feeling. The meetings would take place monthly from this point on. If all went as planned, this would be the first of potentially 120 meetings over the next ten years.

Both Ivan and Sam stood at the very back of the room by two separate doors, their backs to the wall. Sheppard had mentioned to Billy that this was what the security forces always did at their compound in Switzerland. Here, there was no need for security against an outside force, but the two fell easily into that role. Sam had become a favourite of many of the young people—a jovial, smiling uncle who always seemed to have a joke to share. Ivan still mainly wore that same stoic, serious look and spent time with only a few of the children, including Tasha, with whom he played chess almost daily. For most others his seriousness was off-putting. Ivan was like the strange uncle who made everyone nervous. Lars, the only one with any experience in space, had become an important asset and had taken on work around the station. He was even scheduled to pilot the next Earth survey, and it was agreed that he would be part of a three-person rotation with Amir and Tasha. He seemed as straightforward as Sam was friendly and Ivan serious. It would have been so much simpler if the three of them hadn't arrived, but they were here for the long run and had to be watched, understood, managed, controlled, and utilized.

Billy continued to watch everyone very carefully. He wasn't going to make the mistake he'd made with Jennie with anybody else.

Each month, each person on the station was required to meet separately with Saul and also with Billy and Christina. Billy valued the input given to him by the doctor concerning "mental health symptoms," but he valued Christina's opinion much more. Saul understood medical issues and conditions, but his understanding of people was as limited as the rest of the children's.

As the quartet ended its piece, the audience offered polite applause, and that was the cue for Billy to start. He walked up to the podium and shook hands with the four musicians. They then moved off stage with their instruments as those in the air and on their feet all took seats.

Joining Billy at the front were Christina, Professor Sheppard, and Jennie. Jennie was going to share the findings of the latest Earth survey. She hadn't been on that mission—and had only lately been allowed to work unsupervised—but she was the person who, along with Sheppard, had analyzed the data. Jennie's appearance at the meeting would let people know that she was not only well now but rehabilitated and fulfilling her function. And in this small, interconnected world, it was important to demonstrate that everyone—no matter what problems they had or what they might face in the future—was valued and cared for.

Jennie was seated, waiting her turn to speak. Billy took to one knee beside her chair so he could quietly speak to her.

"How are you feeling?"

"Nervous. Really nervous."

"You don't look it at all. I'll tell you something if you promise not to tell anybody." He leaned in even closer. "Talking in front of an audience scares me to death."

"Really?"

"Really." It was a reassuring lie that he was offering her. "But I try not to let people know, because I figure they need to see me calm and in control."

"That is how they see you," she said. "That's how I see you."

"Then it's working. That's our secret, so don't let the others know. I'm going to get the meeting started and have you report almost immediately, because waiting is probably the hardest part. And thanks for doing this."

"Thank you for believing in me again," she said.

Billy gave her a questioning look. "You have that wrong. Nobody ever stopped believing in you."

Billy walked to the front of the stage and waited. It took no more than a few seconds for the crowd to notice and respond, greeting him with complete silence and attention. Every single person in the station was present, with the exception of Lars and Jason, who had agreed to stay and monitor the control room. Even then they were watching by closed-circuit television. Billy was starting to think that Jason lived in that control room. He had thought about ordering him to spend less time there, but really, his presence was reassuring to Billy. Jason had a certain calmness to him. He was in the control room and he was in control. It sort of fit.

"Good afternoon, and thank you all for joining us," he began.

"It's not like we had someplace else to go," Amir replied from the audience, and there was polite laughter.

Billy was pleased by that response. He was trying to encourage the crew to become more relaxed, more playful, and to volunteer suggestions and criticism. So far the response had been very positive.

"We are now sixty-five days into our mission," he began, "and we have successfully completed some of the most difficult steps on our journey. We've left the planet, travelled to and from the moon, and have taken up residence in our new home. By all reports, our home is solid and safe and able to go on providing for us. We have food and water, air and warmth. This is where we will wait out the storm brewing on the planet below us."

Billy had, with Sheppard's and Christina's help, written out that opening and then memorized it. Reading from a script wouldn't work when he wanted to look straight out at them, look them in the eyes and exude confidence. He thought through the next part of his speech.

"I have such confidence in all of you. Over the days and months and years to come, we will use our skills to keep the station and ourselves alive. More than simply living, we will thrive. We will grow as individuals and as a group. We will develop our abilities, learn new skills, and teach each other new things. We will take on any new challenges as they arise and solve them. I'm looking forward not just to the time when we shall again return to the surface of the planet, but to the time we will have playing, laughing, and growing up together. I am proud to be a member of this crew and honoured to be its leader. Thank you all."

The audience broke into applause. Billy turned to Christina and she gave him a subtle nod to signal her approval. It was now her turn to speak. Christina rosc and took Billy's place at the front. While it had taken Billy a long time to memorize his speech, it had taken Christina only a few minutes.

"I'm so pleased to have got to know so many of you so well. I started on this mission believing in the abilities of everybody here. Having got to know you all over the time on the surface and the past two months, it's gone beyond believing to really knowing. I trust you all with my life, as I know we all trust each other with our lives. I want you to know that my door is always open to anybody who wants or needs to talk to me about anything. I'm here for you the way you're all here for me. We're more than just a crew, we are a family."

She emphasized that last word with purpose. She and Billy were both very aware that family was something most of these children had never really known.

"We all need to care for each other. To show consideration, kindness, and love. You are all special members of this large extended family. Thank you all so much."

Again they applauded—possibly, Billy thought, louder than they had for his own speech. That was good. Christina's message was meant to be reassuring. She remained at the front, as she had one more thing to do.

"We're here on this home while we wait for our old home to become ready for our arrival. There have been many questions about the state of the planet below us. We all know the length of our stay in space will be determined by those conditions. Rather than paraphrase the findings of our Earth surveys, we thought it would be best for you to hear this information directly from the person most capable of understanding and interpreting it. Could Jennie please come forward?"

There was more applause. Jennie didn't immediately get to her feet. For a second Billy thought he had miscalculated again and put her in a situation she couldn't handle. He had a terrible vision of Ivan rushing forward to try to contain her thrashing limbs and bring her to the medical clinic so she could be sedated. When Jennie finally rose and walked to the edge of the stage, Billy felt a palpable rush of relief.

"Good afternoon," she began. "I'm a scientist and not really that comfortable talking to a large group of people." She turned slightly to face Billy, Christina, and Sheppard and gave them a reassuring smile. "We have launched two missions to undertake a complete survey of the planet below. I was a member of the first of those surveys, and unfortunately that mission had to be cut short before it was complete." She paused. "I take responsibility for this—the limited data. It means that we have only two samples, one of them incomplete, to compare changes and make predictions on a planetary scale. Fortunately, over two-thirds of the first survey was complete, and I will focus on those swaths of the planet and hope we can project from there."

Billy had already been fully briefed by both Jennie and Sheppard, so he knew what was going to be reported. He was far more interested in how Jennie was going to handle the pressure of giving the report and the reaction of the audience to hearing this information.

Jennie turned back around. "Would it be possible for Professor Sheppard to join me?"

That wasn't the plan, but he slowly got to his feet and moved forward with uneasy steps. Billy couldn't help but notice how old he looked relative to everybody else in the room. He had done well adapting to life in space, though—better than many of the young crew.

"I was hoping that you could explain to them the issue of making predictions based on the limited samples," Jennie said. "Could you explain it to them the way you explained it to me?"

"Certainly. I want you all to think of yourselves as standing on railroad track. In the far distance you see a train."

Billy hadn't heard this story before and leaned forward to listen. He knew what a great teacher Sheppard was—they still had a regular appointment to meet three or four times a week, and often met more informally any time Billy required more information. Sheppard often reminded Billy of something Einstein once said. It was a quote that Joshua Fitchett was also fond of: "If you can't explain it to a six-year-old, you don't understand it yourself."

"At first glance, you can't tell the speed of the train, or if, in fact, it's even moving. Continuing to stand there, taking more samples, gives you a better indication of movement and speed. With each sample, each mental picture taken of the train, you can predict those factors more accurately. Does that make sense?"

There were mumbles of agreement and a nodding of heads in the audience.

"We have undertaken two surveys of the planet. We have analyzed the data over two time frames so we have some idea about the change between the two. So you might say we have seen the train on two occasions. With each successive survey over the coming months and years, we will be able to make more reliable predictions. With that said, Jennie, could you begin your report?"

There was more polite applause for the professor, who once again took a seat.

"We used a variety of methods—including radar, radio waves, and laser—to monitor the density and composition of the cloud cover as well as penetrating to the surface to measure temperature, the ice caps on both poles, and weather patterns, including wind speeds and precipitation. The most reassuring news is that those patterns are all within the accepted parameters of the predictions made prior to the actual collision. In other words, the Earth is acting and reacting as expected and predicted.

"Surface temperatures have plummeted and both ice caps have migrated at a highly accelerated rate. In the south, the ice shelves have extended hundreds of kilometres into the ocean, and in the north heavy snows and the beginning of glacial activity have extended up to eight hundred kilometres southward in the interiors of both North America and the Eurasian continent. There are maps available on our computer system to give clear illustrations of this."

A few people pulled out hand-held devices and were probably pulling up those images.

"There has been, as expected, complete cloud coverage of the entire planet. And while the cloud seems to be less dense than predicted, there is no sunlight penetrating to the surface of the planet."

"Is that coverage spread equally over the entire planet?" somebody asked from the audience.

"The dispersal is still ongoing, spreading north to south, with the heaviest being in the north at this time. We assume that this trend will eventually lead to equalization through the world, with only minor variations in density and composition."

"You said it was less dense than predicted," Saul stated. "What impact does that have on the long-term prognosis?"

"It's too early to tell," Jennie said. She turned slightly to face Sheppard. "Professor?"

"Yes, while we would not hazard a guess that this would lead to an early return, it certainly doesn't indicate a longer waiting period."

"We believe that the density issue is a result of both oceanic impacts, which threw massive quantities of water into the atmosphere and increased precipitation, both snow and rain, cleansing the atmosphere of contaminants."

"What would the surface look like right now?" a girl named Olive asked.

"That depends on the specific location."

"I was thinking of India. I was raised in a collective in India."

"I don't have that specific information available, but if you speak to me later I'll be able to provide it."

"Does that go for all of us?" a young boy asked.

"Yes, of course. All are welcome. I'll talk to everybody."

There was a rumble of response as people talked among themselves. Obviously there were concerns about a specific area because they'd all left people behind. They wouldn't have been natural family, but they were still family in one way or another.

"Throughout the planet there would be a fairly constant twilight appearance, even at noon," Jennie said. "Areas that are closer to moderating bodies of water, most significantly oceans, and those locations farther south or north trending toward the equatorial regions would be warmer. Areas around the equator would be experiencing moderate temperatures, not much different from the constant temperature we have set on the station."

Jennie continued to give more information, some of it very technical, and more and more people were following along on their hand-held devices. This part of the briefing was more complicated than Billy either could, or needed to, understand.

Finally she finished and went back to her seat, rewarded with applause. Her expression was equal parts relieved and happy. It was now Billy's turn again.

"Before we adjourn the meeting are there any questions that can be answered by us or perhaps others in the audience?" he asked.

This component of the meeting had its risks. Unscreened and unpredicted questions could lead in directions that might be problematic. He knew this but felt that the necessity of answering questions outweighed the risks involved.

There was no response at first, and then one hand and a second and third and fourth went up. Billy deliberately went to Tasha because he could count on her for a question that wouldn't be too emotionally loaded.

"Can you tell us the number of casualties and survivors on the planet?"

He had expected that question, even if he hadn't expected it from Tasha.

Billy turned to the professor. "Could you answer that one, please?"

Sheppard got up and on unsteady feet came back to the front to stand beside Billy.

"We are now over two months past the event. It would be fairly certain that up to 95 percent of all species have now reached the point at which they are either extinct or at the very least no longer viable. The primary exceptions would be those scavenger species that can feed on carcasses for sustenance, as well as those in deep-earth or deep-sea locations that provide some degree of—"

"I meant people," Tasha said, cutting him off. "How many people are left?"

Sheppard knew the answer but felt a level of discomfort

saying it. There wasn't much choice but to be honest. "Of the human inhabitants of the planet at the time of the event, approximately 4.5 percent would still be alive."

"How many people is that?" somebody else asked.

"If we assume there were 9 billion people alive on the planet, there are now approximately 2 million people left, with an error factor of 15 percent nine out of ten times."

There was a murmur of response, and Saul raised his hand.

"Dr. Saul," Billy said. He always tried to refer to him and the other doctor—"Dr. Sarah"—with their official title.

"I've been told that efforts to make contact with our Idaho colony have not been successful. Is that correct?"

"There has been no contact as of yet. We are assuming that their radio array was severely damaged in the asteroid showers and they have not, as yet, been able to facilitate repairs," Billy said.

"Or that—"

"That is the most likely scenario and the only one we are prepared to entertain at this time," Billy said, cutting him off.

"And if we continue to have no contact for an extended period of time, will you then consider other options?"

"We'll cross that bridge if and when we need to," Billy said. "We will, as always, share all information with everybody as it becomes available. We're all in this together. Let's call an end to the meeting. Thank you all for your time and caring."

PART II

CHAPTER FIFTEEN

YEAR 4 AAE-DAY 137

Ivan was quietly working on the resistance apparatus—one that relied on elastics—in a corner of the room to simulate weightlifting. He'd have preferred old-fashioned free weights, but in zero gravity there was no point.

He glanced over at Professor Sheppard, who was pedalling away on the stationary bike. Sheppard acknowledged him with a little wave and smile as he continued to pedal, and Ivan gave him the merest of nods in return.

Each person on the station, from the youngest to the oldest, had an exercise program that had been designed specifically for them. Over the more than three years they had now been on the station, these programs, regularly updated to acknowledge fitness goals and add variety, acted to keep them fit, and to compensate for the physical effects of space travel and living gravity-free. Though the special shoes kept the crew members anchored to the floor of the station, their bodies were still affected by the lack of gravity, and three years was a long time to be living without it. They were continually monitored for changes in organ function and bone density. Of course, Sheppard, by this point in his life, would have potentially had troubles with both even on the surface, Ivan thought, but on the station this was critical.

Pedalling on the exercise bicycles also had a secondary benefit. The station's engineers had hooked the bikes directly into the station's batteries. It seemed to make the crew happy, Ivan had noted, to know that the effort they put into spinning the bicycles' wheels was converted to energy to power the station's systems.

The station's solar panels were not as effective now as they had been in the beginning. Over the past three years a constant flow of microscopic debris and micro-meteorites had taken almost 10 percent of the panels' capacity out of production. Plans called for teams to go out and do spacewalks to repair those panels on a periodic basis. While this wasn't crucial—the remaining panels, especially augmented with the pedal power, were producing more than enough energy to meet the demands of the station—it would not have been wise to allow things to deteriorate further. Billy was, as Ivan had observed, somebody who liked to have a healthy surplus of everything.

Of course, Ivan suspected that there were other reasons for Billy's decision to send out the repair crews. When crew members were idle they were more likely to experience mental health problems than when they were working around the station. Although everyone had a job to do, it wasn't possible to engage them fully at all times. Sending the repair crew outside would give them purpose. It would also give them practice and help them to develop skills they might need if they ever had to make a really crucial repair. Better to learn and refine those skills now so they could have them if needed later.

Following their designated fitness routine was another way to help the crew occupy down time. But of all the residents of the station, Ivan was the only one who would not follow his training program. He pursued a fitness regimen he'd chosen himself, and refused to allow himself to be tested. Ivan had spent his life knowing what was going on around him without anybody getting to know what was going on inside of him. He wasn't about to change that now. His isolation had kept him alive so far, and he planned to pursue that course for as long as possible.

Ivan trusted Billy even less than Billy trusted Ivan. And for good reason. Even before the asteroid was known, even before the International Space Agency was founded, Ivan had lived in the shadows in the spy-versus-spy world of international espionage. Knowing who your enemies were was difficult, shifting, uncertain. Identifying your friends was simple, straightforward, and easy—you had no friends, only alliances that came and went. The person you could trust was yourself, and nobody else.

Up here in the closed system everything was crystal clear to Ivan. Billy held power. He was now an ally, but alliances didn't necessarily last. The other potential power brokers were the professor, Christina, Sam, and Lars. Ivan kept a mental dossier on all of them.

The professor was the simplest for Ivan to understand. He'd been watching him closely for years, studying the man at the top of the organization he worked for. He was certain that Sheppard could be trusted. He appeared to be without guile, incapable of hiding things, and handicapped by two basic flaws, honesty and integrity. He would be incapable of doing what needed to be done in a time of crisis. Besides, he was old and frail, and would inevitably become older and frailer before he finally died. Lastly, Ivan didn't believe Sheppard was capable of sacrificing parts to save the whole. If there was a difficult decision or action needed, he didn't think Sheppard would be up to it.

Then again, Sheppard had managed to get himself to the top of the most powerful organization in the history of the planet. He had somehow got himself safely up here in space when so many billions below had died. Somehow he had survived. Either he was one of luckiest men in history, or there was something more going on beneath that bumbling, innocent persona. Was Sheppard an innocent, or was he simply acting innocent? Had he been so skilful a manipulator that he'd been able to control everything without anybody becoming suspicious of his actions?

The door slid open and Christina walked in. Ivan's focus turned to her, although nobody who might have been watching him would have known that. He had a way of seeing out of the corner of his eyes while continuing to look straight ahead.

In some ways Christina was almost as straightforward as the professor. She seemed to be a hybrid member of this mission. She had much of the innocence of the other special children on the ship, but there was something more. It wasn't just that she was smart; she seemed to have extraordinary intuitive capabilities. And the time she spent with Billy also influenced her, and was a factor in her importance as a power player on this mission. They were partners, together a great deal of the time, and Christina was probably the only person Billy told everything to. That meant she was careful around Ivan and would report to Billy anything she saw or heard about him that concerned her. Ivan was always particularly cautious around her.

The most straightforward part of Christina was her loyalty. She and Billy could not be separated or leveraged against each other. In any situation, she would undoubtedly take Billy's side and be prepared to give up her life to do so. She didn't just trust Billy. She wasn't just a loyal soldier. She was his life partner, and she loved him. Love made everything else irrelevant. That's what Ivan had observed in people.

Ivan was in a simultaneously strong and weak position when it came to understanding love, because he had never felt it. Objectively he could stand outside the feeling and study it, but he knew that there was an element of the emotion he might never fully comprehend. He knew he liked certain people, had a fondness or an attachment, and would prefer them to stay rather than leave, but he had never experienced love as they described and demonstrated it. He had, in his youth, wondered about that. Perhaps he hadn't found the right person. He listened to music and read poetry and novels to see if it could be captured, like scooping a handful of water from a basin, but it couldn't. The more he studied it, the more he realized it was simply not within his range of emotions. Perhaps there was some small section of the brain that contained the capacity for love, or a single gene on a long strand of DNA. Regardless, he didn't possess it. The concepts of "head over heels" or "falling" or being "helpless" were beyond his potential to experience, but certainly not beyond his understanding. He didn't have to experience it to know how it affected people. Love could be a strength, but he'd also seen it as a weakness, the downfall of so many people. Ultimately, Christina's love for Billy—and Billy's love for her—were weapons or weaknesses that Ivan could wield against them if necessary.

Christina was talking to Sheppard. She glanced at her watch—for the third time in the last few minutes. Ivan had not only noted it but figured he knew what it meant and what to do about it. He put down the equipment, picked up his towel, and walked over to where the two of them stood.

"How long do I have?" he asked Christina.

"I, um, don't know what you mean," she stammered.

"It doesn't matter," Ivan said. "I know it's happening in just a few minutes."

Ivan made his way through the door and into the common room. He wanted to cross the entire station and get to the ship that was his home before the—Just then the alarm sounded. Everybody across the station stopped whatever they were doing, paused for a microsecond, and then rushed off to their emergency responsibility.

Ivan had two advantages over everybody else: he knew

this was coming, and he also knew that it was a drill and not a real emergency.

Two or three times each month they had an emergency drill. The specific time and date of these drills was decided by only one person so that everybody else would react as if they were real. Christina was that person. Not even Billy or the professor would know whether a drill was real. Andrea, who led the fire brigade, was also always in the dark, and her team had to react to each alarm as if it were a real danger.

Ivan, always watchful, had seen Christina repeatedly checking her watch and had come to his own conclusion. After all, it wasn't as if she had a need to check it that often.

Ivan got to the hatch separating two sections of the ship just as two people were getting ready to close it down. He put his hand in the way and brushed them aside so he could step through, momentarily stopping them from performing their task. All around the ship hatches were being closed as the station was subdivided into seventeen separate airtight compartments. Other crew members readied firefighting equipment, manned communications stations, went to the medical stations, donned spacesuits for emergency spacewalks, and loaded launch and re-entry sequences into the ships docked at the five ports.

They were scrambling to be in position to react to an emergency, with two potential situations being most likely and most deadly. The first involved a rupture in the hull of the ship from either an internal explosion or an external collision. Externally, the station was always vulnerable to being hit by a chunk of space debris, and a puncture would result in the station leaking atmosphere and absorbing the extreme heat or cold of space. Internally, there were numerous chemical operations that could potentially cause an explosion if mishandled, including those designed to filter air and produce water. Both rupture scenarios were unlikely but possible. The second great danger was fire. Smoke billowing into the closed system of the station would become deadly very quickly. It wasn't as if they could exit the station or throw open a window. With both deadly scenarios they needed to react as quickly as possible, and by sealing off sections of the station they could limit the damages and casualties.

The last line of defence if there was a catastrophic problem was the ships. Each ship was a potential escape pod. Even if the station couldn't be saved, the passengers still needed to be. Each ship was supplied with emergency rations and water, and had the capacity to generate oxygen. They were programmed with the necessary launch sequences to get them away from the station and the re-entry profiles to get them down to the surface.

The re-entry profile was crucial; it wouldn't do them any good to escape from a blazing or dying station if they couldn't get down to the planet. Perhaps life on Earth would be difficult or maybe even impossible, but the ships were not equipped to support life on an ongoing basis, not to the extent the space station did. The lifespan on board a ship was definitely limited. For that reason, a re-entry profile was recalculated each day and fed into the ships' navigation computers. If the trajectory was too low they'd bounce off Earth's atmosphere and rocket back into space. Lacking the fuel to make a further attempt, the passengers would eventually die from lack of food or water, or suffocate in an atmosphere that would become too contaminated for them to breathe. If the trajectory was too steep, the results would be equally fatal but far quicker. The ship would simply burn up or explode.

Part of determining the re-entry profile involved identifying the spots where the ships would land. They would all try to reunite on the surface—strength in numbers—and land at the location that was presently looking the most promising for survival. The entire Earth had been affected but some parts seemed to be recovering more quickly.

Ivan sprinted down the last corridor. He had to close the distance before the last hatch was shut, blocking him from his destination. While they were supposed to report to the nearest ship to take refuge, Ivan wanted his own ship—the ship that had originally brought him to the station, the place he now called home. Ivan was sure this was all a drill, but not so completely convinced that he didn't want to get there, just in case. This had nothing to do with any sentimental attachment. Aboard his ship were his gun, two hundred rounds of ammunition, and secretly stowed away so nobody knew, a crossbow he'd manufactured and a dozen bolts—arrows—that he'd made for it. If this was more than a drill he wanted to have those weapons at his disposal if they had to drop down to the surface.

He got to the hatch leading into his ship. Lars was there, looking anxious but still waiting, as Ivan had instructed, before sealing off the hatch.

"I didn't think you'd make it!" Lars yelled out.

"I was most of the way across the station."

Ivan went into the hatch and Lars followed immediately, slamming it shut and sealing them off from the rest of the station.

"I'm assuming this is just another drill," Lars said as he quickly turned the cranks to establish an airtight seal.

"Most certainly, but it was still important for me to practise returning here. It is good that you waited."

"That's what friends do for friends," Lars said.

That might have been the truth but it wasn't the reason. Ivan had no friends, and he knew that Lars wasn't stupid enough to think that Ivan was his friend. Ivan knew he was somebody Lars feared. Standing there at the hatch, certain that it was only a drill but with his adrenalin pumping, he must have wanted desperately to seal off the hatch, but he feared Ivan more than he feared any possible emergency. And Lars was right to be afraid, Ivan thought.

Safely sealed inside, Lars turned his attention to the computer. He fed in the launch sequence and then the reentry profile.

"So what now?" Lars asked.

"We wait."

"Did you smell any fire?" Lars asked.

"It's a drill."

"Or the dry burning smell of space?" Lars continued.

"Stop talking," Ivan said.

Lars pretended to zip his lips together.

They both knew that smell. There were little wisps of the vacuum of space that got trapped every time a ship docked with the station, and they were released when the locks were unsealed. Most people didn't notice it, or realize what it was if they did.

Over the intercom there was a stream of messages as each crew reported in to the central command. Continued reports of "locked," "stabilized," "section sealed," "ship prepared for escape" flowed across the channel. In the rush, Lars had forgotten to report their section. "Ship 1 sealed and ready, locked and loaded for escape."

After three years of living in close quarters, Ivan was tired of Lars. But while he certainly wasn't a friend, he was definitely an asset. He was one of only a few people qualified to pilot a ship, and the only one who was an adult. Ivan had befriended a number of the children—including Tasha, who was a fine pilot—but in the end he wanted an adult at the controls of any ship that was the foundation of keeping him alive. Ivan was capable of killing—quickly, efficiently, and basically without remorse or regret—but what he'd said to Billy years before was true: he had not killed one more person than he needed to. Still, there were times in the middle of the night, when Lars kept talking and talking, that Ivan would start to fantasize it might be necessary. He could simply place his hands around Lars's throat, apply pressure, and cut off his conversation and air supply as he slowly crushed his larynx. Really, though, on the whole, Lars was not a bad person to share a confined space with, he thought.

Ivan's feelings toward Lars weren't very different from Lars's feelings toward Ivan—or for that matter, the feelings running throughout the entire station. People forced to live in close proximity with no relief or escape started to feel conflict with each other. Even best friends needed a break, but there was almost no way to find a space to be separate. Billy and the professor were becoming aware of this.

The professor had told Billy about experiments done generations ago with laboratory rats placed in a closed living arrangement. The way the professor described it, it sounded a bit like the space station, with small, individual compartments connected by passageways.

At first the rats lived together in their little world in harmony. Then more and more rats were introduced into the closed space. With the increased numbers they were given increased food and water so that each received what it needed to live. What they didn't have was more space. The numbers increased but the area they lived in didn't. Harmony decreased as numbers increased, until the rats began to act more and more strangely and the society seemed to disintegrate. The guy who did the experiments called it a "behavioural sink." Some of the rats became overly aggressive. Some of them moved frantically, as though they were searching desperately for escape. Others withdrew and became almost immobile. Attacks took place, and there was cannibalism.

Billy knew the people on the station weren't rats, and he didn't expect anybody to start eating somebody else, but he couldn't deny that they were exhibiting some of the other symptoms. Some of the crew spent almost all of their time in their small sleeping compartments. Others became almost obsessive in their movements, roaming the station from one end to another as if they were looking for a way out, or at least a few square metres of space they'd never seen before. Some just sat or stood by portholes and peered down at the Earth or out into space. At times like that Billy was glad that he had taken Ivan's advice and had all the external hatches locked down so nobody could open one up. There were certainly more arguments, and Christina—along with the medical staff—had intervened to try to solve disputes, most of which seemed far too trivial to be causing so much distress. And really, if people hadn't been in such close quarters, the disputes probably wouldn't have escalated at all.

One way that Billy responded to the stress was by making changes in the sleeping arrangements. Some people complained about having to move, but a change was almost as good as a rest, and it would take time to build up annoyance with the habits of a new person.

Billy had also established a number of solitary cells—small spaces behind soundproof doors where people could spend an hour in isolation. These had to be booked ahead of time, and they were almost always booked for at least five weeks in advance.

Another issue that had begun to emerge had to do with procreation. Over the nearly three years they had all been on the station, many of the children had either begun to go through puberty or matured as teenagers. Naturally, the members of the crew had started to consider potential partners and pair off. It was common knowledge that ultimately they would be part of repopulating the planet—it was no accident that there were fifty males and fifty females on the ship. But that repopulation was not going to start aboard the ship. They had neither the space nor the resources to provide for a population boost.

What only a few people—Christina, Billy, and the two doctors— knew was that they had built in provisions for the possibility of new additions. The projections called for two, possibly three, babies to be born in the ten-year cycle of the station. Dr. Saul and Dr. Sarah had been trained in maternity care, childbirth, and pediatric medicine, and the ship had in its supplies the things babies and growing children would need.

They were now almost one-third of the way through a decade—this was still considered a reasonable estimate of the time they would spend in space. One-third complete was encouraging. Two-thirds still to go was not so encouraging. If there was tension and conflict now, it was hard to imagine how much worse it would become in the coming months and years, if for no other reason than because they all continued to grow. Larger people made spaces seem smaller.

A second alarm sounded—this one to signify the all-clear. Ivan had known the initial alarm was just a drill but still felt a sense of relief when he heard the all-clear.

He advanced to the hatch and began to turn the crank to break the seal and open it up. He wasn't finished before the smiling face of Sam appeared in the small window, peering in at him. He had to fight the urge to tighten the crank back up but continued until the hatch popped open.

"I wasn't able to make it back in time," Sam said. "Were you two going to take off without me?" As always there was a jovial, joking quality to his words and manner.

"Of course not," Ivan said. "We would have opened the hatch and risked our lives because you are so precious."

Sam gave him a slap on the back and laughed. That was how he reacted to everybody and everything. He was in a constant state of good humour. Ivan, of course, knew better than to believe it. Assassins were taught that the best way to catch their target unawares was to walk right up, offering a big smile, a friendly manner, and even an outstretched hand. Then you would "double-tap" your victim, putting the first bullet in through the forehead and the second through the top of the head as he collapsed.

Sam's true expressions and feelings were as hidden to others as Ivan's. The difference was that his mask was good humour. He was always helpful, always friendly, and he was liked by almost all the children on the station. He seemed to go out of his way to help Billy, offer advice, agree with his decisions. In private, Ivan had warned Billy about him, but he had the feeling that Billy hadn't needed the warning. He was pretty able to sort things out on his own.

While Sam didn't fool Ivan, he was still a threat. He was a trained killer. He had the skills and the attitude necessary to take a life, and he was the only person on the station potentially able to kill Ivan. Sam was part of the reason Ivan trained so hard to maintain his muscle mass and coordination. If there was an encounter between the two, he didn't want his lack of training to be the factor that led to his death.

Ivan went through the open hatch, leaving Sam and Lars behind. He had been harbouring a fear that the two of them were conspiring against him but had yet to see any proof to back it up. Regardless, if the two of them ever did try anything against him, he'd simply kill them and have more space of his own.

CHAPTER SIXTEEN

YEAR 4 AAE-DAY 186

Billy stood leaning over the railing, looking at the match going on below on the mats, which had been arranged for the common room. For the past year both Ivan and Sam had been teaching the entire crew different martial arts techniques, and they felt that it would be good if they could engage in a tournament. Activities to break up the time—something for people not only to participate in and watch, but to look forward to—were always beneficial to the morale of the station.

Billy had asked the two men to train people. Right now on the station there was no need for these skills, but when they returned to Earth, those same skills might mean the difference between life and death. It was important that the crew members know how to defend and protect themselves. There was no telling what they might eventually be confronted with on the surface, and Billy wanted them equipped with a range of survival skills.

Everybody on the station—including Billy—was taking part in the classes. Billy had enjoyed the opportunity to do something physical, and though he felt it would be a bad idea, as leader, to compete in the tournament, he enjoyed the training and the sparring. Ivan and Sam weren't necessarily the best teachers—or in Ivan's case, the most patient—but they were incredibly skilled. Billy would have paid money to see the two of them in a sparring session.

Originally Billy had taken his lessons from both Ivan and Sam. Ivan had a way of instructing—and then sparing with—his students to let them know he was in charge, that he could dominate. Billy didn't want that, and he certainly didn't want other members of the crew seeing it, so he had decided to work only with Sam.

There was a round of applause as a match ended—one of the younger girls had triumphed over another. The winner helped the loser to her feet. Ivan stepped onto the mat and gave a signal, and they both bowed as a sign of respect. Then they hugged and, holding hands, skipped off the mat and into the surrounding crowd, where they were greeted with more cheers. It was nice to see, but it certainly wasn't a demonstration of the killer instinct Billy had hoped this would encourage.

The next two contestants entered the ring—Jason and Brian. They were about the same age, but Jason was taller, much heavier, and much stronger than Brian. His work in communications involved mainly sitting, but that had not prevented him from growing into a thick-necked and wide-shouldered teenager. Brian was involved in the external repairs and maintenance of the station, so body control and agility were part of his training and everyday work. Both were wearing mandatory headgear as well as pads on their hands and feet to soften their blows.

Billy had sparred against both of them. Jason was straightforward power. Brian had more skill and used his agility and quickness to his advantage. Neither could have beaten Billy, but there was no telling who was going to win between the two of them. This was promising to be a very interesting match.

Sam walked to the centre of the mat and motioned for the two combatants to come forward. They entered the ring from opposite sides until they were only about a metre apart. The whole room fell quiet. Obviously Billy wasn't the only one who thought this was going to be interesting. The two contestants bowed toward Sam and then toward each other. Sam stepped to the side, and yelled a command, and Jason and Brian took up fighting postures. He yelled again and they began to move.

As expected, Jason lunged straight ahead, trying to use his size to his advantage. Brian sidestepped, sliding to the right, avoiding the rush, and then landed a blow to the side of Jason's head.

"Point, Brian!" Sam yelled out.

That was one of five points necessary for a victory.

Brian continued to circle around Jason. They both exchanged jabs and short kicks that were easily blocked. Jason was going to need to be patient and pick his spots. Brian executed a spinning kick, but Jason saw it coming.

He jumped forward, closing the distance, taking away the momentum of the blow, and instead smashed into Brian, sending him tumbling over backwards. Brian landed on his bottom and right off the edge of the mat, hitting the floor hard.

"Point, Jason!" Sam called out.

Brian got back to his feet instantly, practically bouncing back up. Jason moved in even more quickly and swept Brian's feet out from under him, sending him back down again. The audience roared in response.

"Point, Jason!" Sam said.

Again Brian bounced back up, and again Jason rushed him. This time Brian dropped down, and instead of running into him, Jason flipped over his shoulder, spinning and flying off the mat and landing on the floor with a tremendous thud. There was a gasp from the crowd.

Jason slowly got to his feet. There was blood running from his mouth. He spat and blood hit the floor. He screamed and rushed forward, and before Brian could react he bowled him over. The two of them rolled over and over exchanging punches!

Ivan and Sam leaped forward and grabbed, one each and pulled them apart. They continued to try to punch as they were separated. Ivan wrapped Jason in a bear hug, trapping his arms, and carried him away.

Billy had already come down from the balcony, practically hurtling down the stairs.

"Let them both go!" Billy ordered as he stood between the pair.

Sam and Ivan did as they were asked, releasing the fighters. There was complete silence as everybody watched, too stunned to say anything.

"Follow me," Billy ordered, and he turned around.

Jason and Brian, their heads down, trailed behind him. Ivan decided he was also going to go along, just in case. They headed into the conference room, and Billy took a seat at the top of the table.

"Sit," Billy ordered, and the two took seats on opposite sides. Ivan stood by the door.

"Would either of you two like to explain to me what just happened?" Billy asked.

Neither looked up from the table or offered an answer.

"You are two of my most trusted crew members," he said, "and as far as I knew, good friends."

Again, neither spoke or looked up.

"So you have no explanation? There's nothing you want to say to explain this behaviour?" Billy asked.

Jason shook his head. Brian stared straight ahead.

"People fight and they stop thinking," Ivan said. "It happens."

"Then maybe you both need to go to your quarters and . . . wait, you share quarters, don't you?"

"Yes, sir."

"Can you go there and not fight?" Billy asked.

"Yes, sir," Brian said, and Jason nodded.

"Go, now. I'll talk to you both later."

Ivan stepped aside to allow them out the door, which closed behind them.

"What happened out there?" Billy asked Ivan.

"Asha happened."

"What?"

"They both wish to be with Asha, and she has not been able to decide which should be her partner."

"And they thought that it would be decided by a fight?"

"They were not thinking, they were feeling. Isn't that what you want them to do more of?" Ivan questioned.

"Feeling, yes—not thinking, no." Billy shook his head. "But why should I expect anything less? Put a hundred teenagers or near-teenagers in a confined space for years and years and something is going to happen."

"It will get worse before it gets better," Ivan said.

Billy let out a big sigh. "You're right. I know that."

"They are humans, not robots."

"I'll talk to them both, as well as to Asha. Although I'm not sure what I'm supposed to say."

"You will think of something. In the meantime, I should go back out and help with the tournament."

Ivan exited, leaving Billy alone. He knew that all this was inevitable, that it was going to happen. Somehow he had hoped that their superior intelligence would result in superior behaviour. Maybe he should have been glad that it didn't. Maybe they did have more in them than simply following orders. All their training hadn't eliminated the human being within.

CHAPTER SEVENTEEN

YEAR 4 AAE-DAY 203

From the control room window, Billy, Christina, the professor, and Amir could see the four spacewalkers—or space flyers. Two were attached, tethered by lines to the station, while the other two wore jetpacks and shot across the open spaces between the panels. Throughout the station, wherever there was a porthole to peer through, there was a crowd gathered to watch. Trapped inside the station for so long, they were all experiencing a vicarious thrill in watching somebody leave the closed confines behind, to be free in infinite space. Everybody knew the spacewalkers were out there to do an important job, but it felt more like watching a sporting event or a ballet.

The focus of their work was an old array of solar panels attached to what had previously been the Russian space station. It was the oldest component of the cluster of stations and ships and satellites that had been cobbled together to form their refuge. The Russians had gone on using it well after it was set to be retired, and through a combination of guts, ingenuity, spare parts, duct tape, and binding wire, they had managed to keep it alive.

A great deal of what scientists knew about long-term space living had happened on that ship as the Russians had continually expanded the scope of what was thought possible. They had had cosmonauts and guest astronauts from various countries live in the station for up to eighteen months at a time. And in preparing for those international guests and their shuttles and ships, they had all learned to adapt and design their docking systems and hatches so that they could connect. Without those common connections, the work of putting all these pieces together never would have happened.

Below the station, past the four crew members working in space, was Earth—brownish-green, a hazy cloud of dust and dirt, smoke and soot, particles of the asteroid and the surface of the planet, all suspended in the sky. The curves of the planet disappeared around all the horizons they could see below them. Sometimes it felt as if they could just drop down and the planet would catch them.

Although the surface below was still hidden from view, there was hope. In the three years since the asteroid strike there had been thirty-seven complete surveys of the atmosphere and the planet below. For the first two years the news and the pattern had remained steady. With each successive mission the atmosphere had been found to contain more material; it was thicker and denser. Then a survey came back that showed a marginal, almost insignificant, decrease in atmospheric particles, particularly in the Northern Hemisphere, where levels had always been higher.

The results were discussed among the committee but not shared beyond those few members. There was no point in raising hope for something that was so insignificant. It might have been nothing more than a random sampling error. Then, the next month, results showed a further decrease—again, small but downward. Once could have been an error; twice, that was less likely, but it was still possible that it was an error or an anomaly. Two months did not a trend make.

It wasn't until the fourth consecutive result that the news was finally shared. The Earth was starting the process of cleaning itself, of clearing the atmosphere, of allowing the sun to penetrate just a little bit farther toward—though of course still not reaching—the surface. While this allowed a little bit of global warming, it was not enough to generate photosynthesis. The sun was still being reflected back into space thousands of metres above the surface.

Sometimes Billy stared down at the planet trying to imagine the surface. He knew it was barren, freezing cold everywhere except for the band around the equator, and devoid of animal or plant life, except perhaps deep within the recesses of the ocean.

Scattered in small enclaves across the planet were protected, embedded colonies of humans. Billy and his crew knew they were still down there and alive because they could pick up radio chatter. It was important to pick up real communication as opposed to the mindless automatic signals that still called out for help. Both types had decreased. Batteries had died on some of the automated systems. People had died in some of the colonies. They had called for help when none was possible, and they didn't have the provisions—whether food or fuel or shelter or water—to outlast the nuclear winter that now engulfed them.

Billy still wondered about their Idaho colony. He no longer wondered whether it had survived—he'd abandoned those fantasies after the first year had passed without contact. Now, after three years, he just wondered how they'd been killed. It must have been sudden. Despite all the odds against a direct hit, they had lost. Some powerful parcel of the asteroid must have smashed into their site, sending out rocks and a shock wave so severe that it travelled six hundred metres down the shaft and shattered their world.

In his mind he still had conversations with Joshua Fitchett, in the same way he had real conversations with the professor. Joshua had sent them into space because he'd wanted to have a backup plan if there was a direct hit—"Though the odds against the colony being destroyed are so astronomical I don't even want to talk about them," he had said. There were times, when it was quiet and Billy was alone, that he could almost swear he heard Joshua's voice.

Of course it was probably nothing more than the creaking and groaning of the station. Superheated by direct sunlight or super-frozen in the shade, the metal of the ship was continually expanding and contracting. It was eerie to think about it.

A burst of laughter erupted throughout the ship. One

of the jetpack spacewalkers, Raj, was putting on a show, spinning around as if he were dancing, the yellowish-white exhaust from one of the nozzles of his pack trailing behind him. He was spinning faster and faster . . . but the laughter turned to gasps when everybody realized this was not a game! One of his engines was jammed on and he was out of control! His limbs were fully spread out like the blades of a fan, his body helpless at the hub.

The second spacewalker with a jetpack, Elena, had seen, and two thick clouds of exhaust spewed from the nozzles of her pack as she flew toward him.

"Tell her not to get near!" Billy yelled. "Somebody radio out and—"

Before he could even finish giving the order they came together and the spinning limbs of the one smashed into the second. Both bounced away, one still spinning wildly and the second twirling but limp, like a rag doll. The exhaust on the second jetpack had stopped. Either stunned or unconscious, Elena had released the triggers and stopped the flow of fuel to her pack. Both of them, having picked up momentum through the impact, were drifting toward the outer limits of the "courtyard" created by the appendages of the station.

"Jason!" Billy barked into the intercom. "Have you been able to establish contact with either of them?"

"Negative. I've been trying since I saw the first problem and I couldn't get a direct connection to Raj. When I saw Elena going to assist I tried to warn her off but she didn't listen. She hasn't answered since the impact."

"Get me a direct link with the two tethered spacewalkers," Billy ordered.

The two of them, working intently on the solar panel, were turned away and hadn't even noticed the fate of the other two.

He then turned to Amir. "Get a ship ready for launch."

"But how will that help?" Amir asked.

"You'll retrieve them if necessary," Billy said.

"How would we do that?"

Billy was flustered. "I don't know. Maybe you'll have to nudge them back toward the ship."

Amir looked stunned. Billy turned to the professor.

"That's a long shot," Sheppard said. "Most likely the collision would shatter the spacesuit."

"Do any of you have another suggestion?" Billy asked.

Amir, Christina and Sheppard shook their heads.

"Ship 1, Lars's ship, would be best," Amir suggested. "It's the smallest and most manoeuvrable."

"Then get Lars and the ship ready for launch. Stay docked until you are given the command to go."

Amir rushed from the room, already yelling into his com-link to locate Lars and alert a crew to the potential undocking and launch.

"Go ahead, you're connected!" Jason said.

Billy took a half second to gather his thoughts and his words. "Hello, Brian and Asha, this is Billy. Do you read me?"

"Affirmative," they both said.

"I need you to abandon your task."

"We're almost finished."

"You're finished now. We have a situation. Turn around, please."

They both complied and there was a gasp as they saw the still-spinning spacewalker.

"What's happening?" Brian screamed.

"Is he all right? What can we do?" Asha demanded. Her voice was calmer than Brian's.

"There has been a collision between Raj and Elena. You can help, but I need you to turn your eyes away from Raj and toward Elena. Look to your right and down. I need you to locate her."

Awkwardly they turned, pushing off against the station to gain an angle change.

"I see her!" Brian said.

"We've been unable to make contact with either of them. We believe that the force of the collision or the g-force of the spinning has rendered them both unconscious. Do you think, if you took a position tethered to the bottommost array of solar panels, that you could reach Elena?"

"Unknown, but we can try," Brian said.

"Should one of us go to Raj instead?" Asha asked.

"Negative," Billy said. "Do not, I repeat, do not attempt to intercept Raj."

It wasn't just that his spinning limbs created a hazard to them. It was becoming clear that his spinning momentum, and the exhaust flowing from his jets, was soon going to take him away from any point where the spacewalkers could possibly reach him.

"Okay, Commander, we have it," Brian said.

The two of them quickly put their tools into a bag that was tethered to the side of the solar panel. They began to scramble along the side of the panel and back toward the closest module of the station itself. Like rock climbers, they needed to use the body of the station as their foundation, moving from section to section, clambering along it.

Both were tethered with two lines each—as always, a backup—when they were stationary. To move they had to uncouple one line, while remaining attached by the second, and pull themselves forward. Having gained a metre or so, they then attached the free line and uncoupled the second. It was important that they always remain attached by that one line or they could lose contact with the ship and start to independently orbit. They weren't equipped with any form of compulsion apparatus that would allow them to return to the station if their momentum pushed them away.

They moved, but it was in a halting, jerky manner. They were unable to travel along the structure more than a few metres before they had to reattach and reach back and detach the other tether.

"They're not moving fast enough," the professor said. "They won't be able to get her before she drifts too far."

"I agree," Asha said. She had heard the professor speaking to Billy through Billy's open communication link. "She's gone unless we can move faster, and there's only one way to move faster," Asha said.

Everybody knew what she meant. They'd have to detach both lines and, without a safety in place, pull themselves along the edge of the structure. If they lost their grip on the outside of the station, if they mistakenly gave the slightest push against the structure, they'd lose their hold and start drifting away.

Billy had to decide and decide quickly. They'd already potentially lost a second spacewalker trying to save the first. Did he risk the lives of a third or even a fourth trying to save the second? He tried to weigh the variables in his head but there wasn't time—if he didn't decide almost instantly he'd have already decided, because Elena would be beyond their reach even if they got there and—

Christina hit her com-link. "You do what you have to do. Try."

"Affirmative," Asha replied.

Christina released the com-link and turned to Billy. "We can't just abandon her. We have to try. Everybody is watching. You have to do everything, not just for Elena but for everybody else to know that you won't abandon them without a fight."

He nodded. "I'll send the ship to try to bring back Raj."

"But not yet," the professor said. "The action of the ship launching could set up a bump that would dislodge Asha and Brian from the edge of the structure."

Billy hadn't even thought of that, but of course the professor was right.

Asha and Brian had detached both lines and were moving much more quickly as they pulled themselves along hand over hand, clinging to the outside of the station. She appeared to be the faster of the two, or the one more willing to risk, and was pulling away. They reached the module and now had to travel the length of it to reach the solar panel at the far edge and bottom of the station.

Elena had continued to drift, her momentum carrying her out toward open space. It was difficult to judge the angle of her escape, but it appeared that a walker tethered to the end of that panel would be able to grab onto her and reel her back in.

Billy watched intently as the two walkers pulled themselves away and under the station and disappeared from his view. What if they couldn't reach her? What if something happened to one or both of them? He wanted to contact them, talk them through what they were doing, but that might only distract them. In monitoring them more intensely, he would only put them at risk.

"Jason, any luck in raising either Raj or Elena?" Billy asked.

"Still silence, but there's been a development with Raj."

"What development?" Billy asked.

"We've taken some photos. They're being brought to you right now."

Instantly the door opened and Tasha appeared. She handed the photos to Billy. The first was a shot of Raj's back; the haze of the exhaust was obscuring part of the image.

"They used high-speed exposure to capture the images," Tasha said.

Billy, with Christina and the professor looking over his shoulders, examined the photos.

"There's separation between sections of his suit along the side of the jetpack," Tasha said. She drew her finger along a thin black gap on the white suit. It was clearly visible to all of them. "Either the suit wasn't properly sealed or it was somehow ripped during the mission."

"It was sealed properly," Billy said.

"How can you be certain?" Tasha asked.

"He was out there for almost thirty minutes. Professor, how long could he have lived after the seal was broken?"

"Ten or fifteen seconds, perhaps. No longer."

They all knew what that meant without having to say it. With a rip in his suit he was dead. His finger had contracted on the trigger, perhaps in an instinctive attempt to get back to the station in those brief seconds between realizing there was a rupture and death. His frozen finger remained on the controls.

"It would have been fast," Christina said.

"Almost instantaneous," the professor confirmed.

As they watched, Raj—his lifeless spacesuit—cleared the far edge of the farthest extension of the station. Then the jetpack exhaust stopped! Had he regained control? Was he alive, or—?

"The fuel supply is exhausted," the professor said.

That microsecond of hope was dashed for all of them. The body would continue to spin, the momentum of the exhausted jetpack powering it until it eventually encountered enough resistance or force to slow it down. In the vacuum of space, that would take forever.

"Look! Is that Brian?" Christina exclaimed.

They all turned to see a spacewalker, line trailing behind, floating free of the station and sailing toward Elena.

The walker was getting closer and closer, until the line, still tethered to the station, became taut and the walker could go no farther. Elena was beyond reach, and was continuing to move farther away. They didn't know if she was alive, but they couldn't simply let her drift away.

"We have to send Amir to try to retrieve her," Billy said.

"It's going to be difficult and dangerous and potentially fatal for Elena," the professor said.

"If we do nothing, she dies for sure. Do we have any other choice?"

The professor shook his head, and then his eyes widened, his mouth dropped open, and he pointed out the window. Billy and Christina turned around and couldn't believe their eyes.

A second spacewalker had appeared beside the first. It was Asha. Before their eyes, she pushed off, flying forward, as Brian went back with equal force! Flowing out behind her was a tether either tied to or being held by the first walker. Asha was flying toward Elena, and she bumped against one of her legs, bouncing her body away! Quickly, she wrapped her arms around the very bottom of one leg!

"She's got her!" Billy screamed.

Asha climbed up the leg until they were practically face to face. Awkwardly, a second tether was removed and it appeared that Elena was being wrapped up. She wasn't going anywhere with the spacewalker attached. Asha's tether was attached to Brian and Brian was secured to the station.

They watched, too stunned to speak, as Brian started

to reel the two of them in. Hand over hand, he pulled the tether until finally all three of them were together.

"I have her," came Asha's voice over the com-link.

"Is she alive?" Christina questioned.

"She unconscious but we can see through her face mask that she's breathing," Brian answered.

"Get her back. Get back, all of you," Billy said. He paused. "And thank you. Thank you both of you for what you did."

"Affirmative. We'll be in shortly," Asha replied.

Billy turned back to look for Raj. Well beyond the shade of the station, his spinning suit was reflecting the rays of the sun. He looked like a brilliant, sparkling star. More than anybody else, Raj had loved to be outside the confines of the station. He had been on more spacewalks and free flights than anybody else. There was nobody Billy had trusted more to be out there. And now he was always going to be out there. He was no longer a member of the crew. Instead, he was now a satellite orbiting the planet for eternity.

CHAPTER EIGHTEEN

YEAR 4 AAE–DAY 204

Billy looked up from the official report to find Asha and Brian standing in front of him. They both looked sombre, but Billy noticed a little smugness behind the serious demeanour.

"You've both spoken to Elena, correct?" Billy asked.

"We have," Asha said.

"She'll be observed for concussion symptoms. She was struck in the helmet and the helmet impacted against her head. At least that's what the Dr. Sarah thinks," Billy explained.

"We're just glad that she's going to be all right," Brian added.

"She is alive because of the two of you."

"We were just in the right place at the right time," Asha pointed out.

"A place and time that might well have been fatal for both of you."

"We did what we had to do," Brian added.

"No, that's wrong," Billy said forcefully. "What you *had* to do was make an attempt. What you did was well beyond what was expected or anything I would have ordered you to do," Billy said.

Asha and Brian exchanged a half-look and then both faced forward again.

"We know that, sir," Brian said.

"Which is why we didn't ask your permission," Asha added.

"What?"

"In part, there really wasn't time," Brian said, back-pedalling slightly. "But we knew you wouldn't give Asha the order to free-fly."

"And even if you had given your permission, by then it would have been too late," Asha added. "I knew I had to act instantly."

"Instantly?" Billy asked. "You obviously had enough time to discuss it between the two of you."

"Um, not really, sir," Asha said.

"What do you mean?"

"We really didn't discuss it, sir," Brian said. He turned to Asha as if asking permission to continue.

"I made the decision independently," Asha said.

"But I fully support that decision," Brian added. "And I would have done the exact same thing if I'd been in her position."

"So . . . you didn't know she was going to do that?" Billy asked.

"Well, I knew . . . a few seconds before she passed by," Brian said.

"I told him to catch my line as I flew alongside him," Asha explained.

"You risked your life, took a complete leap of faith, without even your partner knowing what you were going to do until you had done it," Billy said.

"There was no choice if we were going to save Elena's life," Asha said. "Besides, I understood it to be a calculated risk."

"And you simply had faith that he could grab your line?" Billy questioned.

"I trust Brian with my life."

"You *did* trust him with your life."

"And my trust was proven correct," she said.

"I attached the line to my suit as soon as I got hold of it," Brian said, trying to downplay the danger. "And I was attached to the station by my tether."

"If you had missed, we'd potentially be dealing with three deaths now instead of one."

"If we hadn't tried, we'd potentially be dealing with two deaths instead of one," Asha said.

Billy gave her a hard look.

"Sir," she added, respectfully.

"It's just that in the seminars we're having, there's a lot of talk about making decisions and thinking for yourself," Brian said.

"*Thinking* is the key word."

"But we've also been told to follow our guts," Asha added.

Billy laughed. He was the one, with help from the professor and Sam, who had crafted the seminars. They were trying to encourage the crew to make some decisions without waiting for orders—to act instead of react. When they returned to the planet's surface they'd have to be able to act at a moment's notice, without orders, without direction, to deal with the things that were going to happen—things that they couldn't even imagine.

"Apparently you learned that part of the lesson very well," Billy said.

He got up from his seat, shaking his head, and came around the desk to stand right in front of them. He wanted to yell at them for risking their lives. He wanted to take them by the shoulders and shake them both, but he was afraid they'd start to cry. They were just teenagers—teenagers who had followed orders not to follow orders. The irony of that wasn't lost on him. Besides, they'd taken a chance and saved a life.

"How old are you two?" he asked.

"I'm fourteen," Brian said.

"I'll be fifteen on my next birthday," Asha said.

"So the answer is you're fourteen, correct?" Billy asked.

"Yes, sir. I'm fourteen."

"And you were very close to never reaching your next birthday." He shook his head. "I don't know what I should do with the two of you."

"No disrespect," Asha said, "but we didn't disobey an order."

"That's only because you didn't give me the chance to

give any orders that you could disobey," Billy noted. He paused. "As you were taught."

"And technically, we did get permission to take our tethers off the ship so we could move faster," Asha said.

"You show as much guts in here as you did out there," Billy said.

"Actually, I think maybe more," Asha said with an anxious smile, and Brian nodded.

"We will willingly accept any punishment you decide, sir," Brian said. "But I do insist, sir, respectfully, that I receive the same punishment as Asha."

"Believe me, you two *will* receive the same treatment."

Billy reached out his hand and offered it to Asha. "Thank you for what you did."

"You're, um, welcome," she stammered.

He shook hands next with Brian. "You two risked your lives in order to save Elena's life. It's hard to punish you for something that was heroic."

"We weren't *trying* to be heroes," Asha said.

"I know you weren't, but you were prepared to risk your lives for another member of our crew. I hope that if I'm ever in Elena's situation, the two of you will be there to save me."

"Thank you, sir. That means a lot," Asha said.

"But I don't want this to become a habit. Once makes you heroes. Trying it again might just make you dead heroes. Understood?"

"Understood," she said, and Brian nodded in agreement. Billy felt sure that the memory of Raj's death was one that would linger with them forever.

"There's one other thing. I'm going to discuss with the members of the Internal Operations Committee the possibility of you two becoming part of the team."

"That would be incredible," Asha said.

"Yes, thank you, sir," Brian added.

The Internal Operations Committee was a small group of people whom Billy trusted above all others. They met twice a month to discuss all aspects of the station and its residences.

"You're both dismissed."

"Thank you. But we have one question, if we may," Asha said.

"It's about Raj," Brian said. "He was our friend."

"He was a friend to all of us," Billy said.

"It's just . . . we were wondering, are there any plans to recover him, his body?" Asha asked.

"We haven't reached any decision or made any plans yet," Billy said.

"When you do, we'd request permission to be part of that mission . . . if that's all right," Asha said.

"Thanks for mentioning that. Now, both of you go before I decide I should find some way to punish you instead."

"Yes, sir, right away," Brian said.

"You'll have our complete reports within two hours," Asha added over her shoulder as they both rushed through the door.

Billy thought back to the whole sequence of events and the decisions he'd made. If he'd spoken to them first instead of directing a ship to be ready, they wouldn't have needed to take such a risk. There would have been time. He had made the wrong decision, and Amir, Christina, and the professor knew it. He'd apologize to them, although all three would have said it wasn't necessary.

Billy also realized he'd had no choice but to give Asha and Brian a "talking-to." But he was proud of them. And he liked to think that he would have done the same thing—if he'd had the guts.

CHAPTER NINETEEN

YEAR 4 AAE—DAY 222

The members of the Internal Operations Committee all settled in to the conference room. Two new seats had been added, for Asha and Brian. Christina and Billy sat on one side of the square table while the professor and Amir sat opposite them. Jennie, the climatology expert, and Tasha always sat together on the third side. Now, with Asha and Brian on the fourth side, it seemed as though the committee was finally complete.

"Glad you are all here," Billy began.

"Again, not really many other places to go." It was the joke Amir used at almost every meeting.

"We welcome our two new members," Billy said.

They applauded politely while Brian and Asha looked slightly embarrassed. They'd been at least slightly embarrassed for the past two weeks. Being invited to this very important committee was part of it, but beyond that, everybody on the ship had started to treat them as heroes, offering to get them their food, help out with their responsibilities, or give up a favourite seat in the common room. At first it had seemed a little odd. Now it was starting to grate, particularly on Asha.

Billy had observed the interaction. People seemed to need both leaders and heroes, and it was best when the same person could play both roles. Now, as members of the committee, they could do just that.

"I'd like to begin with a discussion about the food production units," Billy said.

"No," Jennie said.

They all looked at her in surprise.

"No, you're not going to want to talk about that first or second or in fact at all," she said.

"I don't understand," Billy said.

"That's because you don't know what I'm going to show you, show all of you." She stood and walked over to a wall-sized screen, clicked a remote, and called up a picture of the planet. "These are the photos taken from our latest planetary survey," she said.

She clicked through the pictures, each showing a similar slice of brown, hazy planet below. Picture by picture went by, all similar swirling clouds.

"Wait!" the professor yelled.

There was no need for anybody to ask why. Jennie smiled and walked over to the picture and touched her finger to the screen. There it was, an irregularly shaped blue circle. It looked like an eye winking through the surrounding brown.

"That's the surface," Amir gasped.

"The Atlantic Ocean," Jennie said.

"Where in the Atlantic Ocean?" Professor Sheppard asked.

Jennie clicked the slides forward and suddenly the outline of landforms was superimposed on the image. The blue dot was off the United States, halfway down the eastern coastline.

"The window is approximately 175 kilometres wide," Jennie said. "It was visible in three successive passes of the planet."

The slide show suddenly became three images side by side.

"The image on the right, during the first pass to the east, shows it at its largest, and I've estimated it to be close to 275 kilometres in diameter there. The size diminished on subsequent passes, as you can see in these slides. By the fourth pass"—a fourth slide joined the first three—"it was no longer visible. It had come and gone."

"This is hardly possible," the professor said.

"Seeing is believing," Jennie said. "I do understand your shock. This was not expected to happen for years to come. But the surveys have shown a remarkable drop in particulate matter in the atmosphere over the past year."

"A drop was expected, but to see that there would be a completely clear shaft in an isolated area is entirely outside the projected models," the professor said.

"Aren't you the one who keeps saying that this is all too complex to fully understand and predict?" Billy asked.

"I am—it is—but this means something even more significant," the professor said.

They all looked at him intently.

"This window opened up and then closed within a three-hour span," the professor said.

"It's unfortunate that it wasn't a longer time frame," Billy said.

"But that's what's so encouraging. We do a monthly survey of the planet. We were over that particular spot for only a few hours, and yet it was captured. This means that either it was a random act captured by chance, or this sort of episode is happening on a regular basis—clear windows through the atmosphere opening and closing across the planet."

"Is that possible?" Billy asked.

"It makes more sense, statistically speaking, than the idea that we just happened to capture that single event in our very infrequent surveys," the professor said. "If you'd like, I can do a complete calculation of the possibility of us being there at that instant to capture one random occurrence."

"Not necessary," Billy said. "What does this mean?"

The professor started to talk and then stopped, gesturing to Jennie instead. She'd come a long way in the last three years—from trying to take a spacewalk without a suit to being one of the most trusted members of the crew.

"Jennie?" Christina asked.

"It means that the planet is healing itself at an accelerated rate, and that our predictions of a ten- to fifteen-year period could be significantly reduced."

"What would cause that?" Christina asked.

"Increased rain or snowfall might be cleansing the sky. Or air currents might be cycling the upper atmosphere into the lower regions. Or perhaps we've simply been wrong in our projections of a more dense atmosphere—maybe, in reality, there were fewer particles but they were much heavier and therefore more affected by the Earth's gravity, and so they fell to the surface more readily. Or—"

"Or we did capture a random, one-time occurrence, and none of that applies," Billy said.

The heightened sense of excitement that was in the air, the electricity in the room, was suddenly gone.

"I need all of this to stay within this room. There's no point in raising expectations if we can't be certain. The thought of another seven or even twelve years aboard this ship is daunting." He looked at the others around the table. "But doable. We cannot raise hopes only to crush them."

"Could we send out another survey team earlier than scheduled?" Amir asked. "I'd be more than willing to captain that trip."

"That change in routine would raise questions," Billy said. "You know that any variation from the normal routine gets people talking—and worse, throwing around theories—on this ship."

Tasha laughed. "Yes, this many geniuses without enough to focus on can be trouble. Nothing goes unnoticed, uncommented on, or unanalyzed."

"Then we just wait until the next survey?" Amir asked.

"There is something we can do before then," Jennie said. "What if we keep a twenty-four-hour watch on the slice of the Earth we can see?"

"And how do we do that?" Christina asked.

"In the old section, the European space station, there is a telescope that was previously used to observe solar flares and sunspots as part of a long-term study."

"And it's still functional?" Billy asked.

"It was inoperable, but I've been fiddling with it in my free time and it now works. I think I can reposition it so that we can capture a view of the Earth directly below us."

"How big a view?" the professor asked.

"I'm sorry, but to have the resolution we'd need it couldn't be very big."

"How big?" Billy asked.

"It would be no larger than an area approximately a thousand kilometres in width and length. I'm sorry it can't be larger."

Billy burst into laughter. "That's one thousand kilometres that we could watch continually. Jennie, you are a treasure. What help do you need?"

"It's pretty straightforward, and I started to do the calculations a few months ago."

"A few months ago?" Billy asked. "You've thought about this before?"

"I thought it might be something to supplement the surveys, but I didn't think you'd want to devote station resources to it," she said.

"Devote those resources," Billy said.

Suddenly the alarm went off. Everybody froze for a second and then scrambled to their feet.

Billy looked to Christina. If this was a drill, she would know, because she would have planned it. He could read her with a look. This was as much a surprise to her as it was to everybody else in the room. This was no drill.

Billy hit the com-link button. “Report, please.”

There was a pause of a few seconds and then an answer. “We’ve detected a satellite.”

“There are hundreds of satellites in the Earth’s orbit. Why was the alarm sounded?” Billy demanded.

“The satellite is on a collision course with the station.”

CHAPTER TWENTY

The alarm had been turned off. There was no point in hearing it now that the problem had been identified, and the incessant chiming got to be annoying and stopped people from thinking, and acting, efficiently.

The control room was alive with activity but all eyes were focused on the radar displays. There was a small blip—more than three hundred kilometres away—that was flashing in warning lights. The automated system had located the mystery object and plotted its course. Once it had been determined that it was on a potential collision course with the station, the alarm had sounded automatically.

"I thought this entire orbital arc had been swept free of all man-made objects," Billy said.

"You're right," Amir said. "I was part of one of the teams that removed, redirected, or destroyed all pieces of debris that could pose a threat to the station."

"All but one, apparently," Tasha said.

"No, all of them. We did a complete scan. We missed nothing. This has to be something new."

"Is it possible that a piece of the asteroid that was in orbit has migrated to a higher orbit?" Billy asked.

"Not unless it has defied the laws of gravity, physics, and inertia," the professor said. "Orbits become lower, not higher, without the introduction of additional power."

"Then either it was in this plane and undetected up to this point, or it has dropped from an even higher orbit," Amir said.

"I don't care where it came from," Billy said. "I just want to know more about it. For starters, just how big is it?"

"Not large. Approximately two metres by one metre."

"And what's the closing speed?"

"Approximately one hundred and twenty metres per second."

"If I'm not mistaken, that's not particularly fast."

"Not for a standard orbital satellite, but it's certainly fast enough to cause serious damage to whatever it hits."

"Any idea about composition?" Billy asked. "Is it rock or metal?"

"We can't tell from this distance. We do know that it's irregularly shaped and it appears to be wobbling within a standard orbit."

"That would explain it appearing in our orbital plane," the professor said. "That wobbling could potentially move an object into a changed orbital path."

"I knew we hadn't missed anything," Amir said.

"Nobody is blaming you or your team," Billy said. "The real question isn't how it got here but how we get rid of it and how much time we have."

"Time is simple," the professor said. His eyes briefly glazed over as he did his human calculator imitation. "Just under four hours."

"Less," Tasha said. "That distance you were given was rounded and close to twenty minutes has passed."

"I'll factor that in and give a more precise time."

"Not necessary," Billy said, "but thanks. What are our options?"

"We hope that it's a near-miss," Brian said. "The odds are against a direct hit."

"I don't like any odds of a hit," Asha said.

"We could intercept," Amir said. "Send a ship out and deflect it."

"That would be like firing one bullet toward another bullet and hoping that you hit it," the professor said.

"I'm a pretty good pilot."

"Even if you did hit the oncoming bullet, it would just destroy you instead of the station," the professor said.

Amir shrugged. "If it hits the station there's a chance I'm not going to survive anyway. Why not try to stop it and save everybody else?"

"That makes sense," Brian said.

"I agree," Asha added. "Maybe one of us could come with you and—"

"This is not being put to a vote," Billy said, cutting her off and silencing everybody else as well.

Billy thought through the two options. Hope that it missed the station and risk being wrong, or send out a ship to attempt to deflect it, possibly killing everybody on that ship in the process. He would be risking the lives of those on the ship to possibly save the lives on the station. Sometimes it was simply best to wait it out. This wasn't one of those times.

"Which ship?"

"Ship 1, Lars's ship," Amir said, and Tasha nodded in agreement.

"Why?"

"It's the most manoeuvrable, has the best acceleration, and is the ship we can most afford to lose."

Each of his points made sense, even the last, tragic one. Ultimately the other ships would be needed to carry the crew back to the planet. Lars's ship was designed to carry three and could be adapted to carry only four or five at best for a short burst to the planet.

"And the pilot?" Billy asked.

"Other than Lars I'm most familiar with that ship," Amir said.

"Do you agree, Tasha?" Billy asked.

"I don't want to agree, but he's right. He'll need assistance, though."

"He will, and it won't be either you or Lars."

The unstated reason was that they couldn't afford to lose two of their three best pilots. Sacrificing one was acceptable. Losing two was not.

"Can I select my crew?" Amir asked.

"I'll go," Asha said.

"So will I," Brian volunteered. He seemed disappointed that he hadn't jumped in first.

"I select the crew. My decision," Billy said. "Brian could you—"

"All right, I'll go get my equipment!"

"No. You'll get Elena. And tell her to bring everything that's necessary for a spacewalk, including her jetpack."

Brian looked as though he was going to argue. "Yes, sir."

"Amir, get the ship ready to go."

"Yes, sir. Will there be a third member of the crew?"

"Yes, there will," Billy said. Everybody looked at him. "I'll be going along."

"You can't do that!" Christina exclaimed.

"She's right," Amir said. "You can't sacrifice your life."

"But you can sacrifice yours?" Billy asked.

"Without hesitation. I'm not essential. You are."

"I'm not going to ask anybody to do something that I'm not prepared to do myself."

"You're the leader. You cannot sacrifice yourself," the professor said.

"I'm not sacrificing myself, or Amir or Elena. I have an idea."

There was a slight sense of motion, and Billy watched as the monitors showed the camera angle from the docking ring as the little ship pushed away from the station. Unseen on both sides of the ship, the small engines were expelling yellow-white exhaust to power their departure.

"Away and clear," Amir said.

As they gained distance they also gained perspective on the station. This was the first time Billy had seen it this way since they had approached it over three years before. He tried to think back—had it always looked that fragile, awkward, unnaturally constructed?

They quickly moved away and the entire station was visible through the screen as well as through the monitor.

"Each time I see it from this perspective I'm amazed at just how small it is," Amir said.

"The farther you go the smaller it gets," Billy said.

"I was in the rear compartment when we arrived, so I've never seen it from this distance," Elena said. "Although if it hadn't been for Brian and Asha, it would have been the last thing I ever saw."

Billy grabbed the radio. "Jason, do we have the coordinates?"

"This is Sheppard here. I've got the starting numbers already programmed into our system. Transmission to your onboard navigation system will commence almost immediately."

"Thanks, Professor. I knew we could count on you."

"Not just me. The whole team is working on it. Before you get to the start point, we'll have the entire routine ready to go," the professor said. "I've just sent the flight information."

"And received," Amir confirmed.

"Professor, is Christina there?"

"I'm here," she answered.

"We're going to be fine, you know that," he said.

"You don't even know that."

"Yes, I do, and you have my word on it. I've never broken my word to you before and I'm not going to start now. In my very brief absence, you know you and the professor have my complete confidence, right?"

"Just be careful. You know how much I love you."

He almost said, "Same," his usual answer, but didn't. "I love you more than anything else in the world, or above the world."

"You want me to re-dock with the station so you two can hug, or can I initiate the flight sequence?" Amir asked.

"Initiate the sequence," Billy said. "And, Christina, no loud parties while I'm gone, okay?"

"Just one when you all return safe and successful. Amir, you take care of him for me."

"I thought he was here to take care of me! I've initiated the sequence."

The thrusters on the port side came to life and the station—the only point of reference—moved to the left as the ship spun to the right. They were on their way to save the station.

The ship would be travelling in a triangular path, with each point smoothed over and curved as they changed directions again. The first two steps were completely pre-programmed—far too complicated for any human to execute as precisely. The final stages of the third step would be where Amir took over the controls. The first step had taken them in the direction of the oncoming object, although they were arcing much higher into orbit.

Fuel was fed constantly into the thrusters to fight against the gravitational pull of the planet. The gravity well was so reduced at this altitude that it always seemed as though they were free of its influence, but obviously it was present enough to keep objects in orbit, stopping them from escaping into space. There was a constant buzz—not from outside in the vacuum of space but from the internal workings as chemicals combined to create fuel to create propulsion to create thrust to create force to push them away from the planet. That sound would soon stop.

According to the programming it would end in seven minutes and thirty-four seconds. That was when they would reach the top of their flight, the highest point of their trip.

"It's all going perfectly according to plan," Amir said.

"That's good to hear."

"I'm just curious. No offence, but you're no astrophysicist—how did you come up with this idea?"

Billy laughed. "I'm afraid it's not mine. It belonged to the Russians. They had to do this same thing in the 1990s to save their station."

"Amazing. I'm assuming it worked, since we have their station incorporated into ours."

"It worked. The station was saved," Billy said.

"And it was exactly the same scenario?" Elena asked.

"Similar, although they had to plot out the entire scheme using human calculation and primitive computing."

"And if what I've read about their MiR station is true, they probably used baling wire and duct tape as well," Amir added.

"I didn't know you read about their station," Billy said.

"Required reading for space junkies. Those people were pioneers."

"We owe them for a lot more than just their station. To think how they survived against the odds is encouraging for us."

"I still think it might have to do with them being Russians," Amir said. "Those people are just too stubborn and stoic and serious to know that they're supposed to stop."

"Like Ivan," Elena said.

"Like Ivan," Billy admitted.

Ivan remained, for Billy, the proverbial mystery wrapped in a riddle locked behind an unblinking expression. He had done everything he'd been asked and suggested some more things that he hadn't, but he was still somebody Billy couldn't trust. He had taken on quiet leadership and was the first to step forward to volunteer information or suggestions, but he still operated as the outsider, in the corner, watching but never revealing. That was partly his temperament, partly his training, partly his background, and partly by design.

"I thought you were going to suggest taking Ivan along instead of Elena," Amir said.

"Why would I do that?" Billy asked.

"I thought he could stare at the object really intensely and make it change directions," Amir joked.

"I'd change directions if he told me to," Elena said. "He's a bit scary."

"A bit?" Amir asked. "If it wasn't for Billy, and Sam too, I'm not sure what would happen. I wouldn't want to get on the wrong side of Ivan."

"Does he have a right side?" Elena asked.

"He's not going to harm anybody," Billy said. "Ever."

"I know that," Amir said. "Well, I believe that. But the guy is unnerving. The only person he seems to get along with is Tasha, and quite frankly, sometimes I'm a little afraid of her too."

"I'm glad he's part of the crew," Billy said. The longer the trip lasted the more grateful he was. Ivan was a steady influence, an outside eye and ear, and somebody who could be trusted to question, at least. Of course that didn't mean that he wouldn't snap Billy's neck one day if he needed to.

"We're coming up to the mark," Amir said.

The clock was ticking down to seconds and suddenly the sound of the thrusters stopped. They were still travelling upward but were no longer exerting force to continue. They had almost reached the apex of their journey—the highest altitude—and now the ship needed to be slowed and redirected downward. This was the slight change in the upward trajectory, the lessening of the arc, as they started to turn the corner on the second part of their journey.

The thrusters on the starboard side came to life—a series of short bursts designed to change the altitude of the ship and aim its momentum back toward the lower orbit and the object of their pursuit. Once the thrusters had aimed them correctly they would no longer be necessary; the energy exerted in escaping from the Earth's pull would be perfectly returned to them in the speed gained as they were pulled back down.

"Perfectly executed," Amir said as the Earth appeared on an angle below them and the thrusters fell silent again.

"Just like playing a video game, or piloting a simulator," Billy commented. "Right, Amir?"

"No, more like watching somebody else do it. I'm just as much a passenger for these parts as the two of you."

"How much time?" Billy asked.

"This will take less than ten minutes. Jumping off a building takes a lot less time than climbing up the stairs," Amir noted.

"And then?"

"We'll be on the third leg, the one where I'm back at the controls and we're chasing the object."

"And our estimated time of intercept?" Billy asked.

"We'll get to it more than twenty minutes before it gets to the station."

"That gives us enough time to know if it's going to hit."

"And hopefully enough time to do something about it. One way or another."

Billy didn't answer.

"It is one way or another, right?" Amir asked.

Billy nodded.

"Just so we know. If nothing else, that allows me enough time to say goodbye to my gods."

"Gods?" Billy asked.

Amir shrugged. "I was raised in India. I guess that makes me a Hindu by default."

"I thought Hindus had one supreme god?" Elena said.

"One main god, but we like to balance things out, sort of like backup gods and goddesses. Extra gods can only help. Especially right now."

"If we have no choice—and you're the best to know that—then I'll give the order," Billy said. "If we can't stop it from hitting the station, then we ram it so it and the debris from our ship all miss the station."

"There it is!" Elena cried out.

At first Billy couldn't see, but then, in a bright shaft of light, it was obvious where she was looking. They'd been following the blip on their radar but now they could see it with their eyes—or at least they could see the sun's rays reflecting off whatever it was. There was now a pattern as every five or six seconds the object's rotation captured those rays and flashed them back, and it became as bright as a star.

"How's the timing?" Billy asked.

"Our closing speed will get us there eighteen minutes before potential impact."

"I wish we had more time," Billy said.

"I can increase speed and reduce closing distance and get us more time, but I wouldn't advise that."

"Why not?" Elena asked.

"The greater the differential between our speed and its speed, the less time we'll have to intersect and react. If we overshoot, we won't get a second chance."

"Understood."

"We have enough time. If we cut it closer to impact

we'll have more time within range, correct?" Billy asked.

"That's correct."

"Then make the calculations and slow us down."

"Will do, Captain."

"No, you're the captain. I'm the commander," Billy said.

"Will do, Commander."

There was a beep announcing an incoming radio communication. Billy hit the switch and static filled the control room.

"Station to Ship 1." It was Jason.

"Ship 1," Billy replied.

"We have command and communication on line."

"Connect."

There was a slight hesitation and then the professor came on line. "We've done our latest calculations and it appears that the object will miss the body of our station."

"Can I assume from that statement that it will hit one of the appendages?" Billy asked.

"The rotational pattern is making it difficult to provide certainty, but we believe it will make contact with the solar array that extends from the former European space station."

"And how would that collision impact on the rest of the station?"

"That array constitutes 15 percent of our total power, so we could continue to function with an acceptable margin of safety with respect to our ongoing power requirements."

"That wasn't the impact I meant. If it hits the solar array, will the array simply crumble or is there potential for it to rip open the side of the station?" Billy asked.

"I can't really guarantee the outcome."

"Then I guess we'll have to guarantee it," Billy said.

"Guaranteed," Amir said in the background.

"In the meantime, could you please prepare the station by sealing off the different—"

"Already done," Christina announced. She was obviously beside the professor. "We've been taking care of business while you and your little crew have been off having an adventure."

"I expected nothing less. We're out now, so let us focus on the task at hand. Please update us on any changes that would indicate a clean miss."

"Will do. Out."

Almost at the same instant that the radio communication ended, the visual communication started. In the distance, just up over the horizon of the planet, the station was "rising." It reflected a steady stream of light back toward them as they chased the body between them.

Billy felt a rush of emotions that he instantly clamped down. That was his home. The place where he lived. The place where everybody important in his life lived. A place he would protect with his life without a moment's thought. He hadn't expected to feel so emotional. There was no time or place for emotions. Or maybe this was the perfect time.

The strongest instinct of any living thing was to survive. Yet here they were, prepared to sacrifice their survival for the sake of the station and its crew. Billy knew this was so much more than weighing his survival against the one hundred lives on the station. Nine billion had already perished below them. What were a hundred lives compared to that? He knew the answer. They were a large fraction of what was left of life. They would live for the billions who had died. One life—or even the three lives in this ship—meant nothing as long as the rest survived.

"We're closing on schedule, and fast," Amir said.

That was obvious through the front screen. It was a much bigger, brighter star, flashing at that same frequency—now calculated to be every 5.3 seconds—as it rotated.

"Any idea what it's made of?"

"The rotation is making it difficult to judge," Elena said. "Small, one metre by two, irregularly shaped, solid as opposed to vaporous."

"It gives some indication of being at least partially metal," Amir added.

"So you think it's some form of rock-and-metal fragment?" Billy asked.

"That would be consistent with the composition of the asteroid that impacted on the planet. It's a fragment—at least it's small enough for us to do something about it," Amir said.

Wordlessly they watched as they closed the distance. Billy counted out the frequency. It was almost calming, like a meditation. They didn't know everything but they knew its routine. Billy quietly smirked. That was what he always wanted to know when confronting a potential enemy—what were its routines, what were its habits, what made it tick?

"There's something about the rotation," Amir said.

"It is strange," Elena confirmed. "I just can't put my finger on the way it's spinning."

"Spinning," Billy said. He gave a small, sad smile. "That's it. It's not rotating. It's spinning."

"Isn't that the same thing?" Elena asked.

"It's not." He shook his head. "And it's not an asteroid fragment. It's Raj."

CHAPTER TWENTY-ONE

They both looked at him, wide-eyed, shocked.

"It's Raj," Billy said again.

"No, it can't be," Amir said. "You can't possibly see that from this distance."

"I don't have to see to know. What else could it be?"

"An asteroid fragment, a piece of space junk, a defunct satellite, a—"

"He's right," Elena said, cutting Amir off. "I can feel it."

"Feel it?" Amir questioned. "Since when have you developed psychic feelings?"

"Since when have you wanted to pray to Hindu gods?" she asked.

"Not pray so much as give my regards, but that's different. We can't know that it's Raj—or at least his remains."

"Doesn't it make sense?" Billy asked. "Metal fragments, the mass and size would be almost identical, and the pattern of rotation, the spinning, isn't that also consistent?"

"Well, yes, maybe. But really, does it matter?" Amir asked.

"It does and it doesn't. If it's Raj, he's not just a piece of space junk," Elena said.

"I know you two were close," Amir said.

"He was my best friend. He was going to be my partner . . . you know, someday. We talked about it."

"I'm not minimizing all of that, any of that," Amir said. "It's just that even if it is Raj, it's still just an object in space that could destroy the station and—"

"You're both right. It's still a danger, and we'll do what we need to do. It's no disrespect to Raj, or to you, Elena. The plan stays the same."

"Can I ask you a question?" Elena asked Billy.

"You can ask me anything you want."

"We all agree that it's acceptable for us to sacrifice our lives to save the station and the lives on it, correct?"

"Three lives lost to save a hundred is completely acceptable," Billy agreed, and Amir silently nodded in agreement.

"Good. We all agree that it might be necessary to sacrifice less to save more," she said.

Billy suddenly realized where she was going with this, and it was going to be hard to argue.

"Then sacrificing my life to save the two of you, this ship, and everybody on the station is a completely acceptable solution," she said. "If I were to go out by myself, then—"

"We're not prepared to sacrifice anybody. The ship will have a greater chance of surviving the impact than you would.

You lived through—but just barely—the impact of your collision with Raj."

"This time I'll know what to expect, to come at it slightly differently."

"This time there's nobody and nothing that could save you," Billy said.

"And maybe that would be okay. We all have to die. At least I'd die spending an eternity with the person I was meant to be with," she said.

"And I'm the one who's crazy for talking to gods?" Amir snapped. "I can aim the ship to just kiss against the outer edge of its rotation."

"It's not an 'it,' it's Raj, and you can't possibly be so vain that you think you can take a ship that close without breaking open a seal or—"

"Both of you stop it. Now!" Billy ordered. His voice had become calm. They awaited his word.

"Amir, follow the procedures exactly as we have planned."

"But I—"

Billy silenced her with a look. "And, Elena, you are to get suited up and get into the space lock with your jetpack ready to go."

She jumped to her feet.

"But there is a condition," Billy said.

"What?"

He gestured for her to come to him. "You're going out there to change the orbital path of the object."

"Of course."

"And to say your goodbye to Raj," he said.

She nodded. It looked as though she was on the verge of tears.

"But you have to promise me you're not going out there to join him, to end your life."

She didn't answer, but she looked as though he had read her mind—she looked a little guilty.

"You were thinking about that, weren't you?" he asked.

She let out a deep sigh. "I was thinking that if it had to happen, it wouldn't be the worst way to go."

"That's just it. It doesn't have to happen. You're going nowhere unless I have your solemn word that you'll do all you can to get back inside this ship alive."

She started to answer and he stopped her.

"Raj probably loved you the way you loved him. I understand that. I get that." He thought about Christina. "I live that. Raj wouldn't want you to die with him. He'd want you to live without him. You know who he was. Well?"

She nodded her head. "I'm coming back. Or I'll die trying. You have my word."

Distance and size and speed meant nothing when there was nothing to compare and contrast it with. How fast and how close were impossible to tell with the naked eye. Instruments told them everything.

The object of their pursuit was 250 metres directly in front of them. Both ship and object were travelling at an enormous speed relative to the Earth—roughly 1,000 metres per second, which translated to 3,600 kilometres per hour. Of course, that was all completely irrelevant. All that mattered was the closing speed—how much faster one object was going than the other.

Their ship was now gaining on the object, closing the distance by one metre per second. Amir had masterfully taken control of the ship, using its thrusters to come behind, adjust speed, and get them ready for a pass—all before reaching the station. It would be 250 seconds before they came alongside. In fifteen minutes, they would both collide with the station.

The size was equally certain to them. The exact size indicated there was no question that it was Raj, or what remained of him. The last molecule of oxygen had been sucked out of the suit and had vanished into space, causing the material to shrink, constricting and showing every curve and nuance of his body. The helmet was still in place, the screen shattered; the only thing that stopped them from seeing the remains of his face was the rotation of his body. As they closed in, even that small grace would be lost, and Elena would certainly be close enough to make out the details. Flesh and blood would be gone, organs exploded—leached and frozen and burned and boiled until only the skeletal remains were left.

"Suited up and ready at your command," Elena radioed in.

"All your seals are secure?"

"Checked and double-checked."

"You have two minutes. Do a triple-check."

"Roger that," she said.

"Jetpack charged?" Billy asked.

"Yes, Mother," she joked.

"That's 'Father,' and answer the question."

"Charged, and equipment secured," she said.

Amir shook his head. "Is that what we're calling it, equipment?"

"Would you prefer if I called it my space tool?" she asked.

"It's a mop. You have a mop. You're going into space with a long-handled mop."

"At least it's long-handled."

"It doesn't matter what we call it. You have it with you and that's what's important."

"Wait," Amir said. "There's a camera in the lock."

He hit a switch and an image of Elena—suited up, jet-pack on her back, mop in her hand—appeared. It did look ridiculous. Both Billy and Amir involuntarily giggled.

"You take that equipment—tool, mop, whatever—and take care of business," Billy said. "And, Elena, say goodbye to Raj from all of us. He was a good person, and we're going to honour his memory by saving the station. He risked his life for all of us, and the last thing he'd have ever imagined was putting us—putting you—in danger."

"Thanks for saying that."

Billy meant it. He also needed to give her one more push toward surviving and not allowing her grief for Raj to overwhelm her desire to live.

"Elena, please engage your internal life-support system," Amir said.

"Engaged."

"I'm going to evacuate the atmosphere from the lock. Starting . . . now."

Amir hit the controls and the oxygen in the lock was vacuumed out and cycled into the ship. That was important. If there was pressure in the lock when the door was opened Elena would be blown violently out into space, hurtled at such a speed that she might even lose consciousness. Billy watched on the control panel as the indicator showed the air pressure going down and down until it reached zero. No oxygen. What was left was empty space inside.

"Pressure zero, opening the outer door," Amir announced.

The top part of the monitor showed the door sliding open and the black of space rushing in. Elena pulled herself along, hand over hand, to the exit. She couldn't use her jetpack while inside or the exhaust might burn or otherwise damage the interior wall of the ship. She moved out of camera range and almost immediately appeared in front of them through the window. She was gliding; her final push away from the ship had increased her speed. Although it appeared that she was motionless, jetpack not yet firing, the mop held before her like a lance, she was actually travelling at the same speed as them—2,400 kilometers per hour—plus just enough extra kick to send her away from them and toward Raj.

"All systems go?" Billy asked.

"Systems go. Am I far enough away from the ship to ignite my jets?" she asked.

"Give us ten more seconds of clearance. I don't want your exhaust tarnishing the ship or Lars will make me wash it," Amir joked. Amir's joking was like whistling as you walked past a cemetery—just a way to lighten things up. This really needed to be lightened up.

"You know what to do and what not to do," Billy said. "And we know you can do it."

"I'll do it," she said, her voice just above a whisper. "And igniting pack thruster."

A little haze of exhaust came out of the central nozzle in her jetpack and she picked up speed, leaving the ship behind and sailing toward her goal—toward Raj.

"Not too fast," Amir warned her. "You don't want to over-accelerate and pass your target."

"You'd better stick to flying ships," she said. "This is my area of experience and expertise, and the only person who can match me is . . ."

She let the sentence trail off—they all knew it was Raj. He was the one who was her match, the person who'd been her partner on all those spacewalks. Now it was just her.

She pulled farther away, getting closer and closer to Raj.

"She's almost there," Billy said. "She has to slow herself down now or—"

Elena executed a complete spin so she was suddenly facing toward the ship and away from Raj. Then there was a blast of exhaust flowing from behind. She was using the reverse thrust to decrease speed.

From that distance Billy couldn't be sure, but it looked as though she had positioned herself so that she and Raj were almost side by side, with Elena ever so slightly away from the outside point of his rotation.

“She has completely matched his speed,” Amir said. “That was amazing.”

“Elena, commence procedure,” Billy ordered.

They watched, waiting for Elena to take action. There was nothing. She floated there beside Raj, just out of range of his rotation, looking at him, but not moving.

Amir turned off the com-link. “What is she doing?” he asked Billy.

“Thinking, or maybe looking for the point of impact.”

“Thinking time is almost over. The closer we get, the more she’ll have to change the path. It has to be now.”

Billy nodded and turned on the com-link. “Elena?”

There was no response. His greatest fear was that she wasn’t thinking, that she’d frozen, that she couldn’t do what she had to do.

“Elena!” Billy yelled.

“Sorry,” she said. “I was just saying goodbye. I’ll engage.”

Elena leaned forward, pushing the mop out in front of her and pushing it into Raj. One of his limbs shot out and smashed against the mop, knocking it out of Elena’s hands. It sailed off to the side, and instantly there were exhaust fumes as Elena chased after it. Within a few seconds she’d reached out and grabbed it by the handle. She spun back around, her jetpack propelling her, and again she pushed the mop against Raj. Once more it was kicked out of her hands, even more violently, and it went even farther. Elena rushed after it again.

“Any change?” Billy asked.

“Rotation slightly slowed, speed slightly reduced.” Amir

looked over the data on the screen. "And orbital path has been altered by almost 1.5 degrees."

"Is that enough?"

"Too close to call. Another degree or two would be nice."

"Roger that," Elena said.

She had retrieved the mop—it looked as though part of it had broken off—and once again she rocketed back.

"I'm going to lean into this one," Elena said.

"Just do the same thing," Billy advised.

Elena positioned herself so that she was right beside Raj. "Here goes nothing." She forced the broken handle forward, pushing Raj as he struck against the mop. Raj bounced to one side, Elena to the other, and the mop shattered into pieces! Elena was spinning, rotating in the opposite direction from Raj as his momentum had transferred through the mop handle before it shattered and into her.

"He's clear, his path has altered significantly!" Amir yelled out.

"Elena, did you hear that?" Billy demanded. "Elena? Elena, are you—?"

"Roger," she said. "I'm here, I'm fine."

"You're better than fine," Billy said. "You did it. You saved the station. Return to the ship."

"No," she said.

"What do you mean no?" Billy asked.

"I'm not coming back to the ship."

Billy was stunned. She'd done the job, she'd saved the station, she'd given her word—and now she was just going to throw her life away?

"I'm going to stay out here," she said.

"You can't do that—" Billy started to say when Amir hit the button to kill the com-link.

"She's gone crazy!" Amir exclaimed. "She thinks she's going to atone for the death of Raj by some misplaced act of—"

"You should really turn off the com-link before you call somebody crazy," Elena said.

"I . . . I . . . um," Amir stuttered. Obviously he'd hit the wrong button.

"He's just worried," Billy said. That forced calmness that felt so unnatural to him came out sounding reassuring to everybody else. "But we do need you to come back."

"No, no, I don't think it's best for me to return to the ship. Don't worry, I'm not sacrificing myself or anything else," she said. "I'm going to dock with the station instead of the ship. I'm on course. I have enough oxygen and my momentum is good, so I hardly need any fuel except for the final entry. And I do have more experience coming in through the docking lock with the ship, right?"

"Of course you do, no question," Billy said. "But still, we're right here." He wanted her safe and sound back in the lock.

"I'm not going to do anything stupid, thinking that somehow it's noble," she said. "Honestly, you don't have to worry."

"Worrying is my job, but I didn't say you were going to do anything wrong."

"You were thinking it, though, weren't you?"

Billy let out a big sigh. "I understand why you'd want to, but you know we need you."

"I know. I understand. It's just, well, this is hard to explain because it doesn't make sense, but I want to escort Raj the rest of the way . . . make sure he goes on his way, and then I'll go on mine." There was a long pause. "Does that make any sense?"

"That makes complete sense."

"So I have your permission, sir?"

"Permission granted," Billy said. "We'll see you back on the station. And please, Elena, say a goodbye from us as well. We all miss him."

Billy's voice choked up over the last few words and it caught him by surprise.

"We're going to close the com-link," Billy said. "Give you some privacy."

Amir hit the button again. This time he double-checked before he spoke.

"You're scared she isn't coming back?" he asked.

"A little, but what could we possibly do if she decided not to come back?" Billy asked.

Amir shook his head. "I'm not sure. We have no other spacesuit, no jetpack. Heck, she even took our only mop."

Billy reached over and gave Amir a pat on the back. "I'll try to find Lars another mop. In the meantime, I want you to fire reverse thrusters. I want to let Elena and Raj get past the station long before we do, so she has time to get inside before we dock."

"Roger," Amir said.

Amir made some adjustments and Billy could hear the thrusters engaging. There was no discernible alteration, no sense of movement or change in speed or position. As they watched out the window, though, they could see the difference in their circumstances relative to Raj and Elena. The two seemed to be getting smaller as they accelerated away. The closing speed of their ship had been lost, replaced by negative momentum. The pair were still speeding through space but with each passing second they were now leaving the ship a dozen or so metres behind. Raj continued to rotate—albeit considerably more slowly—catching the sunlight and reflecting it back at them. Elena was static, floating beside him, just outside the still-rotating limbs.

Beyond the two objects was the station. It was still far away, on the edge of the horizon, but getting larger as they closed in. Home sweet home, Billy thought. He silently listed what he hoped would happen: Raj would miss the station; Elena would go aboard safe and sound; Amir would successfully dock the ship. And then, finally, he would hold Christina in his arms.

CHAPTER TWENTY-TWO

YEAR 4 AAE–DAY 365

"Ten . . . nine . . . eight . . . seven . . ."—the crowd all screamed, louder and louder with each number—"six . . . five . . . four . . . three . . . two . . . one! Happy New Year!"

All around, kids yelled and screamed and threw shredded paper into the air, blowing horns and shaking noisemakers and hugging and shaking hands and kissing. Lost in the middle were Christina and Billy. He wrapped an arm around her, they hugged, and he gave her a small kiss on the lips.

"Happy New Year," he said.

"And to you."

He released her and looked around to see if anybody had noticed or cared. He was always so careful about public displays of affection. Everybody knew he and Christina were a couple, mates—but there was a decorum that he tried to maintain. He also wanted to set a tone. As they got older the crew members were either dating or becoming formal couples, or at least thinking about what would happen in the future.

Christina and Billy were now almost twenty. They'd been together since they first came into space, before they took up residence in the space station. They were like an old married couple—with close to 100 children who were all growing up.

Funny how nine-year-olds became thirteen-year-olds who began to think—and feel—things through. Sheppard had joked to Billy that there seemed to be an excess of pheromones in the atmosphere that even the oxygen scrubbers couldn't remove. He worried that if he continued to breathe in what they were breathing out, he'd start acting like a teenager again. Or, as he corrected himself, really for the first time. Hardly ever a child and even less a teenager the first time through, he was still revelling in being among so many young and brilliant minds. He was constantly amazed by their abilities and intellects. Sadly, as he'd confessed only to Billy and Christina, he also realized that while their minds were racing forward, his was starting to let him down. So far it was noticeable only to him and those closest, but it was becoming more pronounced.

"Happy New Year," Billy said loudly as he offered Sheppard his hand.

"And to you. I didn't expect I'd necessarily be entering into the fourth year."

"Well, I didn't expect to be flying around the planet in a space station, but things happen that nobody could predict," Billy said.

"That's an understatement. Who knows? I might even be there when we touch down on the surface again."

Billy raised a glass. "To the professor. May you be the first one off the ship."

"I might have to be shoved out the hatch in my walker."

Sheppard, Billy, and Christina clinked glasses and sipped their ice water.

"May I join you?" Ivan asked.

"Of course!" the professor replied.

"It's good to be among the adults," he said.

Billy could detect a subtle smell of alcohol coming from Ivan. Ivan had taken vegetable peelings and fermented them to create a crude alcoholic drink. He hadn't asked Billy's permission—or felt that he needed to—and Billy hadn't said anything about it. Billy had learned to pick his battles. Ivan was responsible with what he made and drank, and never offered to share it with any of the crew other than his two shipmates. As well, the production was so small that there wasn't much to go around.

"Professor, I believe you are old enough to have a drink, correct?" Ivan asked.

"I think I just might be above the limit."

Ivan pulled out a silver flask and poured a little bit into the professor's drink. He raised his glass. "*Prosit*!"

"*Prosit*!" the professor said as the two men clinked glasses.

"So, Commander Billy, what is the legal drinking age on this world of ours?"

"We're over the United States, so it's probably twenty-one," Billy responded.

"So only Sam, Lars, the professor, and I can partake of my special creation," Ivan said.

"I guess so. Although we are above Idaho, and I think it might have a lower drinking age," Billy said.

"It can have whatever age you want it to have," Ivan said. "In my country, boys much younger than you would drink with their parents." He paused. "You are no boy. Well?"

Billy nodded his head.

Ivan unscrewed the top again and poured a small quantity of the clear fluid into his glass. They both raised their glasses and clinked them.

"*Prosit*," they said together.

"So in a few years there will be more who can partake," Ivan said.

"In a few years we'll raise the drinking age to avoid that," Billy said.

Ivan laughed. "Alcohol combined with raging hormones confined to a small space is a recipe for troubles." He paused. "More troubles."

There was no need to say anything else.

The crew was maturing, getting older, more of them reaching puberty, trying to discover who they were and who they belonged with, and it was becoming more and more of an issue. Small skirmishes and larger arguments were becoming increasingly frequent. Christina had taken on the role of mediator, counsellor, and disciplinarian when needed. She had also reorganized work schedules and living accommodations to keep things from boiling over.

What they couldn't control was the "shrinking" space.

The station was of course a finite size and the number of crew was fixed, so that didn't change. But each member of the crew—with the exception of the four adult men—was increasing in size. And the bigger the people, the smaller the spaces seemed, as bodies bumped into bodies, beds felt smaller, ceilings seemed lower, and chairs got narrower. Through the course of the last four years the males had grown, on average, 36 percent, and the females 28 percent, for an average of 32 percent. They knew those figures exactly because each month all crew members were weighed and measured to determine the amount of food they were allowed. Projections called for a further 5 to 8 percent growth per year for the next three years, with a 3 to 4 percent increase in growth through years nine and ten on the station.

Increased size didn't just mean larger quantities of food and water. It also meant higher metabolism rates, increased need for oxygen scrubbers, and a greater need to neutralize the moisture coming off their bodies, which condensed on the external surfaces. All those had to be factored into the maintenance of the equipment.

They were also trying to keep everybody busy. Idle time was bad time. But there was always work that needed to be done on the station. The ship was aging even more significantly than the crew, and long-term space travel created mechanical strains and stresses that necessitated constant and increasingly critical maintenance.

There were also numerous attempts to keep the crew busy in other ways, the New Year's Eve party included. There were clubs, card and chess tournaments, music rehearsals and concerts, tutorials, lessons in languages, and cultural presentations. With so many experts, there were lots of teachers and lots of things to learn. And of course physical activities were an important component, and a chance to let off some steam.

Ivan and Sam had continued training everyone onboard in various forms of martial arts, focusing on both the art of self-defence and useful attack skills. Sam had recently initiated a program of meditation to follow each lesson or sparring session to help establish calm and reflection before students were sent out of the "dojo."

Tonight, almost everybody on the ship, with the exception of the five people on duty or watch, was here. Billy scanned the room. One person was definitely missing.

"Does anybody know where Sam is?" Billy asked.

They all looked around.

"He was here earlier," Ivan said. "He might have gone back to our quarters. Would you like me to check?"

"No, no problem. Could you excuse me? I'm going to go to the control room and offer to relieve some of them so they can join the party."

"Do you want me to come along?" Christina asked.

"No, you enjoy yourself," he said, and then turned and walked away.

Of course Billy wanted Christina to have fun at the party, but his motives were actually a bit more complicated. He didn't want her to follow him partly because he wanted her there to watch the room. But mainly it was because the control room was only his first stop. Billy had noticed that somebody else was also missing—Tasha. She had remained one of his strongest crew members. She had also remained one of the most stubborn and least willing to follow orders or do what was expected. Their relationship had fallen into a bad spiral. The less he could predict her behaviour, the less he could trust her. The less he trusted her, the less he could predict her. And she'd been spending more time with Sam. On the surface this didn't seem like a big problem, but Christina had told him that something about their friendship just didn't "feel right."

Billy came up to the open door of the control room. He stopped and leaned in. "All well?"

"SOP, Commander," Jason said.

"Standard operating procedure is what I like to hear," Billy said.

"I'd like to hear more of the party, myself," he replied.

"I'm just checking something out but I'll come back and take a turn so at least two of you can go to the party. You five decide which two."

As Billy walked away he could hear them discussing which two could best be spared. As those voices faded there were none to replace them. He continued down the corridor, moving quickly but quietly, alert to any sound around him. He wanted to hear but not be heard, see but not be seen.

He cut through the food production unit. This was the shortest route to the ship that was home to Ivan, Lars, and Sam. The flow of fresh air practically rushed out of the plants. Normally he would have simply stood and inhaled deeply. There was no time. As he exited out through the other side, the door automatically opened and then closed behind him.

There was a slight wheezing sound that normally wouldn't have been audible but in the silence it sounded ominously loud. He'd ask engineering to take care of that.

Then there was another sound—a voice. And as he moved it became louder, more agitated, definitely female—was it Tasha? And then silence.

Billy made the turn around the corner and skidded to a stop. There in front of him were Tasha and Sam. Tasha was on the ground, and Sam was kneeling next to her with his hands around her throat. His back was to Billy.

Without a word, sound, or thought Billy flung himself forward, smashing into Sam, ripping him away from Tasha's prone body. The two of them tumbled forward together and then flew apart, Billy hitting the far wall. He jumped up, but before he could get fully planted his feet were swept out from under him and he tumbled back down.

Sam stood over him, smiling. "What's the idea, buddy?" he asked.

Billy was confused—why was he smiling?—and then he realized why. Sam had height, size, and position, and he was a trained killer. Billy had to think, or at least delay.

"Tasha, are you all right?"

Tasha was sitting up, rubbing her throat. She tried to answer but only a raspy sob came out.

"She's fine, just fine," Sam said. "We were just talking when you interrupted us. You hurt her when you jumped me. Why did you do that?"

"You weren't talking. Tasha, go, get out of here," Billy said.

Sam jumped back before Tasha could even think to move. He grabbed her by the arm, and she screamed out in pain. Sam spun her around like she was a sack of laundry and then dragged her over and dumped her right beside Billy. She screamed again as she dropped down next to him.

"It'll be okay," Billy said quietly as he moved slightly forward to put himself between her and Sam.

"I think we need to talk this over a little bit," Sam said.

"Sure, we can talk," Billy said. His hand had reached down to the back of his boot—the place where he usually kept his knife. Tonight he'd left it in his quarters.

"People do stupid things when they've been drinking," Billy said.

"As stupid as trying to take me out?" Sam asked.

"That was pretty stupid," Billy said. "How about if we just admit we both made a mistake and call it even?"

"Yeah, I'm sure that will work—until you get free. What then?"

"What do you mean, what then?" Billy asked. "You go to bed and sleep it off and we pretend that none of this happened."

Billy slowly got to his feet and offered Sam his hand. Sam's smile got bigger. Was he going to agree to this or—suddenly there was a knife in his hand!

"You don't have to do this," Billy said.

"You're right," he said, the smile growing. He lowered the knife and Billy relaxed slightly, then Sam lunged forward as Billy stumbled backwards! Billy felt searing pain, like a slash of fire as the sweep of the knife sliced through his shirt and into his side! He grabbed his side. Blood dripped out through his shirt and between his fingers.

"I'm going to kill you. Then I'm going to kill her to keep you both quiet."

"You won't get away with this," Billy gasped.

"Who do you think is going to stop me?"

"Everybody will know what you did."

"Me?" Sam asked. "This was all Tasha's doing. She stabbed you because you had an affair with her and then ditched her, and she was bitter and rejected."

"What?" Billy demanded.

"And then she took her own life with the same knife," he added.

"Nobody will believe that."

"Maybe you're right. Maybe it was a tragic seal leak and the two of you were blown into space, and they won't be able to examine the bodies because you'll be gone."

"The seals are fine."

"I'll arrange it so they aren't. I know how to do all of that. Besides, even if they don't believe me, what are they going to do about it, try to take me down?"

With him gone, Billy thought, it would be up to the professor and Christina to try to seek the truth and run the station.

"I'll work with Ivan and the two of us will be unstoppable, unpunishable, and in control. Nobody can stop the two of us together. Do you think the professor is going to take us on?"

Before Billy could even think to react, Sam leapt forward, the knife slashing down. And then Sam screamed in pain and stopped. His smile was gone. Slowly he turned around, and as he did, Billy saw the handle of a knife sticking out of his back, blood leaking out of the wound. Sam stumbled forward a few steps and collapsed onto his knees, and then onto his face.

As Sam fell, Billy saw Ivan standing there. He stepped forward, planted a foot in the middle of Sam's back, and pulled out the knife. Sam didn't react—no sound, no movement, nothing, not even a rush of blood.

"Is he dead?" Billy asked.

"I don't stab somebody so they can live. I severed his aorta."

"But you stabbed him in the back."

Ivan shrugged. "His back was facing me. Besides, I had no need to even the odds. Sam is deadly with a knife. If it was going to be him or me, or him or you and Tasha, I think I made the right decision. Let me see your wound."

In that instant, Billy had forgotten about the slash on his side. He pulled open his shirt to reveal a long, thin red gash twenty centimetres long.

Ivan examined it. "Stitches, but nothing more. That's the way I heard he always operated."

"What do you mean?" Billy asked.

"He would carve somebody up before he killed him. There would have been another dozen slashes before he finally finished you off."

"He's done this before?" Billy asked.

"I'd heard rumours. No proof, just reputation. I once told you I kill only people I need to. Sam killed people he wanted to. We have to get both of you to the clinic. Get you stitched up and Tasha examined."

Ivan reached down and offered Billy a hand. He hesitated for a just a second. Ivan held the knife in his other hand and . . . there was no point. If Ivan wanted him dead, he was dead. He took Ivan's hand and got to his feet.

Together the two of them helped Tasha up. Her eyes were vacant and her reaction was to not react. Billy had seen this before. She was in shock.

"What about him?" Billy asked, gesturing to Sam.

"He's not going anywhere. Let's take care of the living before we dispose of the dead. I'll make sure it will be done."

CHAPTER TWENTY-THREE

YEAR 5 AAE–DAY 1

Billy sat on a chair outside Tasha's room at the clinic. Christina was inside, offering comfort and support. Tasha had come out of shock, become hysterical, and finally had to be sedated to be examined. Christina wanted to be there when she woke up so she didn't wake up alone.

Tasha was physically fine, although there was bruising around her throat—finger marks—and her larynx was badly bruised. The force of Sam's hands had almost crushed it. The doctor reported that a few more seconds of pressure and the damage would have been irreparable. Emotionally, she was pretty shredded after what she'd seen, and worse, what had almost happened. It was strange—living in a space station they faced the ongoing threat of sudden and certain death on a daily basis, but it all seemed so abstract, so clinical. This was different, because it was right there, brutally real, red, and bloody.

Billy reached down and touched his side. It was tender, stinging, but it would ultimately be nothing more than a thin scar, if it left a mark at all. A little deeper and it would have been fatal. Life and death were just a centimetre or two apart. Billy, the professor, and the team had outlined dozens of ways that death could come on the station and tried to provide a plan and backup for each of them. Being stabbed to death wasn't on the list.

The station had finally gone to bed, the party over, with only a few people knowing what had happened. Only the two doctors, Christina, Amir, the professor, and Lars—plus of course Ivan and Tasha—knew the full story. Tomorrow, when everyone awoke, Billy would have to decide who would know what, what parts of the truth would be told.

Billy heard steps. Ivan appeared and took the seat beside his.

"How's your side?"

"It's nothing."

"A paper cut is nothing. I saw the gash. How many stitches?" Ivan asked.

"Thirty or forty. I wasn't counting."

"My father always said that a good scar is worth a good story."

"I won't be telling this story. At least not all of it," Billy said.

"Another thing my father said was that the only way two people can keep a secret is if at least one of them is dead."

"Your father was full of interesting advice."

"He was, shall we say, an interesting man. I could tell

you a few stories about my childhood . . . and show you the scars that went with them. What was your father like?"

Billy reached into his pocket and pulled out a picture of his family—father, mother, him, and his brother. He handed it to Ivan.

"He looks kind, but looks can be deceiving."

"He was kind. They were killed in a car crash."

"Sad, but life throws us many curves. Undoubtedly their deaths somehow led to you being here alive and today," Ivan said.

Billy nodded. "I've thought that through before. For better or worse, we're only the result of all the good and bad things that happen to us."

"Sometimes I think the bad things have more influence. And how is Tasha?" Ivan asked.

"She's physically fine but pretty shook up."

"If she wasn't it would be more troubling. She's never seen somebody die in front of her eyes, I would imagine," Ivan said.

"I don't think so." Billy paused. "Do you remember your first body?"

"I remember each one of them. You?"

Billy shook his head. "I try to forget, but some stand out. I'm not going to forget this one. Did you take care of it?"

"Lars and I cleaned up the area and disposed of the body."

"Disposed?"

"We put it in the space lock of the ship and opened the door without decompressing. It was flung out into the vacuum and well clear of the station. Sam will never be seen again."

"How did Lars react to all of this?" Billy asked.

"He had to clean up his own vomit as well as the blood. He does not have much of a stomach for this sort of thing. Still, he was grateful for what happened. He was afraid of Sam."

"I didn't know that. He never said anything," Billy said.

"He was too afraid. He also told me more about what I suspected was going on between Sam and Tasha."

Billy had known they were friends. "They were seeing each other?"

"I think there might be other words for their relationship. It would be better for you to hear from Tasha than from second-hand guesses," Ivan said.

"I appreciate that. I appreciate everything. Why were you even there?"

"I followed you, just to be certain," Ivan said.

"But why would you think you needed to do that?"

"I knew Sam wasn't at the party, and I saw that you noticed that too. I guessed that you were going to try to find him," Ivan said.

"But even then, why would that be a concern?" Billy asked.

"Somebody who always smiles and laughs when there is nothing friendly or funny is not somebody to be trusted. I knew that Sam was not a good person."

"But you never tried to warn me."

"Would it have done any good if I'd tried?" Ivan asked. "Besides, you didn't trust him. You don't really trust anybody, do you? Certainly not me."

Billy thought about this but decided not to respond. He was interested to see where Ivan would go with the question.

After a pause Ivan went on. “No, I wouldn’t trust me either. Especially after last night. Don’t worry, I don’t take it personally. After all, you saw me kill Sam before your eyes.”

“Yes, but you saved my life. Tasha’s life,” Billy said.

“Maybe I did it for me as much as I did it for you. Sam was a threat to me as well. That threat has now been eliminated.”

The door slid open and Christina poked her head out. She looked surprised to see Ivan there.

“I haven’t had a chance to say it, but, Ivan, thank you for what you did,” she said.

“I did what was needed. Nothing more.”

“It was a lot more. Billy, do you think you could you come inside, please?”

He got up, trying not to wince in pain, but both Ivan and Christina noticed. He’d have to more careful around anybody who didn’t know.

Billy and Christina retreated into the room, the door sliding closed behind them. Billy was surprised to see Tasha awake and sitting up. She gave him a sad, weak smile. He circled around to the side of the bed.

“How are you feeling?” Billy asked.

“Sore, hurt, sorry. Is he, is he . . . ?”

“He’s dead,” Billy said. “There was no choice. I know you were close to him.”

She shook her head. “I thought we were friends. At least until he—” She burst into tears and began sobbing.

Christina came over and cradled Tasha's head in her arms, holding her until her sobbing subsided.

"Tasha," she said softly, "can I tell him? Would that be all right?"

She nodded.

"Stop me if I'm saying anything wrong, okay?" she said.

Again she nodded.

"Tasha was spending a lot of time with Sam," she began. "He was, well, charming at first. Then he started making advances, suggesting they could be more than friends."

Billy tried to remain neutral, not show any emotions that Tasha might read as upset or disapproving, despite the anger starting to build inside.

"Then, well, she thinks that he gave her something in her water bottle one night, and she woke up in his bed. She was upset, but he convinced her that there was nothing she could do—that nobody would believe her, believe what had happened."

Tasha's tears flowed more freely. She looked down, unable or unwilling to make eye contact.

"He told her that if she tried to break things off, if she didn't go along with what he wanted, it would go badly. That he'd take it out on her or somebody else. That knife was always there as a real threat."

"The threat is gone," Billy said. "He'll never hurt you or anybody else again. It's over."

From the look in Christina's eyes, Billy knew it wasn't over.

"What happened tonight that was different?" Billy asked. "What set him off?"

"I told him," Tasha said, forcing the words out between sobs.

"Told him what?" Billy asked. Did she tell him that it was over, that she was going to tell people?

Christina took a deep breath. "Tasha told him that she's pregnant."

Billy searched for the right words but nothing came. Tasha was pregnant with Sam's child. Sam was gone, dead and blown out into space. There was only one thing he could do.

He reached out and took Tasha's hand. "Tasha, you've been through so much. You have to know that we're all here for you. You and your baby."

CHAPTER TWENTY-FOUR

YEAR 5 AAE–DAY 12

In the end, Billy decided that the advice given to Ivan by his father was correct. There was no point in even attempting to keep a secret—much less a series of secrets—when so many people knew so much.

A meeting was called on New Year's Day for the following day at noon. Everybody who had celebrated the new year with such high hopes was given the cold, dampening information about what had gone on. In simple, direct words they were told about Sam's assault on Tasha and his attempted murder of Billy, Ivan's killing of Sam, and finally Tasha's pregnancy.

They were also told one more thing that was "secret." It was an attempt to balance the bad and unthinkable with the good and hopeful. The facts were still being gathered, and they didn't know yet whether it would affect the timeline for their return to Earth, but there were promising changes going on below. Between the telescope aimed at the surface and the results of the last planetary survey, there was no doubt that the clearing of the clouds, those little circles of blue, was widespread, ongoing, and could potentially become more frequent.

Originally the Internal Operations Committee had thought to wait for data from another two surveys—two more months—before releasing information to the crew. However, in light of the terrible, disturbing events, Billy had decided that the crew needed to be given something more. Maybe they wouldn't be up here for another six years. Maybe. A little bit of hope could go a long way, and right now hope was needed.

Sam had been liked by almost all of the crew. He had fooled most of the crew. His role as a martial arts teacher, the smile, the shared laughter, and the friendliness that he projected had made him popular. Some couldn't believe that he would ever have hurt Tasha and tried to kill Billy. They just couldn't wrap their heads around the whole thing.

Easier to understand was how Sam was killed. Ivan looked and acted the part of a killer. His history was known to people, and although his background in security was similar to Sam's, his demeanour seemed to fit the part of a killer more. He always maintained a cold, detached distance from everybody. While nobody talked openly about it, many of the crew were actually afraid of him, and knowing that he had killed Sam was certainly not going to reassure anyone. His cold, calculated, unemotional response in the days that followed only offered a more powerful reason to fear him.

Today, the Internal Operations Committee was also meeting. People filed into the conference room and took their usual spots: Billy and Christina at the head of the table, Amir and the professor opposite, Brian and Asha on the third side, and Jennie and Tasha on the fourth.

Tasha had offered to resign her spot on the committee but Billy wouldn't allow it. He argued that her expertise was needed, but also her honest opinions. And Christina agreed that Tasha needed to be there. It was important to send a message to everyone on the station that what happened was not her fault. She was a victim and needed their care, support, and help in dealing with what was going to happen next.

"Good afternoon, everybody," Billy began. "I want to start by talking to you about making a change in the membership of this committee."

Judging by her expression, Billy could tell that Tasha was afraid he had changed his mind and decided to accept her resignation.

"I want to add another member," he said.

"That would be great," Tasha said, looking very much relieved.

"Of course," added Brian, and the others nodded, or added their voices in support. Billy hadn't even talked to Christina about this, which was unusual in itself.

"I appreciate your support, but don't you want to know who it is?" Billy asked.

"I'm sure we all do," the professor said. "Who is it?"

"Ivan. I want Ivan to be part of the committee," Billy said. "It's not just that he has something to add, but I think we need to send a message to the entire crew that Ivan carries no responsibility for what happened, that, in fact, his actions saved my life and Tasha's." He paused. "And the life of her unborn child."

"He has my support," Tasha said.

"Can we put it to a vote?" Billy asked.

"Certainly," the professor said. "All in favour of adding Ivan to the Internal Operations Committee, please raise your hand."

Every hand went up.

"I will invite him to the next meeting," Billy said. "Now, down to today's business. Where should we start?"

"I have some good news about the solar panels," Brian said.

"Good news is a terrific place to start. Please."

Brian turned to Asha for the report.

"With the work completed yesterday, we were able to get the solar panels back in full operation," she said.

There was a spontaneous burst of applause.

"We are now back to almost 95 percent of the power we had when we first boarded this station," Brian added.

The projections called for them to lose 5 percent of power per year of operation due to the degradation of the solar panels through micro-collisions and aging. They had managed to cut that loss down to 25 percent of what was expected.

"We'll have to make decisions about how to use the additional power that's back on line," Billy said.

"Our carbon dioxide levels are up," Amir said.

"I can feel it in the air," Jennie said.

"How much?" Billy asked.

"They're still well within acceptable levels, but higher than we'd want," the professor said.

"So does the committee think the additional power should be directed to getting more oxygen scrubbers in operation?" Billy asked.

"Or perhaps we could simply add more growing capacity," Christina said. "Put more plants under cultivation with more grow-lights. That would produce more food and convert more carbon dioxide to air. Natural air scrubbing."

"That is a much slower process," the professor said. "We also have issues around the plants releasing more moisture into the air. As you know, the condensation is starting to cause problems with some of the equipment. The scrubbers also harvest water from the atmosphere."

"Let's ask those with the most expertise to prepare a report to consider the long-term solution that would best suit our needs," Billy said. "In the meantime, are the scrubbers the best solution?"

"Yes, in the short term that's definitely the route to go," the professor said.

"Then let's get those started while we continue gathering information about the long term. Any other specific issues around the station?" Billy asked.

"Things break down and we fix them," Amir said.

"Although things are breaking down more often," Brian added.

"Some of the components of the station are very old and beyond their projected lifespan," Christina said.

"I'd know about that," the professor said. "But somehow I keep ticking along too."

Everybody smiled or laughed.

Unfortunately, Billy was aware that the professor's aging was becoming more problematic. He still buzzed around the station offering advice and information but his movement was slower, his hands less steady. More troubling was the fact that he was becoming more forgetful, and Billy had started to question some of his information. The station's engineers had instructions to double-check critical suggestions that the professor made before acting on them.

The professor's diminishing capacity was a loss for the entire station, and for Billy more specifically. The professor was the person he most relied on for information, guidance, and advice. He had been a last-minute addition to the station, but he was one of its most important contributors.

Billy was already feeling the loss—emotionally, intellectually, and practically. That was the other, unspoken reason for asking Ivan to become part of the committee. Although Billy didn't fully trust him—and probably never would—he was going to need him more in the coming months and years.

"If there's no more station discussion, I'd be most interested in hearing about the latest survey data," Billy said.

"We certainly have more information," Jennie said. "As we discussed with the crew, those windows have continued to pop up randomly across the planet."

"Is there a notable pattern to their appearance?" Christina asked.

"The frequency is increasing, but they are scattered across the planet, and they open and close with varying size and duration."

"So sunlight is able to penetrate to the surface, correct?" the professor asked.

"In the clear windows," Jennie said.

"I don't understand," the professor said, although that had already been discussed. It was yet more proof that he wasn't processing things the same way.

Jennie hesitated, as though she might mention that, but she didn't. "Clear windows are openings that extend all the way to the surface and are easier to see. But the radar is also finding partial—or as we're calling them, opaque—windows, or frosted glass, where the window extends through the upper levels of the atmosphere but doesn't reach all the way to the surface."

"So in the clear windows there is potential for sunlight to produce photosynthesis," the professor said.

"The opening and closing of the windows takes place in far less time than needed for that to happen. The largest window was open for less than twenty-four hours," Jenna said. "However, the light penetrating to the surface has caused an energy exchange."

"The planet is warming?" the professor said.

Jennie gave a slight smile and nodded. "There has been a rise in temperature, globally, of almost two degrees over the past three months."

"That's amazing, simply amazing," the professor said.

"Our laser imaging is showing a major retreat in the ice fields, particularly in the Northern Hemisphere, where it is now summer," Jennie said. "And the implications of this are nothing short of game changing."

"Do you think we could return to Earth sooner than planned?" Billy asked.

"There's not enough data over a long enough period of time to fully judge the overall trend," Jennie answered. "I wouldn't want to make that pronouncement yet."

"But if you were to make a guess, just for the people around this table?" Christina asked.

"It looks very positive. Very positive."

"Let's keep that positive prediction within this room," Billy said. "In the meantime, I want more information gathered."

"Do you want me to lead another survey team prior to the next scheduled trip?" Amir asked.

"Yes, I think that would be warranted," Billy said. "I don't think there's anybody in this room, or on the station, who doesn't dream about the day we can once again set foot on our home turf."

It was the stuff of dreams and hope. So far they'd been able to repair, reroute, or reconceive everything that had gone wrong, even sidestepping critical failures in the station. But what was still to come? And how long could they keep solving the problems? Four years had seemed like an eternity. Six more years might be an impossibility, in spite of all their rigorous planning and extensive backups.

"I asked Jason to prepare a report for Christina on the radio transmissions still coming from the planet," Billy said. "Christina?"

"Thank you. The number of existing, surviving colonies on the surface appears to be constant at approximately one hundred and fifty."

"Originally weren't there more than five thousand signals being received?" Brian asked.

"In those first few days. The numbers dropped off exponentially as those first ill-conceived or badly run groupings failed."

Failed—as in the people there died because they weren't prepared.

"That number went down to less than five hundred by Year 2 AAE, and then an additional two hundred failed within the next year."

"That could be a result of inability to transmit as opposed to overall failure," the professor said.

"Or maybe they just realized that there was no point in transmitting messages. They might even have decided that communication was counterproductive," Amir said.

"What do you mean?" Billy asked.

"Letting people know you're alive might only encourage other groups to come and take your resources. I've been wondering—maybe the failure of some of these colonies had nothing to do with adequate resources or being well prepared. Maybe they were overwhelmed by outside forces."

"We certainly can't rule that out. That's why our Earth colony was placed in such an isolated location," Billy said. The colony on the ground was something that wasn't spoken of very much. It made them feel more alone to think that it was gone.

"I assume that none of the signals we are monitoring originate anywhere near our Earth colony," the professor said.

"There are seventeen separate signals coming from the North American continent, but none within a thousand kilometres of our launch site," Billy said.

"Any estimates of the size of those colonies?" Brian asked.

"We pick up traffic and some content, so we know that some of them are larger, perhaps four hundred or five hundred survivors," Billy said.

"We also make an assumption that they have to have a certain size—a critical mass, you might say—to have the skill set necessary to survive," the professor said. "We think each must have a minimum of one hundred people."

"So we assume that there are at least fifteen thousand people still alive," Brian said.

"I think we're projecting numbers that would be at least three times that, but even that might be a major underestimation."

"I don't understand," Brian said.

"We are monitoring the colonies that are sending out radio signals. Others may, as suggested, have stopped broadcasting, or never had the ability to send signals, or simply chose not to send signals," Christina said.

"Like we don't send signals," Billy explained.

"I'd always wondered about that. Why don't we send signals?" Asha asked.

"It was the protocol put in place by Joshua Fitchett," Billy explained.

"But why?" she persisted.

"He felt that our advantage would be lost by acknowledging our presence."

"But how would that harm us?" Brian asked. "It's not like anybody can get us up here . . . can they?"

The professor shook his head. "The ability to launch a vehicle into space is limited to only a very few people with information, skills, and materials. It is well beyond the capacity of any existing settlements or colonies—or, in fact, all the colonies put together."

"Then what are we worried about?" Asha asked.

"Maybe nothing. But on the other hand, there's not much to be gained by communicating," Billy said.

"Isn't there? Wouldn't most of the settlements be limited in their broadcast range?" Amir asked. "For example, would a colony in North America even be aware of a similar colony in Australia or Asia?"

"The curvature of the planet coupled with the density of the debris-filled atmosphere makes long-distance transmission or reception literally impossible," Jennie explained.

"So as far as we can tell, we're the only ones who are aware of all the colonies. We're the only group who regularly does fly-overs of the entire planet," Amir said. "And it's not just that we're not telling them we're up here—we're not telling them about each other."

"They must feel so alone," Christina said.

"And we could change that. We could let them know that they're not alone, that there are other people out here," Brian said.

"You're right," Billy said. "I've been thinking about this myself."

"So we're going to do it?" Asha asked.

"I think we need to consider this further and make the right decision. Once we reveal ourselves, we can never be invisible again. There are consequences I can't predict." He paused. "I just wish I could ask Joshua about it."

"It's such a tragedy that he was . . . that they were . . . well, you know what I mean. It was such an incredibly implausible statistical probability that they would suffer such a devastating direct impact," Professor Sheppard said.

But Billy had also entertained another thought, one he hadn't shared with anyone, not even the professor or Christina. What if they were still alive down there? What if they'd chosen not to communicate because they—meaning Joshua—felt that their "death" would be greater motivation for those on the station to survive? What if? It wouldn't be the first time Joshua had claimed to have been killed. He had staged a fire at his own home so that he could disappear and escape his enemies. But it was such a wild thought. There was no point in getting hopes up without reason. Besides, as long as the thought stayed in Billy's head there was no way it could be disproved. A little bit of hope—even false hope—was an incredibly powerful thing.

"Our next scheduled survey ship goes out in three weeks," Billy said. "I'd like preparations to be made for us to have the capacity to communicate with each colony on the surface as we pass over."

"We're going to do it?" Asha gasped.

"I'm not saying that. I'm saying we need to be prepared in case that decision is reached. Let's keep this, as with all things discussed in this meeting, to ourselves until we make a decision. If there's nothing else, let's adjourn the meeting."

CHAPTER TWENTY-FIVE

YEAR 5 AAE–DAY 84

For more than four years now, Billy had thought often about what they would have done without the last-minute addition of Professor Sheppard to their mission. His expertise, his presence, had meant so much to everybody. Today, the answer would have to be faced.

Last night, peacefully in his sleep, the professor had died. It was as much unexpected as it was expected. He'd gone to bed complaining about feeling "a little weak." In the morning, when he didn't show up for breakfast and wasn't seen around the station, Billy and Christina went to check on him. They found him with his glasses still perched on top of his head and a reading tablet balanced on his chest. Classical music was playing softly in the background.

Billy called the crew together. They gathered quickly, knowing that emergency meetings never meant good news. There was tension in the air. Billy knew it was going to be hard to tell the others when he was so close to tears himself. They needed to see him in control.

The meeting was called to order and Billy took to the small stage at the front of the common room.

"I brought you here this morning because I need to share some very sad news." He took a deep breath. "Last night, in his sleep, Professor Daniel Sheppard died."

There was a gasp that could be heard across the room, followed by sobbing.

"We don't know the cause of death. He was found this morning, by me and Christina, in bed. Dr. Saul was called and examined him. It is believed that his death was quick and painless for him." He paused. "It will be neither for those whom he left behind. Professor Sheppard was my friend, my teacher, my mentor, a man I looked to for guidance—a man we all came to love."

There were more tears. People were hugging and comforting each other. It was becoming harder for Billy to remain composed when it seemed like every single person in the common room was either in tears or on the verge of crying. Even Ivan, standing in the corner as always, looked less stoic than usual.

"To me he was 'Professor.' Some of you called him 'Grandpa' or 'Grandpa Shep,' and he told me how much he liked those names, how much he loved being the grandfather to so many. I think he liked that as much as he liked being the professor . . . maybe even more.

"Few among us ever knew our parents or grandparents. He became that wise and kind grandfather for us. I know each of you had special moments with him. We need to remember those moments.

"He and I talked many times every day. He helped me to understand technical things about the station, about space, about the universe. About life. About me. I will remember the lessons he taught me about life.

"He told me that as a child he dreamed of being an astronaut, of being in space. To come and live on the station—some of which was his design—was the dream of a lifetime. He also told me that he would never live long enough to return to Earth. Once again, he was right."

Billy's voice cracked over the last few words and he broke into tears. Christina was instantly at his side, her arms around him. He tried to continue and found that he couldn't. Another person he cared for was gone—like his parents and brother, like his street family, like Joshua Fitchett. And now the professor. He buried his head into her shoulder.

Tasha stood up. "Could I say a few words?"

Billy tried to answer but he couldn't. Christina gestured for her to come forward and she climbed the steps to the stage.

"Shep meant a lot to me, as he did to most of us," Tasha began. "I'm going to miss him so much." She wiped away a tear.

"As you all know, I'm expecting. What you wouldn't know is that Dr. Sarah recently told me that I'm carrying a healthy little baby boy. In less than three months he will be welcomed into the world—or, I guess, into above-the-world—my son. He will be named after his grandfather. He will be known as Sheppard. I hope he grows up to be somebody as remarkable as his namesake. Our Grandpa Sheppard is gone but he won't ever be forgotten."

In spite of the tears, applause and cheers erupted. Christina reached out and wrapped an arm around Tasha, and the three of them stood on the stage and hugged.

The escape pod was the closest thing to a coffin that they had on the station. It was big enough for the professor's body with room to spare. It seemed fitting that a man with such expertise, such a love of outer space, would die there.

The professor, in his pod, was in one of the station's space locks. Elena and Brian, in spacesuits, wearing jetpacks, were also there. They were going to be the pallbearers, bringing the pod out of the ship. The whole process was being supervised by Amir from the control room. The images of the pod and pallbearers were being beamed onto the big screen in the common room, where the rest of the crew had gathered.

Billy stood at the back. He wanted to be able to slip out if needed. He didn't want his reactions to be the focus for anybody else. People seemed to sense that he needed to be alone, and even Christina was giving him space.

Ivan entered the room and took his usual spot—right beside where Billy was already standing. For Billy, being in that spot was almost a subconscious way to stay detached, the way Ivan always seemed detached. They greeted each other with a slight nod of the head.

"I will miss him," Ivan said quietly.

"So will I."

"He was a good person," Ivan said. "I don't think I've met many of those."

"I think there used to be more of them before the world changed."

Ivan shook his head. "The asteroid didn't change people, it merely revealed who they truly were. You are the same person you were before all of this."

"I guess that makes us two pretty bad people."

"Us?" Ivan asked. "We are the good guys. Don't you think I'm one of the good guys? Don't you think you are?"

"I think I'm as good as circumstances allow me to be," Billy said.

"What more could anybody ask? Being good doesn't mean being stupid. You and me, we'll do what we need to do and be as kind as the situation allows." He pointed to the screen. "Look, they're leaving the bay."

Billy turned back toward the screen. The big bay door was slowly opening, revealing the blackness outside. The escape pod—the coffin—floated between Brian and Elena as they slowly moved toward the door, their special shoes attaching them solidly to the hull of the ship. Getting to the edge, they deactivated the shoes and pushed off. Brian gave a larger push and the three of them—Elena, Brian, and the professor—soared out, skidding slightly off to one side. The outside camera picked them up and showed them floating away from the station. Now, with enough distance, they both used their jetpacks to take them away.

"Let's watch from the control room window," Billy said, and he and Ivan slipped out the back door and along the corridor.

Entering the control room they now could see the event in real life, the whole thing unfolding outside the window. Jason was working the com-link, communicating with the two space flyers, and Amir was monitoring the overall station condition. He had undoubtedly been the one who controlled the depressurization of the bay and opening of the doors.

"You're almost in position," Jason said to them. "I need you to rotate the pod by about fifteen degrees."

"Roger that, buddy," Brian said.

"Okay, you're looking pretty good on that," Jason said. "I'm going to ask you now to change the trajectory by five degrees and then deliver the package."

Billy didn't like to think of the professor as a package, but that's what the escape pod was—a package to be delivered to wherever in eternity he was going.

Billy walked up to Jason and put a hand on his shoulder. Jason turned slightly around. "Thank you for taking care of all this. You're the centre of this entire station."

"Just doing my job," Jason said.

"No, you're doing much more than that, and I appreciate it. You're a good man. I don't want to interfere with what you're doing right now but can you come and see me later today?"

"Sounds like he's either in trouble or up for a promotion," Amir joked.

"Not in trouble," Billy said. "I'd like you to think about possibly taking on even more responsibility. We'll talk."

Jason looked very pleased.

"Is he being placed in an orbit that will not interfere with the station?" Ivan asked.

"No, he's being placed in a trajectory that will cause him to re-enter the atmosphere," Billy explained.

"But won't the pod burn up on entry?" Ivan asked.

Billy nodded. "Like a cremation. The fragments will be scattered throughout the atmosphere and eventually settle all over the planet."

"I think he would have liked that," Ivan said.

"He told me he hoped that he could return to Earth one day. He's just getting there a little bit sooner than the rest of us, that's all."

The pod was given a large push, powered by thrust from one of the jetpacks. As the pod continued to move, Elena used her thrusters to come back around until she was right beside Brian. Then together the two of them started to fly back toward the open bay door.

Jason began addressing their reboarding of the station through the com-link and Amir began to work the necessary controls. Billy walked over to the edge of the window and watched as the pod continued to move off. It got smaller and smaller until he wasn't sure if he was really seeing it so much as wanting to see it.

If the trajectory was correct it would orbit for another four or five hours, dropping lower and lower until it started to encounter the upper levels of the atmosphere. Those minute particles would start to slow the speed of the pod, and the decrease in speed would cause it to fall lower, where it would encounter more particles. It would be on its journey down toward the surface, the heat increasing as the friction increased, until finally it would burst into flames, the last shreds of it being converted to ash. Part of Billy wished he could see that final burst, to know that the professor's wish had come true.

"Ivan, do you have a moment to talk?" Billy asked.

"Am I in trouble now?" Ivan joked.

"Or being promoted?" Amir added.

Billy gestured to the door. "Please." He followed Ivan out to the corridor and as the door closed behind them he began to talk.

"I'm not sure if it is a promotion but it might mean a lot of trouble," Billy said. "I was hoping you would consider taking on the role that the professor played for me."

"I am not qualified to provide his expertise. Both Amir and Jason would be better suited."

"I'm not asking you for technical advice. We have many people who can give me that. I'm asking for your honest opinion—on everything—including when you think I'm wrong. Maybe especially when you think I'm wrong."

"Interesting. So now you feel that what I will give will be honest?" Ivan asked.

"Your honesty is beyond question. I need somebody I can trust. Well?"

Ivan slowly nodded. "You will have my honest opinion. You will also have my word: here on the station, and when we return to Earth, I will give my life if necessary to safeguard you and the other members of this crew."

He reached out a hand and offered it to Billy. The two men shook.

CHAPTER TWENTY-SIX

YEAR 5 AAE-DAY 251

The alarm sounded and Billy practically jumped out of bed.

"This isn't a drill, is it?" Billy barked at Christina.

"No drill," she said, as she quickly got to her feet and began to get dressed.

The alarm stopped and was replaced by an announcement.

"Code red! Code red! Code red!"

"There's a fire," Billy said, trying to project a calmness he didn't feel. "I'm sure it's not serious."

"But we'll treat it like it is," Christina added.

"Code red! Code red! This is not a drill. Repeat, this is not a drill. There is a fire in R section."

Okay, that was to be expected. The former Russian space station was the oldest and most problematic of all their components. Predictability made Billy feel better. The fact that the fire was in one of the outer wings instead of the central core also gave him a sense of relief.

Fire was one of the most serious things that could happen. In closed, oxygen-rich quarters, with their limited ability to fight it and almost no ability to flee from it, fire was one of the greatest potential threats.

The door slid open and the smell of smoke was in the air. Billy felt the hairs on the back of his neck rise as he pulled on his clothes. He turned back to Christina. "Treat it like a full evacuation," he said, and then he was gone.

The corridor was already filling with people. There was no sense of panic, but there was a definite sense of urgency. They had done fire drills more often than anything else except a hull breach, so they fully knew what everybody had to do. If a breach or fire couldn't be contained, then they had to abandon the station. The ships that had brought them here became their escape routes, their lifeboats.

As Billy moved toward the fire the smell became stronger, more pungent, more powerful. He was soon confronted by people fleeing in the opposite direction.

"Where are you going?" he demanded.

"The route to our evacuation ship is blocked by the fire, so we're going to our secondary ships," one of them said.

"Excellent. Just slow down. No need to run or panic."

Since the fire was sufficiently large to stop them from getting to their ship—no, wait, it was two ships docked together—that meant that forty extra people would be crowding onto the remaining three ships. There would be close to a hundred people on ships that were designed and supplied for sixty. That was an issue that he hadn't even anticipated. At the next committee meeting he'd have to discuss having the ships redeployed to correct that oversight.

Each section of the ship had been sealed off to prevent the spread of fire or rupture. Fire was one of the most certain ways to cause a breach as the flames ate through or melted the outer hull. Billy had to manually open and then reseal the hatches as he passed through each corridor or section door. Unlocking the last door leading to the corridor to the Russian subsection, he was greeted by wisps of smoke. He hesitated at the thought of resealing the hatch—locking himself in with the fire—but there was no choice.

He was quickly greeted by the chief of the firefighting team, Andrea, who was dressed in full equipment, including respirator. One of the older crew members, Andrea was almost as stoic as Ivan, completely dedicated, and she trained her brigade regularly. She didn't believe in leaving anything to chance.

Andrea pulled off her mask.

"Report," Billy said.

"Full-fledged fire, ongoing, originating in the electrical system."

"How bad? How controlled?"

"Very bad and not controlled. We're throwing everything we have at it."

"Is there any way to get somebody to the two ships and detach them from the station?" Billy asked.

"Negative. That docking corridor is the hotspot where it erupted, and the fire is the worst type," Andrea said. "Even in our suits we can't approach it."

"Can you contain the fire? Can you put it out?" Billy asked.

Andrea didn't answer at first. Was she thinking, or afraid to give the answer she already knew? She finally spoke. "If we were on the planet I'd advise that we just abandon the facility. But we'll do our best. Now I have to get back to the fight."

"Of course."

Andrea pulled her mask down and headed back along the corridor. Billy, without a fire suit or respirator, trailed behind.

He stopped at the entrance to the subsection, which Andrea had resealed after her entrance. Peering through the porthole in the hatch, he was shocked by what he saw. The entire scene, as far as he could see, was nothing more than billowing black smoke. Visible were the members of the fire brigade, not much more than shadows moving through the thick black clouds. Billy felt his stomach tightening. This was even worse than he could have imagined. He had to do something, but what? It wasn't as if he could go in there and help. Without a suit, or at least a respirator, he wouldn't last more than a few seconds. Then he thought of something.

He started off toward the control room and hit his com-link. "Jason, do you read me?"

"Roger, Billy."

"Can you externally control the bay door of Ship 4?"

"I can control everything externally," Jason replied.

"Good. I need you to order Amir, Elena, and Brian to the control room immediately, and I need two jetpacks and four spacesuits."

"Who's the fourth suit for?" Jason asked.

"That would be for me."

It had taken less than five minutes for them to assemble and another five to get into the suits and reach the open bay. There had been a great deal of unvoiced concern about Billy's participation, since he'd never been on a spacewalk before. Amir was also anxious—he preferred his trips into space to be inside a ship. But everybody complied quickly. They were told the plan and understood why it had to happen, and happen quickly.

Those crew members not fighting the fire or in the bay were all safely sealed into the other three ships. Hatches throughout the station had been closed as well. The fire wouldn't spread. The danger was an explosion causing fragments of the burning subsection to puncture other sections of the station and cause breaches. They couldn't take any chances. In fact, if things got worse they were going to send the other ships off to orbit a safe distance from the station.

There was one other safety built in. If the station went up they couldn't survive in space on the ships more than a few weeks. Each ship had been given the re-entry data necessary to land on the planet. The environment on the surface was cruel, and perhaps nobody would survive long term, but it was their only chance. The ships were programmed to all land at the same spot, the place that had been deemed most likely to support life. They'd land with the few months' supply of food that was always on the ships and a hope that they could survive.

"Okay, Jason, we're sealed and checked. We're ready to go," Billy said.

"I'll start evacuating the atmosphere. The door will be open in less than two minutes."

"Evacuate quicker. Do it in under a minute, and patch me into Andrea, stat."

There was a click, some static, and then the com-link was established.

"Andrea, this is Billy. Update me."

"Not good, not good." There was a series of hoarse coughs. "I don't think we can control it . . . I don't think we can win."

"If you can't win, I still need you to fight it as long as possible. Can you give us another ten minutes?"

"Doubtful, but we'll try. We won't give up."

"Give us what you can before you have to get out, that's all I'm asking. Over."

The big door at the end of the bay started to open and there was a rush of air pulling them forward. They were held in place by their shoes' grip on the floor. To hurry things, Jason had only partially pulled the atmosphere back into the ship and let the rest rush off into the vacuum of space.

"Let's go. Elena, you have Amir. Brian, you have me," Billy said.

Elena took Amir by the arm and they jumped out of the station and into space. Billy and Brian were next. Brian held Billy's arm.

"You okay, Commander?" Brian asked.

"No, definitely not. Let's just do it."

They jumped out and soared off into open space. Billy felt like screaming, but the scream lodged in his throat. Rather than floating he had the strangest sensation that they were falling.

Brian activated his jetpack and the whitish-yellow exhaust streamed out, pushing him and Billy forward. Billy wanted to close his eyes and pretend he wasn't even there but instead he focused on Amir and Elena up ahead of him. They disappeared around the edge of the station and Billy and Brian quickly followed, rounding the curve and regaining sight of them and the two ships docked with the Russian subsection. Outside all looked normal, while inside a fire was blazing, threatening the lives of the members of the fire brigade and threatening to burn through and destroy that section of the station.

"Jason, is the docking bay on Ship 2 open?" Billy asked.

"Door open and awaiting your arrival," Jason replied.

"Expect us inside in less than a minute. On my word, close the external door and start recompression as quickly as possible so we can get into the ship proper," Billy said.

Amir and Elena pulled up alongside the ship and Elena skilfully propelled them into the gaping opening of the docking bay. Billy and Brian were only a few seconds behind them.

"Start to close the bay door!" Billy yelled as they approached.

The door started to close from the top.

"Duck!" Brian yelled as the two of them shot in and under the door, their momentum pulling them forward until they crashed into Elena and Amir, who were already planted on the floor of the docking bay.

"You might have waited a few seconds before giving that order," Brian said.

"A few seconds might mean the difference between life and death. Jason!" Billy ordered. "Pressurize the bay and get us into the ship as soon as possible!"

"Roger."

The door had slid shut and air was being added to the bay. As soon as the pressure between the bay and the ship was equalized they'd open the hatch to enter.

"The hatch between the two ships is open, correct?" Billy asked.

"Open and ready for a run from where you are to the controls of the first ship," Jason said.

"Good work, Jason. Amir, you know what to do as soon as we get inside," Billy said.

"Get the door open and I'm in."

The plan was simple. Amir would run through the first ship, through the hatch that connected the two, and then take the controls of the ship that was docked against the station—against the section that was on fire. They'd take the ship—and the second ship that was attached—blow the lock, and get both ships away from the station.

"Is the pressure equal yet?" Billy asked.

"About half pressure."

"And if we open the hatch now?" Billy asked.

"You'll be blown backwards."

"There's not much backwards to be blown," Billy said.

"I'm going to open the hatch. Everybody hang on. Jason, increase the tension on our shoes. Get us stuck to the floor as hard as you can."

Billy started working the wheel to open the hatch. At first it hardly budged, but then he got it spinning. He released the latch and the door smashed against him, practically knocking him over as the air rushed in. It lasted only a few seconds.

"Return the shoes to normal!" Billy yelled. "Amir, get going!"

Amir pushed through the hatch and hurried as quickly as he could in the bulky spacesuit. Billy ran behind. They ran through the ship, shedding their helmets and gloves as they went, then slid down an opening to the stairs that led to the belly of the vessel. That was where the docking bay connected them to the second ship. Although Jason had told them the door separating the two ships was open, Billy was relieved to see it with his own eyes.

Amir started to slow down.

"You need to go faster!" Billy yelled.

"I'm a pilot, not a sprinter," he puffed out.

"What happens if the station explodes while we're still attached to it?" Billy yelled.

"Okay, good incentive!" Amir suddenly sped up as they entered the second ship.

Brian and Elena, who were somewhere behind them, would come only this far. Their orders were to seal off the entrance between the two ships so that if something happened to the first, they would still be free to detach and leave it behind.

Billy and Amir ran along the length of the ship and then struggled up the stairs and along the corridor that led to the controls.

"Jason, I need you to get ready to break the seal to release the ship."

"Ready on your command. Just say the word."

"It'll come in less than a minute. Get the fire brigade to evacuate the section if they don't believe it can be extinguished."

"Four are already out. Andrea's still in."

"Get her out too, now!"

Amir, closely followed by Billy, ran into the command room and instantly jumped in behind the controls, his hands flying across the board much faster than his legs had run across the ship.

"Okay, initiate launch," Amir said. "Retro-thrusters ready. Release us, Jason."

"Latches released. You're good to go."

Amir started the thrusters, but the ship didn't seem to be separating.

"What's happening?" Billy demanded.

"Jason, release the latches, release the latches!" Amir yelled.

"I've released them. They might be damaged . . . fused by the heat."

Billy put a hand on Amir's shoulder. "Increase the thrusters."

"But if they aren't released we could rip the front off the ship."

“And if we don’t get out of here we could have the front of the ship blown off. Increase the thrusters.”

“I wish I were still wearing the rest of my spacesuit,” Amir said.

“Don’t be stupid. If the front of the ship is gone you’re going to die either way. At least this way it’ll be faster.”

“Point taken. Increasing power to thrusters.”

He slid his hand along the controls and the ship began to shake, but it still didn’t release.

“Increase them more!” Billy ordered.

Amir slid the controls to the top and the shaking increased. And then suddenly the ship popped away from the station and the shaking stopped.

Billy screamed in delight. “You did it! You did it!”

The ship sailed away, flying backwards from the station, each metre travelled a greater margin of safety for them and the other ship.

“We’re free of the station!” Billy yelled over the radio. “Get Andrea out and make sure that section is completely—”

He stopped mid-sentence as the docking bay of the station exploded, sending a stream of debris flooding out into space!

CHAPTER TWENTY-SEVEN

Tools, generators, supplies, and every piece of equipment that wasn't nailed down had been blasted out as air rushed through the breach and into space. The rest of the station still showed lights. It was still alive, and so were the people in it. They'd lost a section but they'd retained the station, and that's what mattered.

And then they saw something else. Floating among the debris was a body partially clad in a firefighter suit.

"It's a person," Amir gasped.

"It's Andrea," Billy said. "Everybody else had already evacuated the section. It has to be her."

Both of them knew she had been killed instantly. The firefighting suit and respirator would have provided protection from the heat and smoke but could not have saved her from the effects of the frigid vacuum of space. As it was, the respirator and helmet were nowhere to be seen, and the shiny metallic suit was in tatters. There was no question she was dead.

"I killed her," Amir said. "I did that when I pulled away from the station. It's all my fault."

"I did it," Billy said. "I gave you the order. And there was no choice. Jason, report in. What happened?"

"The fire is extinguished," Jason reported. "The evacuation of the atmosphere in the section killed the fire."

That made perfect sense. A fire could happen only if it had oxygen to fuel it. Take away the atmosphere and the fire couldn't live.

"We see a body. Is it . . . ?"

"Andrea. It's Andrea."

"I thought she had made it out. We must have weakened the seal when we pulled away," Billy said.

"No," Jason said. "You don't understand. You didn't do anything. Andrea did it."

"Did what?" Billy asked.

"She told me the only way to stop the fire was to open the seal and remove the atmosphere. Because of the damage I couldn't open the seal remotely. Andrea made the decision to do it manually . . . with a fire axe." Jason's calm, measured voice broke over the last few words. "She said there was no choice. She sacrificed her life to allow the station to be saved."

Billy took a deep breath. He needed a few seconds to absorb what he'd just been told.

"Has the hatch held between the substation and the rest of the station?" he asked.

"The seal has held, and so has the second hatch at the end of the corridor. Andrea did it. She saved the station."

"I want the crew to remain in the ships until we've done a full inspection of the structural integrity of the station. No one, I repeat, no one other than the structural engineers is to leave the ships. Understood?"

"Understood, and will communicate."

"Can you also tell Christina . . . tell everybody that the fire is out, that Elena, Brian, Amir, and I are safe, and that the two ships have been secured."

"Roger. Should I tell them about Andrea?"

"Not yet. There'll be plenty of time to share the tragedy and to honour what she did. Right now they just need the good news."

"I understand. Let's get the ships docked and get you back on board," Jason said.

Billy muted the com-link so Jason couldn't hear him. "Amir, are you okay? Can you bring us around to dock us through the European space station lock?"

"I'm fine. Fine enough to do what I have to do. I'll get us in."

Billy pushed the button again. "Jason, I'm going to leave it to you and Amir to take care of business and get us back home safely."

—

5 AAE-DAY 253

The mood around the table was solemn. The fact that they'd all just come from the ceremony to honour Andrea had something to do with that. And the realization that they had all now come to, about the seriousness of what had happened, explained the rest. There was no need for formal reports when personal knowledge and rumours had already made everybody in the Internal Operations Committee aware of the situation they now faced.

"Let's not waste any time talking about things that aren't essential," Billy said. "As you are all probably aware by now, the structural integrity of the station is not in question. However, the Russian subsection was totally destroyed."

"Although there is potential for it to be rehabilitated to some extent," Brian added.

"To a minor extent, but the risk might not be worth the return. That will have to be decided in subsequent meetings," Billy said. "We need to look at the short term first. Ivan, you had a chance to go over the reports. Could you please share the results?"

Slowly Ivan got to his feet. His expression—as always—was blank, neutral, not revealing much—although everybody already had a pretty good idea of what he was going to say.

"The fire has resulted in the loss of all the resources and benefits that flowed from that part of the station. The attached solar panels are no longer on line, and without them we have experienced a 25 percent reduction in our overall power supply."

"Can they be brought back on line?" Christina asked.

"Asha and I have done a full examination and analysis," Brian said. "The failure is permanent."

"The fire was electrical. The circuits were fried and cannot be replaced. There is no possibility of getting them back on line."

"As they wrote in their report," Ivan said, tapping the paper he was reading from, "there remains enough power to supply the ongoing needs of the station. That is not a significant loss."

"And not to toot my own horn, but we were also able to rescue the two ships, so we have not lost any of our transportation or survey ability, and we retained the supplies from both of those ships," Amir said. "As well, we can obviously still transport our crew back to the surface when that is considered feasible."

"That is a further positive on our long-term projections, but we need to look at the short term. Ivan, please continue."

"The situation, as Billy has indicated, is more of a short-term issue with long-term implications. The subsection was where we generated almost 35 percent of our water. With the subsection gone, we can no longer produce enough water to supply either our crops or the needs of our crew."

"What are you saying?" Amir questioned.

"That we are not able to meet the physical needs of our station," Ivan said.

There was shock and silence as the full weight of what he had just said sank in. Ivan had already shared the report and the implications with Billy, and the initial shock had worn off for him.

"So what does that mean, exactly?" Brian asked.

"We cannot produce sufficient supplies of water to grow enough crops to feed all the members of the crew. We cannot produce enough water to sustain the lives of the hundred members of the crew."

"But can't we do something to generate more water, to grow more food?" Asha asked. There was more than a hint of panic in her voice.

"The engineers indicate that there is no solution available," Billy said, answering for Ivan. "Even with attempts to conserve and reduce supplies, there is not enough water for all of us to live."

"But there has to be something we can do," Christina exclaimed.

"There is," Billy said. He turned directly to her. "I'm sorry I didn't share this with you, and I haven't discussed it with the members of the committee." He paused. "I want you to know that I have great respect for all of you. I care for all of you deeply. But sometimes a decision has to be reached, and it isn't something that can be decided by a committee. This is my decision to make as the leader and I hope you'll all respect what I'm going to say to you, because, well, there is no choice."

There was complete and utter silence.

"We cannot sustain life for the one hundred people on this station. To attempt to have all of us survive is to doom us all," Billy said. "The projections say that sixty-five people—sixty-five lives—can be maintained. Is that correct, Ivan?"

"Perhaps seventy, but sixty-five is optimal," he said.

"Then that's how many people will remain on the station," Billy said.

"But the others . . ." Christina gasped. "You can't just end their lives. You can't expect people to volunteer to sacrifice themselves."

"I'm not asking for volunteers. I've already decided the people who will remain."

"And the rest?" she said. "You can't just have them—"

"Yes, I can. The remaining thirty-five people will no longer live . . . on the station. They will be going down to the planet."

CHAPTER TWENTY-EIGHT

YEAR 5 AAE–DAY 259

Billy stood at the door of the corridor leading to the ship—the ship that was going to take them down to the planet. Normally each of their five ships held twenty passengers. This one had been reconfigured with thirty-five seats. They weren't going far, a one-way journey through the atmosphere and to the surface. Billy wanted to leave the extra ship at the station just in case. Everything always had to be just in case; there had to be a backup plan. He'd learned that well.

Already onboard the ship, strapped in and ready to go, were most of the people who were going on the mission. Tasha was at the controls. Billy needed a good pilot, and Tasha wanted to come along. Giving birth in space was possible but had been done only three times before. There were risks. Of course, there were risks where they were going as well, and having a pregnant woman and then a newborn in the party wasn't ideal, but it was going to happen. Billy would defend them both with his life.

Amir had wanted to pilot the ship but he was told that he had a more important ship to pilot. He was being left in charge of the space station. He and Jason. They were being left as the co-leaders.

Originally Billy had wanted to leave Christina on the station, not just to be the leader but because he didn't want to risk her life on the surface. It was safer on the station; they would always have the option of going down to the planet if they needed to. Those who reached the planet would never have the option of returning. But she had simply told him no, in no uncertain terms. He'd tried to talk her out of coming, told her that they'd be reunited in four or five years, when surface conditions were better. She wasn't buying what he was selling. She was clear that her place was with him, that he needed her if he hoped to survive. In the end, he didn't need much convincing. He couldn't imagine living without her, or wanting to live that way. He would have preferred to die beside her than live without her. His plan, though, was for both of them to live. For all of them to live.

They stood side by side saying goodbye to everybody on the ship. Their last gift was to give each person a message, something that would help them to go forward. It was important that they not think of themselves as abandoned, or believe that they weren't chosen to go down to the surface because they weren't "good enough." Each person remaining on the station had an important role to fulfill. They had the expertise needed to keep the station going. They needed to keep the station crew alive for up to another five years.

With the exception of Tasha, all pilots were staying on board. They would be flying missions, conducting surveys, and eventually bringing at least three of the other ships back to Earth. Lars was included in that group because he had shown himself to be reasonable, kind, and a grownup who could help provide stability.

All those like Brian and Asha and Elena with skills necessary to repair or maintain the external parts of the station were staying. Those finely honed skills were essential for the station to survive and useless on the surface. Flying and floating weren't going to be options there. In fact, walking and running might be beyond the crew when they landed. No human had ever lived in space as long as they had, and while all sort of plans and programs had been implemented, they had no idea how their bodies would react until they reached the surface.

Those who had horticultural skills were placed in both groups. The food supply on the station had to continue, but they would definitely need to try to grow food on the surface. The doctors, engineers, and experts in all earth sciences were also divided into two groups, with two-thirds of them staying on the station.

Ivan stood by the door, carefully watching as always. He was returning to the surface. Billy didn't know what or who they would encounter, but having Ivan with him gave him an ace in the hole, somebody who could handle whatever was to come. It was certainly possible that they'd need to defend themselves, and potentially kill others who threatened them.

Billy had also revealed to all of them his final ace in the hole. Unknown to anybody except him and Christina, he had knowledge about Joshua's backup backup plan.

One hundred kilometres away from the underground colony, in four different directions, Joshua had made separate depots. They were isolated, away from any civilized settlement, in the open, wild country. Buried beneath rock and hidden among trees and forest, Joshua had placed enough food and supplies to provide for four hundred people—one-quarter of the people who were in the underground colony—in the event that the colony had to be abandoned. Now, one of those would be the refuge for the people forced to abandon the space station. It was the depot to the south of the colony that they were aiming for.

Billy and Christina continued to work their way down the line. They had spoken to everybody except the last two, Amir and Jason. Christina gave both a hug and a kiss, whispered something in their ears, and then walked away down the corridor, leaving Billy alone with them.

"I guess this is goodbye," Billy said.

"For now," Amir said. "We'll be down there sooner than you think."

"He's right. The first five years have passed quickly. We might even be down there earlier than planned if you find the circumstances are right," Jason added.

"You're right, and it's not like we're not going to be in communication with each other."

They had agreed that they would check in with each other on a regular basis. Just as significant—even more significant for the rest of the world—the station was going to move forward with the decision to start communicating with every known colony on the planet. This was, in part, to avoid having the communication between Billy and the station stand out, but also to start establishing a network. Those still alive on the planet would need to work together if the world was ever to return to any degree of organization and normalcy.

"I guess I should mention this right now," Amir said. "If we do a really great job up here, we might insist on staying in charge when we land."

"I'm more than prepared to share leadership. The same way you two are going to share leadership. Amir, you need to allow Jason's stability, his care, his thoughtfulness to be moderating forces. Jason, you need to allow Amir's sense of adventure and daring to influence your style. Together you're going to offer great leadership. I know that."

"We won't let you down," Jason said.

"You know you can count on us. We'll keep the place running and people safe until you tell us it's time to reunite on the surface."

Billy shook their hands. "Until we meet again, my friends."

He turned and walked to the hatch. Ivan gave him a nod and headed down first, leaving Billy as the last to enter the ship, the last to leave the station. As he reached the door he turned and waved, and all those assembled burst into applause. He smiled, gave another wave, and entered the corridor leading to the docking bay. The hatch was sealed behind him.

Slowly, deliberately Billy walked down the corridor, through the docking bay, and entered the ship. Once again the door was sealed behind him and he went toward the control room. All along the way the crew was strapped in, ready for launch. He shook a hand or gave a pat on the back, saying a few short words to each of those he passed.

In the ship were two months' supply of food, almost no water—it was needed for the station and hopefully would be readily available on the surface—extra clothing, seeds, tools for cultivation and building, and weapons that they might need to defend themselves.

It was time for Billy to take his seat. He entered the control room. Tasha was at the controls. Ivan and Christina occupied the two seats in the back, leaving the seat beside Tasha open. Billy took that seat and belted himself in.

"We're ready to go, Commander," Tasha said.

"I'm ready for you to pilot us to a soft landing on Earth, Captain Tasha. Shall I signal departure?"

"Roger."

Billy opened a channel to the station. "Ship 1 is ready to go."

"We will release the docking latches." It was, of course, Jason, already at the command centre of the station. "Release on five . . . four . . . three . . . two . . . one. And latches have been disengaged."

"Retro-thrusters engaged," Tasha said.

The camera in the nose of the ship showed them moving slowly away from the docking station. Separation was complete. Billy turned his attention back to the window, where he could watch the real station instead of the video image of it.

In the corner of the window he caught sight of wisps of exhaust coming from the retro-thrusters. He thought back to the first time he'd seen those whitish-yellow exhausts coming out of a spaceship. It was less than five years ago but it could have been yesterday or a hundred years ago, or both. This was for sure the last time he'd see them. Once they had sufficient separation from the station they'd engage the main engines, the ones that would deliver them back through the atmosphere and down to the surface.

The station got smaller and smaller. It still looked delicate, but now he could see the place where it had proven most fragile. The Russian section was dark and damaged, with no lights and no life. It was why they were leaving, why they had to return to the Earth, why their lives were in jeopardy. He stopped himself—there was no time for that sort of thinking.

"We have sufficient separation," Tasha said. "I've entered the re-entry data and the engines will automatically be engaged." She moved some of the dials and pushed buttons on the control console. "And engaged."

There was slight change in rotation as the view of the station out the window vanished and the Earth below started to move into focus. The ship's orientation continued to change as the ship rotated. The bottom of the ship had the thickest plates, to absorb the heat of re-entry.

"How long before we hit the upper atmosphere?" Billy asked.

"Less than two minutes."

"And then?"

"It will take less than ten minutes for our descent through the atmosphere to slow us to the point where I can fly the ship again."

"And then?"

"Our glide will be approximately another thirty minutes while I get us in position over the target. At that time I'll engage our chutes, and we'll fall to the ground two minutes later."

"Good." Billy turned to Christina and their eyes locked. She gave him a reassuring smile. "I'm going to address the crew." He opened the com-link to the ship.

"We are starting our descent to the planet, to Earth. I don't know what we're going to encounter. Nobody does. What I do know is that on this ship are the people who can overcome whatever challenges we will experience. We will survive. We will succeed. We will excel. And I want to be the first to say one more thing." He paused. "I want to be the very first to say to all of you . . . welcome home!"

Don't miss the action-packed prequel to REGENESIS:

DOUBLEDAY CANADA